Chasing Nightmares

by Nicole Aisling

Phoenix Flight Press

For Grandma and Grandpa.
Thank you for supporting my dreams. I wish you were here to see them come true.

Part I

Asleep

Chapter 1

T HE DARK STREET WARPED and shifted as Ashlin raced down it. Buildings and dead streetlamps cast twisted shadows that seemed to fall in whatever directions they felt like. They moved as she passed, following her like fingers outstretched to catch her.

Footsteps thundered after her, far enough away that she couldn't see what caused them, but close enough that she shouldn't keep pausing to glance back. She didn't know what pursued her, and she didn't want to.

Because Ash knew one thing for certain: monsters are real. They live inside our minds, our demons and worst fears hounding us when we close our eyes and try to find peace. You can't hide from your nightmares, can't outrun them, because they're part of you.

Except it wasn't Ash's own demons that she ran from down that dark, empty street. They dwelled in someone else's head, someone else's nightmare, and she had no power here. Just because the monsters didn't stalk the waking world didn't mean they couldn't hurt her. It didn't mean they couldn't kill her.

At least, Ash assumed they could kill her. When she died in her own dreams, she would startle awake, but she didn't care to find out what would happen if she died in someone else's.

She followed that someone down another street, this one even darker than the last. It narrowed with every step she took, until it became nothing more than an alley. The dreamer finally stopped running and fell to his knees on the pavement. A single flickering light erratically illuminated his hunched form, yellowing his brown hair and white skin.

She reached his side and grabbed his arm, trying to tug him back up. "Come on, we have to keep moving!" She didn't know why she bothered. They could run and run and run, but the nightmares always caught up, no matter how fast she ran. Sometimes it was better to let them catch her. Less exhausting, certainly.

The problem for Ash was that sometimes getting caught woke people up, and she didn't like what happened when a person woke before she found her way out of their dream. There was always a delay between the dream ending and her waking up, and she feared someday her mind might not return to her own body. She would be stuck in someone else's head forever.

When the dreamer didn't move, Ash looped her arm under his and hauled him to his feet. "Keep. Running."

He followed orders, staggering forward at a slower pace than before. They made it to the other end of the alley and emerged onto a main street that, like the ones before it, was devoid of cars. Behind them, thuds echoed off the brick walls of the alley, a storm of sound unlike anything Ash had ever heard.

She couldn't resist the urge to turn and face what they ran from. She wished she hadn't. Twenty paces away, illuminated by the golden light overhead, was a stampede that might start haunting Ash's own dreams.

The hippos moved single file down the alley, arms raised over their heads so their forms could fit between the walls. More accurately, they had their front legs raised, since the creatures shouldn't have been walking on two. Leathery skin wrinkled around their thick necks. They all had their mouths open in huge grins, showing long, yellowed teeth set into jaws that could snap a person's arm off. Ash could even see the gleam of thick whiskers on their cheeks.

They were horrifyingly lifelike, aside from being upright. Well, that and the lacy tutus that fluttered around their waists as they turned in slow circles down the alley. Their steps were unhurried, but the chorus of thuds sounded like something very big running very fast.

Ash was fleeing from dancing hippos in tutus.

She gaped at them until hands pulled on her arm. "Come on!" the dreamer said. "They're going to catch us."

She followed him away from the alley but glanced back when the thudding of footsteps changed. As the hippos emerged from the alley one by one, they dropped to all fours and charged forward. Their biped steps might have been slow, but now they galloped down the street twice as fast as Ash could run, their gaping mouths ready to swallow the hapless humans whole.

They caught up easily. Instead of trampling the humans, the hippos formed a ring and returned to two legs. They started dancing around Ash and the dreamer, who cowered beside her with tears streaking his face. The hippos moved with remarkable grace for such bulky creatures, smooth pirouettes and elegant jumps. Although they seemed to float through the air, the whole street shook when the three-thousand-pound animals landed.

Each time the dancers circled, the ring grew smaller, the hippos closing in. *I need to get us out of here.* The thought cut through Ash's panicked mind. In her own dream, she could have lifted herself and the dreamer over the heads of the hippos. She could have brought some light back to the world, returned the stars to the black sky.

But this wasn't her dream, and when Ash tried to focus on changing it, nothing happened. This dream may as well have been the real world. It refused to bend to Ash's will.

The first press of surprisingly hot skin had Ash shrinking away. Strangely, her panic faded into one grim realization: she was going to die smothered by hippos in a dream world. She longed to go soaring upward, or for the street to drop out from under her. Anything to escape the hippos.

"I'm so sorry," she said. "I wish I could save you." She didn't know why she apologized, when she was the one who would actually die. The dreamer didn't even look at her, weeping on his knees while massive gray bodies pressed him against Ash. She squeezed her eyes shut and prayed for a miracle.

Ash's stomach jolted as the two of them fell straight through the pavement, leaving the hippos behind. When she opened her eyes, they stood in the middle of an abandoned theme park. *Did I do that?* she wondered.

The dreamer had stopped crying, but when he lifted his head and saw the theme park, he looked even more frightened. Ash turned in a slow circle, her eyes roaming their new surroundings. The light remained the same, pale white illumination that didn't come from a moon or stars, as well as yellow streetlamps that flickered in and out of life.

The scenery may have changed, but the dream hadn't, not really. They were still in the nightmare. Skeletal roller coasters rose around them, the metal tracks pocked by time and wooden slats covered in moss. An empty Ferris wheel turned haltingly, too stubborn to quit when all the other rides had, producing a rhythmic squeak with every lurch.

Ash also heard the patter of rain against pavement, but she couldn't identify the source. The sound drifted closer, until she could smell water as well, except it wasn't the scent of fresh rain.

It smelled like a lake, slightly fishy and mixed with wet pebbles, tufts of grass, and a summer breeze. She didn't know why those things had a specific and identifiable scent, but in the dream, they were as distinct as fresh-cut lemons.

When the source of the splashing water stepped out from behind a weathered pillar supporting the nearest roller coaster, Ash realized the hippos had been nothing more than a weak attempt at covering up what really haunted him.

The girl's clothes clung to her skinny frame, her wet hair tangled and splayed out over her shoulders. Water dripped from her pallid face. It ran down her arms and splattered the pavement in an endless stream that came from nowhere. Her head lolled to one side, like she couldn't quite hold it up straight, but her eyes... her eyes were bright, focused, and angry.

"You didn't save me," she said, her voice tight and raw, the voice of someone who had been choking on water. She took a step forward, unsteady and slow, but persistent. She shambled along with the determination of water slowly wearing away at rock.

The dreamer shook his head, then turned and ran under the dip of a coaster track while the dripping girl inched forward. She didn't look at Ash, even when she drew close enough that some of her water splattered Ash's shoes.

Ash backed away from the girl slowly, worried that sudden movement might draw her attention, but the girl took another step, her eyes still focused on her one and only target: the dreamer.

The smart thing would have been to turn and run in the other direction. The dangers here plagued the dreamer, so it logically followed the safest place would be far away from him. Ash could climb a maintenance ladder and hide on top of a roller coaster while she tried to get out of the dream before he woke up.

Instead, she ran after him. If she could talk to him, maybe she could calm him down enough to dispel the nightmare before it consumed him. It was always easier to get out of a good dream than a bad one, swimming up through calm waters rather than being dragged under by a storm.

So focused on finding the dreamer, Ash nearly crashed into someone who stepped into her path. She veered aside to avoid collision, only to run into a food cart instead. She tripped over the locked wheel of the cart and pitched forward. Rough pavement scraped her palms when she threw out her hands to break her fall.

She rolled over to face the person who was *not* the dreamer. He had bronze skin and a round face. She had no idea how old he was, but his face and small stature made it hard for Ash to imagine he was any older than sixteen. He wore a blindingly red t-shirt, a bright spot of color in the otherwise dreary setting. It had a multi-colored brain on the front, along with the words "I get psyched for psychology."

When his brown eyes fell on Ash, they widened.

Most beings conjured by dreams, like the girl Ash could still hear pattering through the park, paid no attention to Ash. Even if they noticed her, their focus was always on the person who belonged in the dream. This boy saw her, though. *Really* saw her, with the surprise of someone who didn't expect to find her and the clarity to realize she shouldn't be there.

"You're really here, aren't you?" he said.

A girl dropped to the ground beside him, startling Ash. She must have jumped from the roller coaster track at least a hundred feet above them, a height that should have resulted in a broken leg. The girl straightened from her crouch, perfectly fine. She blended into the night, thanks to her black clothing, dark hair pulled back in a ponytail, and skin nearly the same color as her shirt. She looked older than the boy beside her, early twenties like Ash. She wore a bitter expression, but there was something odd about her face, the details uncertain. The shape of her nose, the line of her jaw. The edges blurred and reformed, unable to make up their minds.

"What are you doing? We need to reshape it now." She followed his gaze to Ash and seemed to notice her for the first time. The new girl looked Ash over with scrutinizing eyes, which made Ash feel like some science experiment gone wrong.

They were interrupted by footsteps, followed by the rush of a dozen wings. The dreamer ran between them, pursued by a flock of birds. They were the size of ravens, but instead of having black feathers, their bodies and wings were made of fluid water. They left trails of luminous mist as they swooped by, briefly obscuring Ash's view of the other two intruders in the dream.

A few steps away, the fleeing dreamer tripped and went sprawling on the dead grass. The birds circled above him, their triumphant cawing like the crashing of a waterfall.

"I don't have time for this," the girl muttered. She held out an arm and a length of wood appeared in her closed fist, starting in the middle and rippling outward. A wide paddle formed at one end. Surprise flickered over her face as she regarded the oar she held, but then she spun the thing in her hands like a fighting staff and struck at one of the water birds.

The oar's handle cut the creature clean in half. The bird's form hung in the air, liquid rippling, then it burst into a cloud that dissipated on the wind. The girl swung the oar like a base-ball bat as one of the birds dove at the dreamer, who had curled into the fetal position on the ground. The bird exploded into mist when it collided with the broad paddle.

The rest of the flock raised their voices in a thunderous chorus as they flapped their wings out of reach of the deadly oar. The birds hovered in the air, pale light filtering through their translucent bodies while they judged whether they could get to the dreamer faster than the oar-wielding girl could get to them.

"TJ, *now!*" the girl shouted.

"Right, sorry!" the boy called back. His forehead scrunched as he concentrated. One by one, the remaining birds burst like water balloons. The droplets hung in the air, rather than falling like rain or turning to vapor to be carried off by the wind as the remains of the others had. The boy lifted his hands, palms up, and the water rose with them. When he threw his hands apart, a fine spray arced through the air. A bright spot appeared in the sky, a sun sparking to life to push back the darkness. Light rippled outward, turning the sky a brilliant blue. The misted remnants of the birds became a rainbow when the sunlight hit them.

All around, the dream changed. Light washed over rusted roller coasters, turning them shiny and new. Moss and rot receded, leaving wood planks as pristine as the day they had been cut. The squeak of the Ferris wheel vanished as the ride began to turn at a smooth, leisurely pace.

Ash rose slowly, in awe of the previously abandoned theme park that now thrummed with life. Cars full of delighted, screaming passengers rumbled along roller coaster tracks. Lights flashed on other rides. Voices and laughter filled every corner of the park. The patter of the girl's endless dripping was either gone or covered up by the new, joyous sounds.

Ash jumped when someone grabbed her arm. She turned toward the boy, who stood by her shoulder, a few inches shorter than Ash.

"Meet us at the Studio. Wednesday," he said. He joined his companion, who now waited in front of a free-standing door of dark-stained oak. "Remember, the Studio!" he called before the two of them joined hands and stepped through the door together.

"Hey, wait!" Ash shouted. She ran toward the door, but it vanished the moment her fingers curled around the knob. She stood in front of empty air, thriving grass beneath her feet and the dreamer nowhere to be found. People still surrounded her, but they were products of the dream.

Ash was completely alone.

Chapter 2

ASH WOKE TO HER blaring alarm clock, but she didn't open her eyes right away. The dream still lingered in her mind, the drastic change from nightmare to vibrant life and the way the boy had looked at her. *Meet us at the Studio. Wednesday.* She didn't know what he meant by "the Studio," if it even existed. She told herself they were probably part of the dream, but even as she thought it, she knew it wasn't true. They hadn't belonged, same as her.

She forced her eyes open, fighting through the headache that usually followed falling into someone else's dream. She felt like she'd only gotten a few hours of sleep. Nights were never restful when one's mind traveled somewhere else. First day at a new job, and she was going to show up half dead on her feet. Maybe she could go for a record this time, see how quickly she could get fired.

Ash sat up and rubbed at her palms, which still stung from when she had scraped them in the dream. When she glanced down, though, the skin was intact. The pain faded a few seconds later, her brain realizing her body wasn't actually damaged. She had gotten injured in dreams a few times and woken up still hurting. The pain usually didn't linger long, thankfully.

She was more worried about the possibility of dying and not waking up at all.

She pushed aside her comforter, along with the two throw blankets draped on top of it, and dragged herself out of bed to close the window she often left open at night. It was only cracked a few inches, the most it would go before jamming. It had been that way since they moved in, but Ash had never bothered asking her uncle to fix it. She had no intention of using it to sneak out, even if there were an easy way to reach the ground from the second story.

She paused at her desk on her way out of her room and picked up the sketch she had been working on well past when she should have gone to sleep. The mansion home had lived in her head for months, until she had finally sat down to draw it. That happened sometimes. Images in her head would demand to come out, nagging her until she relented. She had probably seen the house at some point and not really noticed it at the time, but it had stuck in her mind all the same.

She added the sketch to the dozen others above the desk, pinning it on the cork board beside the profile of a man with his head bowed, the shadow of stubble on his face. Like the house, the face had lingered in the back of her mind for months. She was still trying to figure out who he was, or if he were simply a fantasy.

She was on autopilot as she got ready for work. While she showered and brushed her teeth, the dream replayed in her mind—specifically, the way the boy had completely reshaped it. He had made turning a nightmare into something beautiful look so effortless, when she couldn't even get rid of some hippos with a love of ballet.

Once she was ready, Ash twisted her still wet hair into a bun so she wouldn't have to deal with the unruly curls. People always complimented the auburn color, but Ash hated managing her hair. There were times she was tempted to chop it off and be done with it. Between her hair and the freckles that dusted her cheeks and forehead, she often felt far too Irish.

Downstairs, her uncle waited for her in the kitchen with a plate full of pancakes. "What's that you say?" he said when he saw her, even though she hadn't spoken. "Pancakes for breakfast? You'd batter believe it!"

Ash rolled her eyes and sat down. He must have worked on that one all morning, planning his pun while whipping egg whites.

"First day," Tiernan said as he set pancakes on the kitchen table, along with a bottle of warm syrup. "Are you nervous?"

"Not really," she lied. It had become a ritual, his making pancakes on her first day of work, something that had happened far too many times since she'd moved back in with him. First the restaurant, then the bookshop. She had liked the latter better, but that hadn't stopped her from zoning out, usually from lack of rest, or prevented interactions with customers from going south. Her next endeavor, a little clothing boutique, had somehow been even worse than her waitressing job.

Really, what Ash needed was to get out of customer service. She was terrible at it.

"You'll do great," Tiernan reassured her. "This time will be different."

She almost wished he would stop saying that. The unwavering encouragement was meant to be reassuring, but it had gotten to a point where it felt empty.

It wasn't the new job her mind kept wandering to as she ate, though. The pair from the dream. The Studio. She had two days to figure out what this studio was, and whether she wanted to go. Everything inside her screamed the interaction had been *real*, and that meant the two strangers might have answers.

"What's going on up there?" Tiernan asked. "You look exhausted. Did you get enough sleep last night?"

Lying to him twice in one morning felt wrong, so she shook her head. "Couldn't sleep. Maybe I am nervous."

"Ash." When she continued to stare at her pancakes, he said, "Ash, look at me."

She reluctantly lifted her eyes to meet his gaze. She hated his serious face, the one that meant he was about to say something that would make her incredibly uncomfortable.

"You are brilliant. You're creative. And you're going to find somewhere to work until you find the job you really want. Okay?"

"Okay," she muttered, but in her head she responded, *If the job I want will even hire me.* Photography wasn't an easy field to break into. She had picked up a few gigs, taking senior pictures or wedding photos for family friends. It wasn't enough, though. She needed to work for an actual established business, but she hadn't found one yet that was interested in hiring someone with so little experience.

She told herself to stop moping and enjoy the pancakes her uncle had put effort into making for her. He had been there for her every step of the way. Raising her after her parents died, paying for the college degree she had never finished, supporting her efforts as a photographer, and then letting her move back in after the falling out with her roommate.

And yet part of her resented him for it. She wished he would get angry at her, for dropping out of college or getting fired or forgetting to clean the kitchen after making herself dinner on the nights he had to work late.

"Oh, and don't forget to stop at Capture It after work," he said. "You should get off before they close."

"Yeah, I'll try." She should have shown more enthusiasm for dropping off her resume at one of the few places that might hire her.

They were halfway through cleaning up when Tiernan's cellphone beeped, mimicking the sound of a pager.

"Shoot," he murmured after checking it. "I have to go in early. Are you okay finishing on your own?"

"Of course. Go. I'll see you tonight."

Tiernan pulled her into a bear hug, ignoring her squeak of protest. "Remember, be Ashlin, not a goblin. You'll do great."

She squirmed out of his grasp and stepped over to the sink, trying to hide her red face. She still wished the goblin thing hadn't become a permanent fixture in her life. Children should get the chance to live down being a terror as a child. "Get out of here," she told him. "Go cut people open or whatever you do."

"You know full well that's not what I do," he said. She did, of course, but she still thought it would be cooler if her uncle were a surgeon, not a pediatrician. "I'll see you tonight. Love you."

"Love you," Ash echoed.

Fifteen minutes later, after setting the clean plates in the dish drainer to dry, Ash was out the door and on the way to her next failure. At least it wasn't too far away, a ten-minute walk to the nearest Metro station and another ten-minute ride from there. The April morning was pleasantly cool for her travels.

The solitary trip gave Ash far too much time alone to dwell on her dream, so she ended up distracting herself by focusing on her surroundings. She had left her camera at home, but she still took snapshots in her mind for drawing later. The houses and storefronts she passed, the palm trees, the way the sun slowly brightened the sky over Los Angeles.

But most of all the people. Oh, the people. She loved watching them go about their busy lives. Ash didn't think there was anywhere else on the planet where people were in such a hurry to get to their destinations, whether they were driving, walking, or zipping by on their bike. Everyone had somewhere very important to be.

Ash, on the other hand, was rarely in a hurry and therefore often late. Walking through the door five minutes late was actually ten minutes early for her.

"Ah, there you are!" a woman said the moment Ash stepped inside Crystal Caverns. Trish, the woman who had interviewed Ash last week, leaned against the front counter. A young man Ash hadn't met yet stood behind it. He was in his twenties like Ash, with a nose ring and gauges in his earlobes. The sides of his blond head were shaved, and he looked entirely in place amongst the displays of gemstones, candles, and handmade jewelry on the counter in front of him.

"This is Desmond," Trish said. "You'll be working most of your shifts with him. Des, this is Ash."

He gave her a smile and a little wave. "Please, just call me Des."

Ash couldn't resist scratching at the back of her hand, her nerves going haywire. Her nervous habit was interrupted by Trish hurrying over to take her hands, and Ash had to resist the urge to pull away. "Now this is really important," Trish said, looking her dead in the eyes. "What's your star sign?"

Ash blinked at her. It wasn't a question she had never been asked before, but it still caught her off-guard. "I'm sorry?"

"Trish needs to look up your horoscope before she assigns you," Des said. "Mercury is in retrograde so if you're an Aries, you *cannot* work the counter today."

Ash knew she shouldn't be surprised at the question, considering what the store sold. Among the racks of clothing were displays of crystals and tarot cards. "Okay... I'm a Pisces," she said, keeping her tone neutral. She had always thought of astrology as complete nonsense, though perhaps someone who kept falling into other people's dreams should keep a more open mind.

"Hmm, that's all right then," Trish said. "You can help Des up front."

The realization that she could have lied and perhaps avoided interacting with customers that day struck Ash too late, though she supposed it was for the best. Dishonesty was not the best way to start a new job.

"My first client is already here. I'll be in the back if you need me!" Trish called, already in the process of disappearing through the door with a glittery sign that read "Employees Only."

"Client for what?" Ash asked Des.

"Trish is a dream guide," he said. "She helps people analyze their dreams and glean meaning from them." He waved for Ash to join him behind the counter, so she stepped around the display case of geodes and glass figurines. A small portable speaker sat on one side of the register, playing out a guitar solo from some classic rock song.

Des drummed his fingers against the side of the cash drawer, humming along with the music. "You've worked retail before?" he asked when the solo ended. She nodded. "And you know how to count change?"

She pulled her eyes away from a book entitled *How to Interpret Your Tarot Cards!* and blinked at Des. "Uh... yes?"

He grinned at her reaction. "You'd be surprised how many people *can't*. Good help is so hard to find these days. I'll show you how our system works and you'll probably be good to go."

True to his word, Des walked her through their inventory system and how to run payments, then turned her loose on the public while he went to reorganize a rack of colorful dresses in the corner. It wasn't difficult, checking out the handful of people who wandered into the store. Ash didn't know if this was a slow or normal day for Crystal Caverns, but she slowly sank deeper and deeper into boredom.

There's something insidious about boredom. It seeps in and leaves you wishing you could be doing anything else, but you don't have the energy to seek out something to do. If she were a better employee, she might have gone over to Des and offered to help with whatever he was working on, but instead she pulled her small sketchbook out of her purse and set it open on the counter in front of her.

On a whim, she started sketching the same face that had lived inside her mind for months now. She drew the harsh angles of his chin and cheekbones, the tight curls of his dark hair, then the shading of stubble on his chin.

The man's expression came next, and for the first time, the hint of a smile graced his face. She didn't know why she usually drew him sad or angry—if it were indicative of her own mood or something else—but that day he needed a smile. Not a full grin with teeth showing, but the subtle sort of smile you give a loved one when they do something cute and you think they aren't looking.

"What's that you're doing?"

Des's voice at her shoulder made Ash jump. She'd been so wrapped up in her drawing that a customer probably could have stepped up to the counter and she wouldn't have noticed.

She tried to slide the sketchbook out of his view, but Des leaned over her shoulder to take a closer look. She expected him to call her out for slacking on the job, but instead he said, "Oh my gosh, you're an artist? That's really cool."

She continued to eye him uncertainly, ever reluctant to accept compliments. "Thanks?" She couldn't help the accidental question mark attached to the word.

"Have you ever been to the Studio?" he asked. Ash had been avoiding his gaze, but now her head snapped up. "It's in midtown. Used to be an art studio before a new owner bought it and turned it into a bar. They lean into the whole art thing and might buy some of your stuff. They support local artists and all that."

"Of course," she murmured. She *did* know the place, from before they closed down, though she hadn't visited since the conversion.

Des might be right about them buying art, but that wasn't the source of the excitement that coursed through her. The bar *had* to be the place where the guy from the dream had asked her to meet them.

Des beamed, pleased to have given her an epiphany. "So who is he?"

"What?"

"The guy you drew. He's pretty. Is that your boyfriend?"

Ash glanced down at the drawing and frowned. "No, he's... I don't know, actually. Just a face I see in my mind sometimes when I close my eyes."

"Ah, your dream boyfriend, then," he said with a grin.

She smiled back, but it was tinged with sadness. "No, not that either."

"Sure, sure. Whatever you say." He winked at her, clearly not buying her claim.

Ash let it go. It didn't matter what Des thought, though she did wish she could figure out where she had seen the man.

"Ooh, you think maybe you can make signs for the shop?" Des asked. "We could use a little artistic flair around here. You know, for promos and sales and stuff. Draw attention to things like the crystals."

Ash glanced around, the gears already turning in her mind. "Can I... make a suggestion?" she asked cautiously. The last time those words had left her mouth, the owner of the restaurant had curtly said he would "take it under consideration" and she'd never heard about it again.

Des, however, bobbed his head eagerly. "Whatcha thinking, art girl?"

She pointed to one of the racks that held a collection of colorful shirts. "If we move that maybe a foot to the right, then pull the crystal display around to sit in front of it... it'll be much more noticeable. You might sell a lot of them just as an impulse buy because they're *right there.* And it'll open up that section of the store a little, I think." Then she could add an eye-catching sign, like Des had suggested. Even if she didn't believe in the healing power of crystals, they were pretty, and something that random tourists looking for something New Age-y to bring home from their trip to LA would buy. But with the way they were tucked in the corner, you were hard-pressed to notice them unless you were looking for them.

Des stared at the clothing rack, his forehead furrowed, then nodded slowly. "We can run it by Trish. She's usually up for changing stuff around in the shop. Let me tell you, reorganizing is a weekly thing around here." It was essentially the same thing as "we'll take it under consideration," but it sounded so very different. Des made it sound like a real possibility, rather than a polite dismissal of her ideas.

When Trish finished up with her client and emerged from the back room, Des told her about the idea to move displays around. She was beyond open to the suggestion, eager to implement it even, so Ash and Des spent the next several minutes reorganizing.

After helping close at the end of the day, Ash left the store feeling buoyed, happier than she had been since she moved back in with her uncle. It felt amazing, optimism rushing through her. She still wanted her photography business, but it wouldn't be so bad working at Crystal Caverns in the meantime. A place where her voice was heard, with friendly coworkers and a relaxed vibe, despite her initial skepticism at the store's theme.

Plus, she had a meeting at the Studio on Wednesday that might hold some much-needed answers.

Chapter 3

E VERY TABLE AT THE Studio was full that night. The TV at the far end of the dining area proclaimed "Nivia Tright!" in big letters. Someone was probably very proud of that truly terrible name, not to mention the garish font.

The clamor of voices and press of bodies reminded Ash why she didn't go to bars, especially on trivia nights. Perhaps an odd sentiment from someone who wanted to be an event photographer, but it was different when she could lurk in the background with her camera and not interact with anyone.

She almost turned around and walked right back out, but the overenthusiastic waving of an arm caught her attention.

"Hey, you! Dream girl," the boy shouted. "Over here!" He didn't look much different than he had in the dream. His dark hair was a bit messier, and he wore a blue t-shirt instead of red, but he still didn't look old enough to be in a bar. The girl who had jumped from the top of a roller coaster sat beside him, watching Ash through narrowed eyes. Her face, though uncertain in the dream, had finally made up its mind and settled into pretty features, even if her expression remained hostile. She had her straight black hair pulled into a ponytail.

So they hadn't been figments of that dreamer's imagination. They were real, the boy *had* asked Ash to meet them at the bar, and she had somehow found herself lured onto a trivia team.

Ash made her way over and sat across from the boy, who grinned at her like she was an old friend he hadn't seen in years. The attention made her shift uncomfortably in her chair. "All right. I'm here," she said. "Are you going to tell me what's happening?"

The boy bobbed his head. "We'll get to that. First, I'm TJ. This is Cat, my sister."

Ash glanced between them. With Cat's obsidian skin, she didn't look much like a sibling to TJ's Southeast Asian features. One or both of them had to be adopted. "Ashlin," she said. Then, as always, she quickly added, "But please call me Ash."

"Great to meet you, Ash!" TJ said. "I've never randomly met another dreamwalker in the wild like that. Not often someone appears in the same dream."

"What he means is, 'what were you doing there?'" Cat said, her voice as chilly as her stare. She was probably an unwilling participant in this meeting, dragged to the bar by her brother. "We were supposed to be there. *Paid* to be there. Don't you know dreamwalking without cause is against Committee standards?"

Ash stared at her, wondering if pretending like she understood any of what the girl had said would benefit her at all. Unfortunately, she was a terrible liar, and even she knew that. "Sorry, what Committee would that be?"

TJ cocked his head. "The D.O.C.? Dreamwalker Oversight Committee?"

"Clearly she doesn't know anything," Cat said. "You were in that dream by accident, weren't you?"

Ash folded her arms over her chest, shoulders curled forward in some strange cross between defensive and wanting to shrink. She didn't like Cat's accusatory tone and felt compelled to apologize, but she bit back the "I'm sorry" and nodded.

TJ's eyes widened in amazement while Cat scowled. "No one ever taught you?" TJ said.

"No one could have taught me!" Ash snapped. She didn't mean to, and TJ's hurt expression made her regret it immediately. "I don't know anyone else who can do this. I don't even know what *this* is. It only started last year."

The others exchanged a glance, even Cat's annoyance replaced by bewilderment. They continued to watch each other, and Ash had the fascinating experience of witnessing a silent conversation. TJ's eyes turned pleading. Cat's scowl returned. She shook her head, and TJ's puppy-dog eyes intensified. Finally, Cat made a sound that must have been concession, because TJ's face brightened once more.

"You're a dreamwalker, like us," he said to Ash. "It runs in families. At least one of your parents is one too, and they should have taught you when your powers started showing, which is usually around eight or nine. Weird that yours didn't show up until now. And that no one ever told you. Are you an orphan?"

"My parents both died when I was little," Ash said quietly. "I was raised by my uncle, on my dad's side. I guess he didn't know." If she had inherited this *power* from a parent, Ash thought, it had to be her mom. She was certain her uncle would have told her about dreamwalking if he'd known the power ran in their family.

"I'm sorry," TJ said, with the depth that only someone who had shared a similar loss could muster. Not pity or sympathy, but true understanding. "But at least you have us now! We can teach you, so you don't end up in any more dreams unintentionally. Wouldn't want you getting in trouble with the Committee, now would we?"

"What exactly is this Committee?" Ash asked.

Before he could answer, a waitress showed up at the table to take any orders. For a second, Ash had forgotten they were even in a bar, despite the flurry of activity around them. She decided one drink would be safe, something to calm her nerves. Cat passed on the alcohol, ordering a soda instead, while TJ asked for some cocktail Ash had never heard of.

"Can I see your IDs?" The question was for both TJ and Ash, but the waitress looked straight at TJ when she said it. She checked Ash's ID first, then TJ's, her eyes lingering on his face before she handed it back to him. TJ kept his gaze trained on the table the entire time. The curse of having youthful features. Ash wondered how often people assumed he was underage.

"They make sure dreamwalkers don't misuse their abilities," Cat said as soon as the waitress left. "You need a license to do what we do. The Committee keeps tabs on people who use their powers on a regular basis."

"And... what exactly do you do?"

"We're dream therapists!" TJ said with no small amount of pride. "People come to us to help them with their nightmares. I mean, Dad's the real therapist, but we can enter dreams and dispel nightmares in the meantime."

Dream therapists, Ash thought. *Only in LA.* Out loud, she said, "Do people know what you can do? Actually... enter their dreams like that?" She would have thought this conversation would feel more surreal, but she rolled with it like she'd expected every word.

"Some do," TJ answered. "Those who actually believe. We tell people what we're doing, but some don't want to accept it, and that's okay. They still let us help them."

Ash thought back to her first day at Crystal Caverns and her skepticism toward horoscopes and healing crystals. She could understand why someone desperate enough might go to a person who offered such New Age-sounding solutions, even if that someone didn't believe.

Ash wanted to ask a dozen more questions, but a voice over the intercom interrupted.

"All right, trivia folks, we're going to get started." The guy went over the obvious rules—no looking answers up on the internet, no phoning a friend for help. Basically, no cellphones. Then he touched on some more rules specific to their set-up.

"So... I'm not actually any good at trivia." Ash somehow felt like she was confessing her biggest secret. Ironic, considering these people already knew her biggest secret.

"That's okay. You don't have to be," Cat replied. When the first question popped up, TJ patted his hand against her forearm rapidly in excitement, but she didn't spare the TV a single glance.

In the 17th century, the bulb of this flower got so valuable that it was sometimes used as a type of currency.

Ash hadn't even finished reading the question when he wrote out an answer in tiny, block-like letters. She barely had a chance to glimpse the word "tulip" before he sprang out of his seat and brought his answer to the trivia host.

While he did, Ash leaned over the table so she could talk quietly but still be heard. "Can I ask you a kind of personal question?"

Cat raised an eyebrow. "Sure. No guarantee I'll answer."

"How old is TJ?"

"Twenty-four," she said. "He gets that a lot."

"Gets what a lot?" TJ said as he slid back into his seat.

"Nothing," Cat and Ash said together.

Ash studied him while his attention thankfully remained on the screen, awaiting the next question. He really didn't look twenty-four, but he wouldn't be the first person not to look their age.

Regardless of age, his brain was clearly stuffed with information. The second question fell into the science category. "This moon of Jupiter is the most volcanically active world in our solar system," the host read for them aloud.

TJ wrote down two letters—Io—without hesitation. When the next question appeared, he scrawled an answer just as fast and was off again like a squirrel up a tree.

It went on like that. All talk of dreamwalking ceased. Ash knew a few answers, but TJ always wrote them down before she even had a chance to voice them. He would absolutely have *destroyed* any game show he managed to find himself on.

Sometimes he would elaborate on answers to Cat and Ash. After a question about Tycho Brahe, he eagerly informed them that the astronomer had lost his nose in a duel after getting into an argument with his cousin about who was the better mathematician. He had also died because he held his pee too long, refusing to breach etiquette at a banquet, which sounded like an unfortunate way to be remembered.

After the final question and a break to add up points, the trivia host announced third and second places. "And first place goes to... the Dreamcatchers," he said, in a tone that told Ash it wasn't the first time. "The top three teams can come up to collect their prizes. Everyone else, thanks for playing and have a good Tright."

TJ went to retrieve their prize, which turned out to be a $30 gift card for the bar. He wagged it at them with a big grin on his face. When they got their check, he put an identical gift card on the table to pay for their drinks, along with a couple bills to cover the extra. Ash pitched in for the tip, despite protests from TJ.

They shuffled out with the rest of the crowd, then stood awkwardly in the parking lot for a few seconds. Ash wasn't sure what to say to them. A friend she would have hugged goodbye, but these two weren't friends. A handshake would have been terrible. A thank you might have been in order, but TJ spoke before Ash could find the words.

"You should come over. We can start teaching you how to control it."

"Tonight?" Ash said, sounding more alarmed than she meant to.

"Sure, why not?"

"I can't. I need to get some sleep." Because she hadn't the last three nights, most recently because of anxiety over meeting these two rather than being dragged into someone's nightmare.

TJ looked disappointed, but he nodded. "Another time, then."

They exchanged numbers while Cat watched Ash like a parent trying to figure out if her kid's new friend was trustworthy. After an awkward goodbye, Ash headed home. Her head still spun with words like *dreamwalkers* and *Oversight Committee*, along with persistent worry about whether she should have used the restroom before leaving, thanks to the knowledge that someone had died because they'd waited too long to relieve themselves.

———

The lights were on when Ash got home. After a stop in the restroom, she found her uncle in the kitchen, sitting on the counter with his legs dangling a few inches above the floor. He had a quart of mint chip ice cream in his hands and was eating directly from it with a spoon.

"I wasn't expecting you to be here when I got home," she said.

"I wasn't expecting you to be gone." He tilted the carton toward her and held up a clean spoon. "Ice cream? I'm skipping dinner and getting straight to the pint."

"That's a quart, not a pint, you weirdo." Ash took the spoon and hopped on the counter beside him. She dug out a massive spoonful and bit a chocolate chip from the middle. "Rough day?"

"You could say that." He looked tired, and not only physically. A deep emotional exhaustion dragged at his shoulders.

She frowned at him. She couldn't remember the last time she had seen him look like that. "Did something happen with one of your kids?"

He forced out a smile that didn't reach his eyes and bumped his shoulder against hers. "Nothing you need to worry about. It's my job to worry about you, not the other way around."

"I'm not twelve anymore." Ash licked the rest of the ice cream off her spoon and went in for another bite.

Tiernan huffed. "Don't I know it. Things were easier when I didn't have to worry about you walking to work or behind the wheel of a car."

"Hey, I'm an excellent driver!"

"Ash," he said flatly. "Let's not tell lies."

She rolled her eyes. She had only gotten into an accident *that one time*, but she still couldn't refute him. She'd had more than a few close calls. "Yeah, well, at least I don't eat ice cream out of the carton like a heathen."

He raised an eyebrow. "No?"

"This doesn't count. You're a bad influence."

He plucked her spoon out of her hand when she reached for another spoonful. "That's it. No more ice cream for you."

"Hey!" Ash made a grab for the spoon, but he pulled it out of her reach, so she took the whole carton instead. She jumped off the counter and stuck her tongue out at him like she really was twelve again.

"Okay, okay!" he said. "I surrender. Just give me the ice cream back." He offered her spoon in trade. Ash took it, but she set it down on the counter. She needed to get some sleep, and a sugar high wouldn't do her any favors.

He only took a few more bites himself before setting the ice cream aside. "Did you at least stop by Capture It?"

"Shoot," Ash murmured. "No, I forgot."

"Ash. It's on your way home. That's three days now."

"I know, I know! I'll do it this week." It was possible her "forgetting" had an intentional component. As much as she wanted that job, she was worried they wouldn't want her, and she didn't think she could take the rejection at the moment.

"So, what *did* you do tonight that had you out so late?"

"I went to trivia with some new friends."

"Ash, that's great! When do I get to meet them?"

"Never. You'll just embarrass me."

Tiernan put a hand over his heart, a mock look of shock and hurt on his face. "I would never! I'm the cool uncle."

"Keep telling yourself that." She stood up on her toes so she could kiss him on the cheek. "I need to go pass out now. Love you, 'cool uncle.'"

"Love you, goblin. May you dream of wonderful things."

Ash only hoped that her dreams stayed her own. All she wanted was a full night's sleep, undisturbed.

Chapter 4

T HE NEXT DAY AFTER work, Ash still didn't go to Capture It. Instead, she followed the address the siblings had given her to an office building in midtown. TJ waited for her outside and gave a cheerful wave when she got out of her car.

"Where are we?" she asked after joining him outside the door.

He opened it for her and gestured her inside. "Our office. Our dad's office technically, I guess. We do work here, though. Anyway, he won't be here tonight. We're just helping one of our clients sleep."

Once inside, he darted past her to lead the way up a flight of stairs while Ash followed slowly, looking around with no small measure of awe. The place was *nice*, all sleek shades of gray, with a shiny directory on one wall by the elevators. Individual businesses were listed next to room numbers, except for the 2nd floor. Only one entry sat beneath the heading: Dr. Robert Knight, Dream Therapist.

"Coming?" TJ called from the top of the stairs, practically bouncing on the balls of his feet.

"Yeah, sorry." Ash started up the stairs, her hand sliding along the smooth handrail. She wondered what it must be like to work in a place like this. It felt so... *official.*

The wall that faced the stairs had a plaque that said "Dream Therapy" in big block letters. Beneath it were the words "Reception" and "Sleep Lab" with arrows pointing in opposite directions. TJ turned down the hallway toward the sleep lab. They entered Room 204, which opened into a lobby that reminded Ash of a doctor's waiting room.

"Come on, this way!" TJ hurried her along, not giving her time to take in the space. He ushered her into another hallway lined with several closed doors. He headed straight for the only open one.

Cat looked up when they entered. She sat at a desk that faced a wall lined with screens, like in a security room. Each screen showed small rooms that looked nearly identical, aside from the subtly varied comforters on the twin-sized beds.

TJ plopped himself down on one of the two unoccupied rolling chairs beside Cat, who glanced at the watch on her wrist. "You're late," she said, sounding like a disapproving teacher rather than a girl who couldn't be much older than Ash. Then again, Ash had thought TJ might still be in high school, so it was hard to say.

"Sorry. I underestimated traffic," Ash said. She meant to sound genuine, but Cat's tone put her on the defensive, and the words came out sharper than she'd intended.

"Dad always says in LA you should *over*estimate traffic," TJ said. "That way you'll be on time."

"Worst-case scenario, you're early," Cat finished. "Sit down. We have some things to go over before our client gets here."

"Wait, am I supposed to go into the dreams of one of your clients?" Ash asked. "Isn't that... intrusive?"

"She won't mind," Cat said. "We have permission to bring you with us."

"Why can't we use one of your dreams?" Ash asked.

"Because we can't," Cat said flatly, with a finality that left no room for argument. She looked pointedly at the third chair.

TJ pushed it toward Ash, so she took a seat. "Top three rules of dreamwalking: one, don't enter someone's dream without permission or a special license from the Oversight Committee."

Ash didn't know what reason someone might get a license to invade people's privacy like that, but she nodded.

"Two," Cat went on, "don't get stuck. Get out before the dreamer wakes up. Sometimes their waking will break the connection, and you'll simply wake up too, but not always. And don't let either body get moved while you're in the dream. The distance makes it harder to get back to your own body, and you can get trapped in the dreamer's mind."

"Your body will end up in a coma, your mind stuck somewhere else," TJ said. "It happened to Cat's grandma once."

Cat rolled her eyes. "Yeah, it did. My parents loved to tell me about that like a creepy fairytale you tell your kids so they behave. They needn't have bothered."

"Tell her the story, Cat!" He sounded like a kid asking for a bedtime story he had heard a hundred times.

Cat pursed her lips, but once again she was powerless against his pleading eyes. "She was just a kid, still learning to control it, and accidentally fell into someone's dream. Luckily, she lived in a small town, and nearly everyone came to the hospital to give their condolences to the family whose daughter had fallen into a coma. The moment the man came into the room, she was yanked back into her body. She said the whole day was surreal, trapped in someone's head while they were awake. Said it was like viewing the world through their eyes, feeling everything they did while privy to their every thought, but she couldn't do anything."

"A prisoner in someone else's body," TJ said.

"The bottom line is don't get stuck. You have no guarantee the person will re-encounter your comatose body."

Ash let that unnerving thought settle in. She could imagine all too easily what it might be like, how powerless one would feel. "And what's the third rule?" she asked.

"The obvious one," Cat said. "Don't die. Your mind will be severed from your body, and that's a coma you'll never wake up from."

Ash had always assumed that, but the confirmation left her feeling cold. All the times she had been seconds away from really dying came rushing back.

TJ clapped his hands together, loud enough that it made Ash jump. "Alright! Now that the boring part is out of the way, you ready to try it?"

Ash rubbed her arm. After hearing all the ways dreamwalking could go wrong, she was very not ready to try it, but she had come to the siblings for a reason. She had to learn to control it so those bad things didn't happen to her. Existing as a prisoner in someone else's mind was a terrible fate. Ash didn't know which was worse, that or dying. Reluctantly, she nodded in confirmation.

A moment later, a ding like a doorbell ringing sounded in the small observation room. "That'll be our client," Cat said with another glance at her watch. "Right on time. At least *someone* knows how to be punctual." Ash glared at her back as Cat left the room.

"Don't mind her," TJ said. "She's not so scary, once you get to know her."

"If you say so." Ash scratched at her forearm, trying to be subtle about it, but TJ noticed anyway.

"You okay there?" he asked.

"Fine. I'm just allergic to cats." She waited for him to smile first before cracking a grin at her own joke. "I guess I'm nervous."

"Hey, don't be nervous. We're here to help. Okay?"

Ash nodded and leaned back in the surprisingly comfortable chair. "So this is what you do? Just... watch people sleep?"

"Pretty much. And help them if needed. Normally we only go in when they're having a nightmare, but hopefully we'll get at least an hour of peace so you can practice without the added danger."

Ash didn't miss the use of the word "hopefully." She thought back to the last nightmare she had found herself in, seconds away from being crushed by hippos. She still didn't know how she and the dreamer had gotten out of it and assumed instinct and adrenaline had kicked in to let her change the dream.

She frowned at TJ. "You said distance makes it harder to get out of someone's mind, right?"

He nodded. "Harder to get in, too. The closer you are, the easier it is."

"Then why were you in that guy's dream? The one where you met me. There's no way I ended up getting pulled all the way here."

TJ grinned at her. "Good! You're asking the right questions. Not everyone comes here to sleep. Sometimes we make house calls, so to speak. That patient lives pretty far south of here. Must have been close enough to you, the nightmare strong enough to drag you in. Nightmares are like that. It's like the dreamer is crying out for help, and any dreamwalker nearby can get ensnared."

"But I can learn to prevent that, right?"

"Sure. At the very least, you can learn to get back out right away."

Ash wrapped her arms around herself and looked at the screens in time to see Cat and another young woman step into one of the rooms. They exchanged words that Ash couldn't hear, then Cat hooked the woman up to a machine to monitor brainwaves.

"Hey, TJ?" Ash asked quietly.

"Hmm?"

"Why are you doing this? Helping me."

TJ glanced away from the screen. "Do I need a reason?"

"Everyone needs a reason."

He held her gaze for a moment before he shrugged. "Okay. We don't want you to die or get in trouble because you dreamwalked where you shouldn't. You're one of us. We want to make sure you're safe."

"Safe," Ash murmured. She would like that, to feel safe again.

In the other room, Cat handed over a small pill and a glass of water, then turned the lights off and left the patient to settle down as much as anyone could with wires suctioned to their forehead.

"What did you give her?" Ash asked once Cat had rejoined them in the observation room.

"Something to help her sleep," Cat said. "And keep her asleep. We don't want her waking up while we're in there."

"It also makes the dreamer more receptive to us changing their dreams," TJ added. "Dad developed it."

"Non-dreamwalkers are usually pretty easy anyway, but yeah, it does help."

"It's harder to change a dreamwalker's own dreams?" Ash asked.

"They're usually more aware of what's happening and can fight you on it," Cat said. "Whether they mean to or not. Overall, their minds are less suggestible than normal people's when they sleep."

Ash nodded and looked back at the monitor. The patient had situated herself in the bed and closed her eyes. A jagged line sketched out her brainwaves along the bottom of the screen, but the frequency decreased as she relaxed and fell into a light sleep. There was something hypnotizing about watching that line move up and down, and soon Ash found herself drifting off as well.

She startled when an elbow nudged her arm. TJ nodded toward the monitor but didn't say anything, which Ash was thankful for. Cat probably would have given her grief about her falling asleep before the patient did. Cat hadn't noticed, however. She watched the screen intently, waiting for a change in the brainwaves that would indicate the right stage of sleep.

"It's been almost an hour," Cat said. "We should be getting close."

"Close to what?" Ash said.

"REM sleep," TJ replied. "Rapid Eye Movement. That's when the most vivid dreams happen. It's not the *only* stage where dreams occur, which is a common misconception, but dreams that happen during N-REM are rarer and usually less intense. Brain activity is higher during REM, so it's much easier for us to craft a dream."

Cat gave him a flat look. "Are you done?"

"Fun fact: somnambulism, more commonly known as sleep-walking, actually happens during N3, the deepest stage of sleep. People used to think sleepwalkers were acting out their dreams, but it's been found that people aren't dreaming when they sleep-walk."

"TJ," Cat said.

"It's still not really known exactly what causes—"

"*TJ.* That's enough."

"But it's interesting!" TJ said.

"She's hit REM. Time to go."

Cat ignored TJ's pout and gestured Ash toward the cots in the back of the room. "Time to see if you can do it on purpose, without getting dragged in by a nightmare. You should be able to reach out with your mind. Find hers and make a connection."

Ash sat down on one of the cots. The beds in the patient rooms looked a lot more comfortable. "What do you mean *find* hers?"

"You'll know it when you feel it," TJ said. He flopped down on a second cot and pulled a blanket over himself, snuggling down with a smile on his face. He dragged the blanket up to his chin and closed his eyes. "See you in there."

Cat gave her head a small shake and claimed the remaining cot. She didn't bother with a blanket. "It's different for everyone. But like TJ said, you'll know it when you feel it." After a pause, she added, "Good luck."

Ash settled down and reached for the blanket at the foot of the cot. The thin mattress was about as comfortable as it looked, but the weight of the blanket helped. She tried to relax and reach out with her mind, but whatever she was supposed to be searching for she didn't find. Instead, the steady sound of breathing from the other two lulled her to sleep.

She woke, groggy and disoriented, to someone shaking her shoulder. She opened her eyes and found Cat scowling down at her. Ash sat up but shied away from Cat's irritation, which radiated from her like heat from a fire. Ash was certain if she got too close, she would get burned.

"You were supposed to enter her dreams, not fall asleep yourself," Cat said.

"Leave her alone, Cat. It was her first try," TJ said.

"I'm not convinced she actually tried. This isn't preschool nap time." Cat stepped back and looked at the monitor. "She's in

N2 now. We'll have to wait for the next REM cycle. Hope your little nap was worth it."

"Maybe if you told me more than 'you'll know it when you feel it' I'd have a little more success!" Ash took a deep breath and exhaled her anger, the way her uncle had taught her. "You really can't give me anything else?"

Cat shrugged. "It's different for everyone, but if you're falling into people's dreams by accident, this *should* be easy."

"Don't overthink it," TJ offered. "Dreamwalking is instinctual for people like us. Maybe you're trying too hard."

Ash pulled her knees up to her chest and tried to figure out how not to overthink something. Her efforts only made it worse, though. She focused on her breathing instead, trying to clear her mind rather than stressing.

Not stressing was about as easy as not overthinking.

She felt similar to how she had the last time she'd been fired, even though this wasn't her job. Failure felt the same regardless.

She remained on the cot while they waited through the next N3 stage, which took nearly an hour. Ash's next try didn't go much better. Or the next one. The hours ticked by, and Ash only got more and more exhausted, which made it easier and easier for her to fall asleep. A few times she found herself dreaming and hoped she had somehow managed to dreamwalk accidentally, but she quickly realized she was in her own dreams, not the patient's.

She would have preferred to stay there and get some real sleep, instead of waking up to Cat's judgmental stare, but at least she felt less out of it when TJ woke her. Like before, Ash found Cat peering down at her through narrowed eyes, but now she looked more curious than angry.

"Were you dreaming?" Cat asked.

Ash blinked at her, struggling to keep her eyes open. She wanted to go back to sleep. "Yeah. Why?"

"Because you were only asleep for like five minutes, which means you were dreaming in N1. Is that normal for you?"

Ash glanced at TJ, a plea for help, but he remained silent. "I have no idea," she said. "How did you even know I was dreaming?"

"I felt your mind and tried to go in so I could pull you over to her dreams. Maybe getting back out would be a better place to start."

"You can do that? Take people between dreams?"

"She's the only person I know who can," TJ said proudly. "Pretty cool, right?" Cat didn't seem the type to brag, so apparently TJ did it for her.

Cat ignored his praise. "That's the other weird thing, though. I couldn't do it. I couldn't even get into your head. I could feel your dreams, but it was like walking into a wall when I tried to enter. Like something was blocking me."

Ash waited for her to go on, but Cat only stared intently. So did TJ. Ash was starting to feel like a science experiment again.

She shifted on the cot, wishing for a way to get out from under their stares. "So what does that mean?"

"I don't know. I've never had that problem before."

Great, Ash thought. *Now I'm broken in two ways.*

"It's not a bad thing, necessarily," TJ said, as if reading her thoughts. He didn't have to, though. The dismay was all over her face. "A lot of dreamwalkers would love to be able to keep others out of their head."

"Well right now it's preventing us from helping you," Cat said. Some of her irritation might have been directed at herself for failing. "We're done for the night. If you're going to keep falling asleep, this is pointless."

"But we'll try again tomorrow?" Ash asked. She needed this. She needed a good night's sleep without worrying about falling into someone's dream or dying the next time she got stuck in a nightmare.

"Yeah," Cat said. "And the day after. I have a feeling it's going to take you a *long* time."

Chapter 5

"**F**ALLING ASLEEP ON THE job your first week?"

Ash's head snapped up and she blinked at the woman in front of her. It took her a moment to remember where she was: at the shop, supposed to be working. But the week had been full of sleepless nights, and Ash was more tired than she had ever been in her life. The sleep deprivation had her dead on her feet, barely able to focus enough to count change.

Trish stared down at her disapprovingly. Ash had never seen that look on her boss's face before, and it didn't fit quite right. Trish was all kind smiles and genuine laughter, flapping of hands when she got talking. She could chat endlessly with customers, a mystical skill that Ash would never comprehend.

"I'm sorry," Ash said quickly. She rubbed her eyes and realized with surprise that the exhaustion had faded. She wondered if it were possible the tiny nap had actually helped.

"Sorry doesn't excuse it," Trish said. "There's always something to do around here. You can sleep when you get home."

Can I? Ash thought. She worked with TJ and Cat most nights, but she still hadn't been able to enter a dream intentionally. The only time she ended up in a dream during their sessions at the clinic, it was because a nightmare had sucked her in. That hadn't been a fun time. The man's mind had been a tangle of fears, unnerving in an untraditional way. Ash had seen things she never wanted to see again.

Ash clearly took too long to answer, because Trish put her hands on her hips and gave a withering stare. "Three strikes, Ashlin O'Shea. That's all you get." Then she shoved a broom into Ash's hands.

Somewhere nearby, hidden behind a rack of knit shawls, Des snickered.

Ash stepped out from behind the counter and started sweeping while Trish stood nearby and watched like a gargoyle. Every swish of the broom seemed to pick up nothing but air, making the task feel entirely pointless. Des had probably already swept that morning, judging from the lack of dirt on the floor.

This is all wrong, Ash thought. Trish wouldn't look at her like that. Des wouldn't laugh at her humiliation. The two had shown her nothing but kindness, even though Ash felt horribly out of place.

She let the broom fall from her hands, and it clattered to the tiled floor. "What do you think you're doing?" Trish demanded. Ash ignored her. She closed her eyes, imagining another scenario, another place far away from the shop and the worries that plagued her. When she opened them again, her surroundings had changed.

She stood in her favorite place, a stretch of tall cliff overlooking the Pacific Ocean. It wasn't a stretch of real coastline, more a combination of areas she had visited with her uncle, now mashed together in her imagination. The bottom of the setting sun barely brushed the horizon, scattering color over the ridges of wind-sculpted clouds. Oranges and reds reflected in the rolling waves below.

Tall grass tickled her bare ankles. The breeze carried the crisp, salty scent of the ocean. Ash inhaled deeply and closed her eyes, letting her racing heart settle. She listened to the crash of the waves and the cries of ocean birds in the distance, the rustle of grass in the wind.

"It's nice," said a voice behind her. Not entirely familiar, one she had heard only in dreams, but with traces of a voice she knew very well.

Ash stiffened. *No, no. Not again,* she thought. She kept her eyes squeezed shut, as if he might go away if she didn't look at him. She knew this dream. She didn't want to live it again. But when she tried to send him away or bring herself to another place, nothing happened. The fear that had brought him there was too strong. Sometimes nightmares latched onto the mind and refused to let go.

He stepped up beside her, not quite touching but his presence close enough to feel. She prayed for him to vanish, for this to go back to a pleasant, soothing dream. When nothing changed, she pried open her eyes.

His head was wreathed in shifting shadows, obscuring a face that—like the voice—would have been both familiar and different. She could only see the profile of a strong nose, the hint of sharp cheekbones and a pointed chin.

"You are lost to me," she murmured. "Why won't you leave me alone?"

"Why didn't you leave me alone?" he said. "Some things are meant to be private."

"It's not what you think!" She screamed the words she had said a dozen times in person, a hundred times in her dreams. They never made any difference, not in real life and certainly not here.

"What is it, then?" he asked. "Explain it."

"I can't! Why can't you just trust me?"

"Because you broke that trust!"

The wind picked up around them, a gentle breeze transforming into an angry gale, the kind that ripped trees up from their roots. Lightning split the sky, accompanied by a crack of thunder that rattled Ash's bones. The storm leeched away the warm colors of the sunset, replacing it with ominous black clouds. Ash shivered when the temperature dropped. It was like stepping from a warm summer day into a freezer.

"You broke us, Ash." He took a step toward her, and she instinctively backed away. "You lied to me." They walked the line of the cliff, him advancing like the oncoming storm. The air crackled around him, and a jagged bolt of lightning shot out to strike Ash on the arm. She cried out and pressed a hand over her stinging skin.

"I never lied!" She had kept secrets, though. Secrets break relationships, no matter the reason for keeping them, no matter how good that reason is. In the end, secrets tear at the foundation, eating away until the whole building comes toppling down.

The storm broke then, blanketing them in rain so thick that a dam may as well have opened overhead. Ash could hardly see through the downpour. Water flooded her eyes, and no amount of blinking could clear it away. Just like no amount of pleading could erase the damage she had done.

A gust of wind lifted Ash from the ground. It swirled around her, pulling her out toward the ocean and holding her aloft for a few weightless seconds. Then it dropped her.

Ash flung out an arm and caught the edge of the cliff, her fingertips curled desperately around a rock that jutted from the earth. But the rain still came in sheets, slickening the stone beneath her fingers and softening the ground that held it in place. Eventually, one or the other would slip free. He stared down at her, a dark figure shrouded by shadows and endless rain.

"Help me, please." She choked on the last word, water flooding her mouth. The rain tasted salty, like the ocean poured from the dark clouds. Or maybe the sky was crying.

He leaned forward, like he might actually reach down and grab her, but then he straightened again and took a step back. "You're on your own." He turned away and vanished into the storm.

Ash lowered her face from the rain. Her skin felt raw from the barrage of cold saltwater. It should have gone numb long ago, but instead it felt like she had rubbed her cheeks on sandpaper. Her free hand ran along the top of the cliff, grasping for something else to hold onto so she could pull herself up, but she found only drenched grass that ripped away in useless clumps.

She knew she should let go. It was only a dream. She would fall into the roiling waves below and wake up safe in her bed, panting and drenched in sweat but alive.

Instinct chased away logic. Her every sense told her she was about to die, so she clung to that one rock, unwilling to surrender even though she could feel her fingers weakening. The rock shifted in the loosening earth, then came free completely.

Water rushed down Ash's throat when she made the mistake of screaming. She started to drop, but then a hand caught her wrist, halting her fall.

"Hold on tight."

Chapter 6

ASH'S FINGERS CURLED AROUND my wrist, clinging to it for dear life. I tried to haul her up and over the edge of the cliff, but some force prevented me from doing so, no matter how hard I pulled. The gravity of her own fear dragged her down.

"Focus, Ash!" I shouted. The storm still whipped around us, the gale threatening to send me tumbling over the cliff along with her. "The worse the nightmare, the harder it is to change. But you can do it if you *focus*."

She shook her head, staring at me in confusion, and I realized my presence was more distracting than helpful. Maybe I should have let her die and approached her another time. We wouldn't get anywhere with the nightmare raging around us.

"This is just a dream," I tried again. "Clear your mind. You're in control."

"I'm in control," she repeated, quietly enough that the wind almost stole the words. The confusion slid away, replaced by hard determination. The storm started to settle, the wind dying back down to a gentle breeze.

I let out a breath and smiled at her. Then I let her go.

Her eyes widened in shock. She dropped toward the water, but that brief panic at the start of the free-fall faded into calm. She twisted her body so she faced downward, and wings the color of the ocean froth sprang from her back. They caught the air, bringing her soaring upward before she even came close to the water.

She flapped her wings once, twice, to bring her higher. The light-weight scarf draped around my neck fluttered in the breeze while I watched her bank and return to where I waited. She landed a safe distance from the edge, but a safe distance from me as well.

"Well done. What you just did isn't easy." I knew what it was like to have nightmares run away from you. It was hard for people like us, so used to being in control, to have that control wrenched away by fear and self-loathing.

Her breath still came in quick, unsteady pants. She watched me like I was an enigma given solid form. I stared back at her calmly while her breathing returned to normal. The long silence started to get to me, but I held my tongue. My father would have been so proud.

"Who are you?" she said finally. "Are you real?"

"You mean am I more than a handsome fantasy conjured by your imagination?" I flashed a smile. "Yes, I'm real."

She didn't laugh, which I found rude, but also understandable considering the circumstances. Her mind was still reeling from the nightmare, and now a strange man stood in front of her. It was a lot to take in.

"You're a dreamwalker. Like TJ and Cat," she said.

"Like you." Of course she didn't include herself in that. She was still getting used to the idea. "I'm a friend. I come with a warning... and a plea."

She continued to eye me warily but said, "I'm listening."

"A great danger to all dreamwalkers is stirring."

The wonderfully cryptic message annoyed the hell out of her, which only made me grin. She scowled, but her lips twitched like she was trying to hold back a smile of her own. I had that effect on people.

She struggled for a second but managed to keep her lips firmly in a flat, unyielding line. "Can you elaborate on that?"

"Eight years ago, the Committee created a prison to hold a very powerful dreamwalker," I said. "That prison is weakening. You have to find it. If he escapes, no one on the Committee will be safe."

"The Committee specifically?"

"He holds a very strong grudge against them. He tried to destroy them once, but they beat him and crafted a prison that would prevent him from ever coming after them, not even in their dreams. Or so they thought."

"Enough about this prisoner," Ash said. "I want to know who *you* are."

I didn't answer right away. How much could I tell her? Enough to get her to trust me. If I said too much, she would only have more questions. In the end, all I said was, "Someone who got caught up in it all."

"And why can't you tell me this in person?"

"This was the only way to reach you."

"Ever heard of a phone?"

My lips twitched. "This is better. Face to face, even if I can't come to you in the waking world."

"So you're far away? I thought dreamwalking didn't work over long distances."

"It usually doesn't."

She waited several seconds for me to explain, but eventually she realized I wasn't going to and gave me an exasperated look. "Fine. How about why you're telling *me* this. Surely there's someone better suited. Like, I don't know, maybe one of the people who created this prison."

Instead of answering, I turned and stepped up to the edge of the cliff. Now that the nightmare had ended, the ocean had turned into a vibrant blue expanse that stretched out until it touched the pink horizon. I watched the white waves crash against the sheer rock far below for a few seconds before turning back to her. "Ashlin," I said. "It means 'dreamer.' Did you know that? Your parents were a bit on the nose."

She glared at me. "Why me?" she said again.

"You're the only person who can do this. The Committee... they wouldn't listen to me. I couldn't reach them even if I wanted to. It *has* to be you." The dream shimmered like air above desert sand distorted by heat waves. "You're waking up," I said softly. I had to be fast. "One more thing. You can't tell anyone except TJ and Cat about me. Understand?"

Ash frowned. "Why not?"

"Understand?"

Reluctantly, she nodded.

"Until next time, dreamer. I'll be in touch."

Chapter 7

"**A**RE YOU OKAY?"

Ash lifted her head, for *real* this time, or at least she hoped it was. Des stood over her, looking down with worried blue eyes rather than the disapproval she had seen on Dream Trish's face.

"Don't take this the wrong way, but you look like trash," he said.

She mustered a weak smile. "I feel like trash." She ran her hand over her forehead, brushing aside the curls that had come loose from her bun. It wasn't too bad, a few stray strands. "Sorry. I haven't gotten much sleep lately."

"Bad dreams?"

"Something like that." Ash rubbed her eyes and tried to shake off the drowsiness. The dream lingered. Not the nightmares, but what came after. The man who wouldn't give his name. The story about a weakening prison. *Was it real?* she thought. She supposed it was better for the world if some dangerous dreamwalker weren't about to escape his special prison, but a part of her wanted it to be real.

She wanted *him* to be real.

Now that she knew other people could enter dreams the same way she entered theirs, Ash thought she could spot the intruders. He'd had that same innate sense of *not belonging*.

Furthermore, Ash had this weird feeling she couldn't shake, that she had seen him before.

"You should go home and get some sleep," Des said, bringing her back to the waking world.

She blinked at him. "Really?"

"You're useless like this," he said, doing his best impression of a stern tone. It was, as impressions go, mediocre. "Trish would tell you the same thing. Go on, get out of here."

Ash eyed him, still trying to spot the trick, but after working with the man for nearly a week, she had come to the conclusion he didn't have it in him to be so deceitful. "Thank you," she said, with as much gratitude as she could put behind those two words. "I'll make it up to you, I swear."

Des waved a hand. "You'd do the same for me, right?"

"Definitely," she said, a promise she fully intended to keep. As she stood, a pair of customers entered, accompanied by the tinkle of the bell. Ash snatched her purse from behind the counter and started toward the door.

"Hey, wait," Des said. She turned back to him slowly, afraid he would rescind his offer to let her leave, but instead he stepped around her and walked to the crystal display. Ash had taken a photograph of different crystals fanned out in a colorful array, and a blown-up version was now displayed above the rack. Des looked over the various crystals before plucking one out and handing it to her. She hesitantly took the chunk of white stone from him.

"White chalcedony," he said. "It wards off negative influences. It might help your nightmares." He quirked a smile at the skeptical look she couldn't keep off her face. "It can't hurt, right? On me."

She knew he was trying to help, even if she didn't believe in the power of the crystal in her hand. Even if it *did* work, she doubted it would ward off someone else's nightmares. If only he had a crystal that would magically make it so she could intentionally enter someone's dream—and get back out.

"Thanks," she said again. "The last thing I need is for Trish to fire me because I'm falling asleep at work."

"I don't think she'd fire you. Tiernan asked her to—" He broke off when her eyes narrowed. "Uh... I mean..."

"How do you know my uncle?"

Des blinked nervously and looked away. "I don't." He was even worse at lying than Ash.

She leaned closer, intentionally into his personal space. "How. Do. You. Know. Tiernan?"

"I don't *know* him, okay?" Des tugged at the gauge in his ear. "I saw him once, that's all. He came in, and I overheard him talking to Trish... about you."

She took a step back and stared past him blankly. "I got the job because of him, didn't I? He pulled a favor."

He was the one who had encouraged her to apply for it. A new age shop wasn't really her first choice. But he had insisted, so she had agreed, and the moment she walked in, Trish had acted like she'd already been planning to hire her.

Ash had thought she had made a great first impression, but clearly that wasn't the reason at all.

Some rational part of her, lurking in the back of her head, knew his intentions were good. He wanted her to succeed. But Ash wanted to succeed or fail on her own, not because her uncle pulled favors on her behalf. She wasn't a teenager anymore, and she didn't need his help getting a job.

It stung that he didn't seem to think so.

She quelled her anger, because none of it was at Des, and pressed her hand against the side of her aching head. "I... I need to go home. I'll talk to you later."

"Yeah. Okay. I'm really sorry." He looked so apologetic, his blue eyes wide and pleading, that Ash felt bad about prying it out of him.

"It's not your fault." The only mistake he'd made was letting it slip. Clearly he was bad at keeping secrets. "I'll see you tomorrow, Des." She tucked the stone in her pocket, then hurried past the customers before he could change his mind.

She should have gone home and gotten some sleep. Doing anything else felt like a betrayal of Des's kindness, but she knew she would only end up lying awake in bed with the mystery man's cryptic warning playing over and over in her head. Plus, she couldn't face her uncle yet. He was probably still at work himself, but she would rather focus on anything but that confrontation.

As much as she needed the rest, it would have to wait.

She pulled out her phone and texted Cat and TJ instead, doing her best to indicate the urgency of the matter without explaining what was wrong. TJ responded first: *We can talk at our apartment,* he wrote, followed by an address.

The apartment complex was only a few blocks away from the Studio, close enough to Crystal Caverns that Ash could walk, instead of trying to figure out public transportation. For once in her life, Ash felt a sense of urgency, the need to get to her destination as fast as possible. If only she felt it were so imperative to be on time for work or a class.

By the time Ash climbed the stairs up to the fourth-floor apartment, she was wishing they could have met at her house instead.

TJ answered the door and ushered Ash inside to where Cat waited in their cozy living room. A lot of furniture and decorations looked like they had been bought at a thrift shop, from the old corduroy couch to the frayed area rug. The coffee table had a few dings in the wood. TJ sat down beside Cat on the couch, leaving Ash to take the antique-looking rocking chair.

"What's so urgent?" Cat asked immediately. Straight down to business, as always.

Ash rocked back and forth slightly instead of answering right away. She had been mulling over what she would say to them the whole way over, and she *still* hadn't figured out the best way to broach the topic.

"This might sound crazy, but hear me out," she said. The siblings sat in silence, waiting, but it took Ash several seconds to find the courage to continue. "I had a dream today. This man showed up in it. I think he was real, another dreamwalker, and he had a message for me. For us."

Cat's face remained blank, but TJ looked curious. "What message?" he asked.

"He said eight years ago, a prison was created to hold a powerful dreamwalker," Ash said. "A man who posed a threat to the Committee. He said that prison is weakening and we have to find it before the man escapes."

TJ's eyes went wide, and even Cat's stoic expression cracked. She looked *afraid,* which scared Ash as much as any nightmare. Their reactions confirmed that the prison really existed. The truth of the warning, however, remained to be seen.

"You've heard of this before," Ash said. Not a question.

"He's talking about Griffin," TJ murmured.

Ash raised an eyebrow. "Is that a first or last name?"

TJ shrugged. "No one knows. Legend has it the Committee made a very special prison for him, like your dream man said. Nobody even knows where it is. The secret's been buried to prevent anyone from finding and freeing him."

"What exactly did he do that made everyone so terrified of him?"

"Killed people," Cat said. "They say he was so strong that no one could stand against him in a dream. Entering his own dreams was suicide. He could swat you like a fly."

"I heard that he's actually a foreign prince from a royal line of powerful dreamwalkers," TJ said.

Cat rolled her eyes. "A prince? Please. The story about him being raised by the mafia is more likely. *Regardless*, it doesn't matter where he came from. He was a dangerous person, and the Committee put him away for good."

"Or maybe not for good," Ash said. "If this man from my dreams is right."

"How do you know you can trust him?" Cat asked. "You don't even know who he is."

"I don't know. I just... I *do*." Ash didn't know how to explain why she trusted the stranger from her dream. "The really weird thing is I think I've seen him before. He looks familiar. Like the face of a person you haven't seen in years but you're *sure* you know them."

"What did he look like?"

Ash thought back, trying to remember. Even with her most vivid dreams, sometimes the details faded. She didn't think "he was handsome" would help them at all, so she dredged up other features. "Tall. White. Blue eyes. Wavy black hair." Thinking back made her face flush. Not so long ago, she would have assumed she had dreamed up such a face. High cheekbones, dark hair long enough to reveal the lazy waves. And those eyes... a deep blue the color of the ocean on a sunny day. He gave "man of her dreams" a new meaning.

"Is that all?" Cat said. "Could you be any more generic?"

"I don't know! He was clean shaven. And wearing a scarf. Not the kind for warmth but the thin fashionable kind."

TJ looked at Cat, his eyes shining with excitement now. "You don't think?"

"No, TJ." Cat's voice was hard, her jaw tense. "He's dead. Don't even go there."

"What?" Ash asked. She really wished she were privy to the thoughts these two shared. They seemed to communicate without *saying* anything far too often. "Who's dead?"

"None of your business," Cat snapped. "It's not important."

Ash thought it probably was important, based on the look on TJ's face, but she pressed her lips together and didn't push. Something about the way Cat talked left no room for argument.

"I say we trust him," TJ said.

"What if it's a trick?" Cat asked.

"What if it isn't?" Ash said. "If he's right and Griffin escapes, that's on us."

"We could at least talk to Dad, find out what he knows," TJ said. "He was already on the Committee when it happened. If he knows where the prison is, maybe he can check on it. See if Griffin really is in danger of breaking out."

"Your dad is on the Committee?" Ash asked. "When were you going to mention this?"

TJ shrugged. "I'm mentioning it now."

They both looked at Cat, who stood there with her arms crossed, looking like she was still searching for some argument. Finally, she groaned and dropped her arms back to her sides. "*Fine.* We'll talk to him. See what he says about all this."

"Oh, one more thing...." Ash said. "He asked me not to tell anyone but you about him."

Cat snorted. "Because *that's* not suspicious."

"Please, Cat."

"All right, we'll keep your new boyfriend a secret."

"He's not—"

"I would hope not, since you barely know him. He could be a serial killer for all you know."

Ash stood, suddenly wanting to get herself and her burning face out of that room as quickly as possible. "Great. We have a plan. We'll go tomorrow?"

"Probably best to wait until next week," TJ said uncertainly. "He's technically on vacation and won't like us barging in."

Ash wanted to argue that it had to be sooner, but she didn't think she could take one more skeptical remark from Cat right then. "Next week, then."

"He's back next Monday. You can stop by the office after you get off work?"

Ash gave a sharp nod and grabbed her purse, then fled the apartment and Cat's judgmental stare. She didn't want to wait until next week, but she didn't know how to convince them going now was worth it, not unless something changed. All she could do was hope she could find some peaceful nights in the coming week and stick to her own dreams.

Chapter 8

ASH'S DREAMS MIGHT HAVE remained her own that night, but a peaceful sleep wasn't in the cards.

Her subconscious conjured a dream that could have been any weekend morning at their house. The TV in the corner of the living room played the type of true crime documentary she often watched with her uncle, and Ash could hear the familiar sounds of Tiernan making breakfast in the kitchen. Bacon sizzled and filled the entire house with an aroma that made Ash's mouth water.

She smiled and settled back against the comfortable couch. The documentary was one she had seen before, but she only watched for a few seconds before her mind began to wander. Even in her sleep, she couldn't stop thinking about the prison, the warning, and the fact that she had to *wait* to find answers. Did TJ and Cat really expect her to sit tight for a full week? They clearly didn't know her very well.

Ash blinked when the sound from the TV cut off. The screen had frozen on the image of a half-finished basement where a kidnapper had kept his victims. It flickered a few times before the TV shut off.

Only then did she realize the kitchen had gone silent as well. Ash's skin prickled. She had enough experience with dreams to know when one started to veer toward nightmare territory.

"Tiernan?" she called, her voice thin. She summoned the clang of pans and the sizzle of bacon back to the dream, but when she made her way to the kitchen, the sounds lacked any source in the pristine, empty room. The stove was cold, even though Ash could still hear the spatter of grease and smell the bacon cooking.

Fear crawled up her spine, and her fingers curled around the door frame. It wasn't the eerie dream or the missing Tiernan that rattled her, though. Something was *wrong*. She recognized her own nightmares, whatever stressed her out during the day coming to haunt her at night, but something else was going on. She could *feel* it.

Someone was messing with the dream.

"Mystery guy?" she said to the silent house. "If this is you, it isn't funny."

When no answer came, she stepped around the kitchen island and pulled a knife from the block on the counter. She didn't know what she might need to defend herself against, but the knife made her feel safer.

The knife didn't do her any good when the house itself turned against her. A drawer nearby shot out of its own accord and slammed into her hip. She jumped away, only to collide with the corner of another open drawer. Silverware, whisks, and knives flew upward, like the ceiling had turned into a giant magnet. Ash narrowly avoided getting impaled by a fork that flipped through the air. The various kitchen objects hung suspended, a few inches shy of the ceiling, then clattered against counter tops and the tiled floor when the force that held the metal released.

Ash threw herself out of the rain of utensils and into the hallway. She started toward the stairs, but the floorboards shuddered and groaned. The sound of splintering wood echoed through the house. The floor dropped out from under her, and Ash plummeted into darkness.

A solitary light bulb flickered on overhead, casting a soft yellow glow over the basement Ash had found herself in. It was the same basement from the documentary, with pink insulation poking out from unfinished walls. A staircase with old wooden steps that looked like they might collapse beneath Ash's weight led upward to a closed door.

She picked herself up from the cold, concrete floor, relieved to find herself uninjured from the fall. "I know someone is doing this!" The walls seemed to swallow her voice, and when she spoke again, she sounded less confident. "Show yourself."

Only silence met her demand, so she started up the stairs. The third one gave way beneath her. She hurriedly rocked back to avoid falling through, her hand clutching the railing for balance. She let out a slow breath and carefully passed over the ruined step.

When she reached the door, she was unsurprised to find it locked. "This is still your dream," she said to herself. She had changed her nightmares before. She could change this one too.

The door gave a soft click when she rested her fingertips against the knob again.

She exited the basement, not to the house that belonged with it nor to her own home but to a vast field with no end in sight. She felt like she was standing in the middle of the ocean, only instead of water, she was surrounded by golden grass that rose to her hip. She waded forward, and when she turned around, the door had vanished.

Ash took steadying breaths to slow her heart rate. She was safe, she reminded herself. Whatever was happening, it couldn't hurt her in her own dreams.

She lost concentration when flames erupted all around her. Panic washed over her as the heat seared her arms and face, but there was nowhere to run to escape the fire. It blazed over the surface of the field, and Ash waited with her eyes squeezed shut for pain to consume her.

Instead, the heat vanished after a few seconds. Ash cautiously cracked open her eyes. The once beautiful sea of golden grass now bore the aftermath of the fire, entire sections of the field burned to ash. Patches remained untouched, though, the lines between grass and blackened ground too clean to be dismissed.

Ash turned in a slow circle, surveying the damage around her. She stood in the surviving grass at the middle of a burned ring, an identical one beside her. It wasn't until she lifted herself into the air that she could read the words scorched into the field.

STOP LOOKING.

She touched back down in the middle of the first O and looked around wildly. She knew now, without a shadow of a doubt, who was messing with her dreams. All logic and rationality fled the knowledge like a hare from a predator, and fear coursed through Ash, powerful enough to make her dizzy. Suddenly, she forgot her earlier conviction that she couldn't die in her own dreams. Cat and TJ had said the almighty Griffin was unbeatable in the dream world. What if the rules were different with him?

Wake up, Ash thought. She desperately needed out of the dream. *Wake up, wake up, wake up.* She tried pinching her arm hard enough that it would have bruised in real life. She tried seizing control of the dream, but her panic whisked away her focus like a gust of wind.

The fire flared up around her again, a ring of flame that swept inward, eager to burn Ash away to... well, ash.

Chapter 9

A TIDAL WAVE WASHED over the blazing field. Steam hissed into the air as water battled flames until both dissipated, leaving only blackened earth in their wakes.

My boots crunched on the charred ground as I made my way toward Ash. She looked around in wonder, her eyes widening when they finally settled on me. I smiled at her surprise—at the way she *saw* me. That was the thing about lurking in the dreams of others. Most people didn't realize you were really there.

"It looked like it was getting a little heated, so I thought I'd step in."

"Took you long enough." She glanced down at her arms and grimaced. Angry red patches had appeared where the fire had gotten close enough to burn her skin.

"Looks like I got here in the nick of time." Would it kill her to say "thank you"? That was twice now I had prevented her death. In a dream, yes, but the deed still seemed gratitude-worthy.

Ash clasped her hands behind her back, probably to keep herself from rubbing at her stinging arms. "Why are you even here?"

"I wanted to check in. Make sure you took my warning seriously. Did you talk to TJ and Cat?"

"I did." She narrowed her eyes. "They told me about Griffin. Which you could have done, instead of being all mysterious."

My lips twitched. "It's more fun if you find out on your own."

"Fun for who?"

The earth around us erupted, thick roots shooting out of the blackened ground. They stretched toward sky, then snapped downward and launched at us like torpedoes.

A sword materialized in my hands at the same moment Ash threw her arms in the air. A wall of stone shot up with the motion, blocking the root in front of her, but she didn't see the one coming from behind. I threw myself into its path and swept my sword through the air in a high arc, chopping through two roots the size of building support pillars like they were made of nothing more than paper.

The severed roots dropped to the ground with thuds that shook the whole field. I spun around to face the root that tried to strike at my back and split it right down the middle before it could impale me.

Ash was faring well on her own, using the resources around her to fend off the attacks. She had grabbed one of the felled roots and was using it as a bat, knocking root after root aside. They kept coming, though, bursting from the ground until we stood surrounded by living pillars.

The roots didn't strike right away. They writhed around us like the tentacles of a mutant octopus. Following Ash's example from earlier, I pulled a chunk of earth from the ground to duck behind when needed. It took all my concentration to hold onto my control over the dream. Ash's dreams were special, and though I could affect them, doing so still wasn't easy. The tidal wave, the sword in my hand. It all took everything I had in me.

"What do we do?" Ash called over the creaking of many roots.

"You need to take us somewhere else!"

I saw her shake her head out of the corner of my eye, though I kept my gaze trained on the roots. "I... I can't! He has control over the dream!"

"No, he doesn't. *You* have control over it," I said. "It's your dream. You fought off the nightmare before. You can do it again."

One of the roots surged forward, but I cut it down before it could reach Ash. Two struck next, on Ash's other side. She summoned her own sword to slice through one, but the other glanced off her shoulder with enough force to knock her to the ground. Ash cried out in pain as she fell.

I clapped my hands together over my head, and stone slabs shot out of the ground at a diagonal. Four triangular walls, coming together in a point to form a pyramid around us. The stone walls shuddered as a root slammed into the side, but they held.

"You need to get out of here," she said. "I can't die in my own dream, but *you* can die here."

"I'm not leaving you. Who knows what he can do to you?"

"He *can't* really kill me in my own dream, can he?" Fear crept into her voice, undercutting her earlier certainty.

I glanced away, my lips pursed. "Probably not." Another root struck our hiding place, and jagged cracks shot through the stone.

"*Probably?*"

I shrugged. "There's no evidence that someone can die in their own dream unless they're scared into a heart attack or something. But there are a lot of stories about Griffin that shouldn't be possible, so who's to say?"

"Stories like what?"

"Besides, he can hurt you without killing you," I went on. "Pain in a dream feels as real as when you're awake. I'm not leaving." Another assault on the other side of the pyramid created new cracks. Two more thuds, and the cracks grew. "Although I really don't feel like dying, so now would be a good time to get us out of this."

Ash closed her eyes and took a deep breath, but she flinched at the next thud. Pieces of stone crumbled away and showered down on us.

"Focus," I said softly. "You can do this, Ash."

I felt her power sweep through the dream, fighting off the foreign influences. The storm of sound outside fell silent. No more roots crashed into my stone pyramid. When I tried to reach out to change the dream again, I found her blocking me.

Ash pushed the stone walls back into the earth and stood. All around us, petrified roots reached toward the sky. One was frozen mid-strike, halfway to delivering the blow that might have brought the shelter down around our heads.

"See?" I said. "I knew you could do it."

Ash glanced back at me. "Why did I *have* to do it? I thought you said Griffin was locked away in a prison that prevented him from coming after people, even in their dreams."

"It's like I told you. The prison is weakening." I tilted my head to look up at the points of the roots far above us. "If he can get to your dreams, it's even worse than I thought."

Ash turned in a slow circle before refocusing on me. "Why can Griffin control my dreams when Cat can't even get into them? Why can *you,* for that matter?"

I considered how I wanted to answer that. "Griffin is powerful," I said finally. "There are almost always exceptions to the rule. You might have shielded dreams, but that doesn't mean *no one* can get into them. Clearly." I gestured at myself to illustrate my point.

"Shielded dreams?"

I leaned against one of the petrified roots and crossed my arms. "Some people's dreams are easier or harder to control. It depends on the person, their personality, and how well you

know them, among other things. It's complicated. But essentially, your dreams are harder to control than most."

"But you can control them."

I gave a slight smile. "I'm not most dreamwalkers." And even I
had a hard time shaping her dreams. "Listen to me, Ash. Do not
underestimate Griffin. He can do things no other dreamwalkers
can do. Some say he can even control people... when they're
awake."

"What, like mind control?" she said skeptically.

"Something like that. The point is, don't make assumptions.
Just because you normally can't die in your dreams doesn't mean
he can't kill you in them. You have no idea what he's capable of."

"You're really good at not answering my questions, do you
know that?"

I let out a slow breath. "I want to help you, but I need you to
trust me."

"Why? You've given me no reason to trust you."

"I just saved your life."

"In a dream I would probably wake up from."

I rolled my eyes. She had an answer for everything, didn't
she? "I saved you from your nightmare, then. Isn't that worth
something?"

"I guess." She looked me over, eyes narrowed, like she could
somehow decipher my existence if she stared hard enough. "I
believe you about the prison, okay? We're going to Cat and TJ's
father next week to ask him what he knows."

I pushed away from the root, my shoulders tensing. "You
can't tell him about me, remember? You can't tell anyone."

"Yeah, I remember that part. Feel like telling me why not?"

I shook my head. "I need you—"

"To trust you," she finished dryly. "I heard you the first three
times."

I grimaced and looked around. If she wouldn't give her trust, then my efforts would be pointless. "Can you release your control of the dream? I want to show you something." She still held the dream in a chokehold so tight I could hardly keep myself visible to her.

She blinked, like she hadn't realized it, and I felt my ability to influence the dream return. I focused on what I wanted, and our surroundings faded from the charred field to a dimly lit warehouse. It was mostly empty aside from a few crates in one corner. The warehouse belonged to a Committee member but hadn't been used for years, even before the fight that had taken place here.

No one stirred in the warehouse, but the aftermath of the fight was evident. Pieces of a broken chair lay scattered over the concrete floor. A handgun had been carelessly left behind, along with a hunting rifle.

The latter sat on the floor beside one of two bodies.

Their faces were turned away from us, but the sight was still enough to make Ash press a hand over her mouth.

"This is what happened eight years ago," I said. "It's what will happen again if Griffin escapes. More people will die." Seeing it, being in this warehouse, made me feel like I was suffocating. I brought us back to the cliff overlooking the ocean where we had met.

I stepped closer to Ash, my eyes intent. I think that scared her a little, because she backed away. "You *have* to find the prison," I said. "Do you understand? It has to be now, not next week. If he can reach your dreams, then he's closer to escaping than I thought. We might not have much time."

Ash nodded slowly. "Okay. Okay, fine. I'll talk to TJ and Cat."

"And you won't tell anyone else about me," I prompted. She gave me an annoyed look that I took as confirmation. "I don't think Griffin will disturb your dreams again tonight. He made his point. But be careful. I'll be keeping an eye on your dreams in case he tries to attack again."

The urge to take her hand and give it a comforting squeeze drove me to lift my arm before I remembered that she hardly knew me. There wasn't much comfort I could offer. I curled my fingers into a fist and tucked it at my side. "Be careful, dreamer."

Chapter 10

I T WAS STILL NIGHT when Ash sat up in her bed, pale moonlight streaming through her cracked window, but that didn't stop her from immediately grasping for her phone and dialing TJ's number. She wiped sweat from her forehead, her hand shaking, while she waited for him to answer. The panic from the nightmare had faded, but the anxiety over what it meant had not.

"Please pick up," she whispered. The phone rang and rang, so many times that Ash began to give up hope.

When the ringing stopped, she waited for the voicemail, but instead she heard rustling background noise, finally followed by a sleepy voice. "Ash? Is everything okay? It's three in the morning."

"I know. I'm sorry." She hadn't known what time it was, actually, beyond *too late to be calling someone.* Or too early, depending on how you looked at it. "I need you to wake up Cat. It's important."

A long silence met her request. "Okay," he said reluctantly. "But you're the one who will have to pay the fine."

She fidgeted with the corner of a throw blanket while she waited. She imagined TJ throwing back his covers and shuffling down the hall to Cat's room. His voice sounded far away, like he had lowered the phone, when he said, "Cat? Wake up."

"This had better be good," came Cat's muffled reply. When she spoke again, her voice was louder. "You're aware it's three in the morning?" TJ must have put the phone on speaker.

"Sorry," Ash said again. "It couldn't wait. I think Griffin was just in my dreams. He was trying to scare me and left me the message 'stop looking.' I think it's true, that his prison is weakening. If he was able to get into my dreams..."

"Ash, you had a nightmare," Cat said, the irritation in her voice palpable. Ash didn't need to see her face to know she was scowling. "That doesn't mean it was Griffin. You're just stressed out, sleep deprived, and paranoid."

"*No.* You don't understand." Ash's fingers curled into a fist around her blanket. "It was him. I'm sure of it."

"Don't take this the wrong way but... how?" TJ asked. "Did you even see him in the dream?"

"No, but I could feel it. And the guy who warned me about the prison helped me fight off the nightmare and confirmed it was Griffin attacking my dream." Ash slumped back against her pillows. "We can't wait until next week to talk to your dad. What if he escapes before then? We need to go *tomorrow.*"

"He'll be about as happy about us disturbing his vacation as Cat is to be woken up at 3 a.m.," TJ said.

"A risk I'm willing to take."

"Clearly," Cat muttered. "TJ, a word?"

A rustling sounded on the other side, probably TJ turning the speaker off and setting the phone down on the bed instead of muting it. Almost like he wanted Ash to hear what happened next.

"Are you really going along with this?" came Cat's hushed voice.

"Please? Come on, Ash is really freaked out. We owe her this."

"We don't *owe* her anything. We've already helped her enough. I didn't even want to go to the Studio. What if he finds out we've been keeping her a secret?"

"We won't tell him how we really met," TJ said. "It'll be fine."

"I don't want to talk to him about this at all, let alone interrupt his vacation."

"And what if she's right and Griffin escapes?" TJ asked. "You know what happened back then."

"Not really. Because they refuse to tell us anything," Cat muttered.

"Maybe this is an opportunity to get Dad to tell us more. We're older now."

"We shouldn't be getting involved in anything concerning Griffin." Cat's next words were even quieter than before, barely audible. "I don't want to lose you, too."

"Then help me stop this," TJ replied. "We'll find out what he knows, and maybe we can convince him he needs to check on the prison."

A long pause followed, maybe one of their silent conversations taking place. When Cat spoke again, TJ had put the phone back on speaker. "Fine," she said. "We'll go talk to him tomorrow morning."

"Wait... tomorrow morning? No, I have work."

"I thought you were in a hurry," Cat said.

Ash ran her fingers through her tangled hair. She did want to talk to their father as soon as possible, but she wasn't skipping work to do it. "*Look*, you might feel secure in your dream therapy or whatever the hell you two do, but I finally found a place I like working and I'm *not* getting fired from it. So I'll see you tomorrow evening."

"It'll be better if we go in the morning," TJ said. "He'll be less likely to slam the door in our face if we join him and Mom for brunch."

"The following morning, then," Cat said. "Happy now? Can I go back to sleep?"

Ash let out a slow breath. "Yes. Thank you."

"Mmm hmm" was Cat's only response. The call ended before TJ or Ash could say anything else.

Ash flopped back against her bed, her phone still clenched in her hand. She didn't think she could go back to sleep, so she spent the rest of the night fervently sketching, including scenes from the dream. Her kitchen with its wayward utensils scattered through the air, the basement, the man with his ominous warnings, and finally the field with the words STOP LOOKING drawn in dark hatched lines.

Part II

Dreaming

Chapter 11

ASH MANAGED TO AVOID her uncle both that night and the following morning. She had gone to bed before he got home and slipped out before he woke up. She still felt frazzled from the nightmare and her lack of sleep, but she spent the morning taking pictures of the city at twilight, then just after dawn. She got a few gorgeous shots of the sunrise, too. Taking the pictures helped calm her mind and killed time before work.

She still got to Crystal Caverns ten minutes early, a first for her. Des was already inside, the door unlocked, so she let herself in.

His head popped up from behind the counter when the bell rang, and his blue eyes widened. From his expression, she already knew what he was going to say. "Hey, about yesterday—"

"I don't want to talk about it." She set her purse and camera down on top of the counter. "Can we just not?"

He bit his lip and nodded. While he counted the cash drawer, Ash went around turning the rest of the lights on. When she finished, she leaned against the front counter to watch him.

"Why are you always here so early?" she asked.

Des paused in counting the quarters and glanced up at her. "I don't like being late." Quarters clanged together as he tossed them into the slot one by one.

"Isn't on time enough?"

His forehead scrunched as he stared at the last few quarters in his hand. After a few seconds, he gave Ash an exasperated look. "You made me lose count!"

She gave him a sheepish smile. "Sorry." She forced herself to stay silent while he finished, though doing so was like asking a three-month-old puppy to sit still. Her eyes wandered around the quiet store, lingering on the clock as the seconds ticked toward opening. Still six minutes to go.

The sound of Des sliding the drawer shut brought her attention back to him. "I live in Westlake. I leave early enough that I can get here on time still if something happens."

Ash gave him a long look. "You and I are very different people."

He laughed and tugged at the sleeve of her thin sweater. "Tell me about it. Why are you wearing a sweater in LA in spring?"

She glanced down at the floral pattern, then at Des's tank top. "Because it's pretty," she said defensively.

"Yuh huh." Des hopped onto the back counter and tapped his heel against the cabinet below him. "Still weird."

Ash crossed her arms. "You're one to talk. Why work here if it's so far away? Surely you could find a job closer to home."

"Because I really like this job, which makes the drive worth it." He cocked his head slightly. "So why were *you* here early? You're normally rushing in the door right before opening."

"I felt like leaving early," she said.

"Avoiding your uncle?"

"You're annoyingly perceptive sometimes."

"I think what you mean is I'm incredibly wise and you should listen to all of my advice."

Ash shook her head and turned away so he couldn't see her smile. She walked around the crystal display to find something productive to do, or at least *pretend* to.

Des turned on the speaker and started some music. He had been playing classic rock the first day, but now the twang of country songs filled the store. Earlier in the week, it had been classical. Ash was starting to wonder about his taste in music and whether there was anything he didn't listen to.

For the first several hours of the day, Des kept darting glances at her, like he wanted to say something. She could feel the tension building in him, until the dam finally broke.

"It's not like he bribed her or anything, okay?"

Ash sighed and paused in organizing behind the counter so she could turn to face him. It had been too much to hope she could get through the day without talking about it.

"I just don't want you to be mad. At either of them," he said. "All he told her was that his niece was applying and he would really appreciate it if she considered you for the position."

Ash understood it from Tiernan's perspective, but she still couldn't shake the feeling of betrayal. "He still shouldn't have gone behind my back. He should have *told* me they knew each other." Keeping secrets wasn't done in their family. At least, she'd thought so.

"Just... talk to him before you let it fester for too long," Des said. "Please. For me?"

Ash narrowed her eyes at him, but he gave her a pleading look that could rival TJ's. She tried to resist, but in the end she slapped her hands down on the counter and said, "Fine! I'll talk to him. Happy?"

Des did indeed look happier, perked up like a dog with a bone. "Good. Communication is *key* to any relationship. You gotta talk it out." With that settled, he went back to putting out new merchandise from the box at his feet.

Ash tried to resume her own work, but what Des had said hung over her like a persistent storm cloud. *Communication is key.* She had lost a friend because she couldn't bring herself to talk to him. She hadn't been able to tell him the truth. Ash promised herself she would talk to Tiernan, but it wouldn't be that night. He would probably be working late again, and she had her own plans for tomorrow. More important things than sorting out her family drama.

———

Ash did her best to escape the house again without running into her uncle, but he was waiting for her in the kitchen when she tiptoed down the stairs. He had a smile for her, like he always did, but Ash couldn't muster one in return.

His own smile faltered when he saw the look on her face. "What is it? What's wrong?"

Perhaps Ash should have weighed her options before speaking. She could have lied and pretended like everything was fine, but with him standing right in front of her, the frustration and sense of betrayal came flooding back. "You got me the job," she blurted before she could stop herself.

Dismay flickered across his face before his expression turned guarded. "How did you find out?"

"It doesn't matter how," she said. "Why would you do that? Do you think I'm not capable of getting myself hired anymore?"

"Of course I do." He sounded genuine, but actions spoke louder than words, didn't they? "I just thought it would be a good place for you and wanted to make sure you landed the job. I didn't mean—"

"I can't talk about this right now." Ash glanced down at her phone when it vibrated.

Leaving in 30. Are you on your way?

TJ's text gave her the perfect excuse to slip away. "I'm meeting friends. And I need to go before I'm late."

"Since when do you care about being late?" Tiernan's smile said he meant the words as a joke, but considering everything else, they felt like a slap instead.

"I have to go," she said again before spinning away and rushing out of the house.

It took her longer than thirty minutes to get to TJ and Cat's apartment. It wasn't far away, but she hadn't figured out her public transportation route ahead of time, so it took longer than she had hoped. Cat radiated her usual impatience when Ash finally arrived, but they piled into TJ's sedan without exchanging words and carpooled to Pasadena.

The Knights lived on a picturesque street. If you searched the internet for images of "Pasadena suburbs," you might turn up a picture of their neighborhood. Flourishing camphor trees shaded the street and the cars parked along the curb. Perfectly manicured green lawns and colorful gardens welcomed visitors to each two-story house on the block.

It was the kind of place where broken families hid behind the artificial beauty of happy middle-class homes.

TJ parked in the driveway of a white house with stormy blue trim. They passed under the shadow of a palm tree on the way to the porch, and Ash's eyes lingered on the blooming lilacs and morning glories that lined the path to the front door. She wished she had her camera with her, or time to pause and take pictures.

It felt strange to Ash that Cat and TJ would have to ring the doorbell at their own parents' house. Even when she had lived elsewhere, Ash had still carried a key to her uncle's house and would let herself in whenever she wanted to visit, but TJ pressed his finger against the button and the three of them stood in silence while they waited.

The door opened to reveal a middle-aged woman. She had brown hair with hints of silver at her temples, and her fair skin was faintly tanned from the California sun. A bright and genuine smile broke out over her face when she saw them.

"TJ, Cat! What a wonderful surprise." Her blue eyes lingered on Ash curiously. "I'm Celia, TJ and Cat's mother. Come inside. I'll fetch us some lemonade."

Cat glanced at Ash for the sole purpose of rolling her eyes, then followed TJ inside. Ash trailed after. A small entryway awaited them, with a narrow table on the wall across from the door. Atop the table sat a glass vase of purple flowers, perhaps picked from the garden out front. The rug beneath Ash's feet seemed too fine, in her opinion, to catch the dirt from visitors' shoes. A railing ran along the right side of the entryway, separating them from the stairs that led downward. Beyond the stairs, Ash could see the living room.

"Robert, we have guests!" Celia called as she hurried through an open doorway to the left that led to the kitchen.

Both Cat and TJ started removing their shoes, so Ash followed their example. The siblings slid their shoes into the top shelf of the shoe rack beneath a desert painting. The two levels were labeled—the top one had a strip that said FAMILY, and below it was GUESTS. Ash set her own ballet flats beneath TJ's and Cat's shoes.

Heavy footsteps descended stairs out of sight, somewhere behind the wall with the entryway table. A white man with dark brown hair peppered with gray appeared in the living room. Robert Knight was large, over six feet tall with broad shoulders and muscles that filled out his business suit. He was far too imposing for someone with the job title of therapist. Contrary to his wife's welcoming smile, his face tightened into a disapproving expression.

"Hey, Dad," TJ said nervously.

"You should have called first," Robert said.

Celia appeared behind him, a tray with three glasses and a pitcher in her hands. She gave Robert a pointed look. "Don't be ridiculous. You can stop by whenever you like, dear." His narrowed eyes said he didn't agree, but he didn't argue with his wife.

She waved them into the living room and set the tray on the coffee table. "Come have a drink. It feels like it's been ages since I've seen you! Let's catch up."

They joined the couple in the living room and sat down in a line on the couch, Cat in the middle. She radiated tension, her eyes focused intently on her mother. Or intently *not* on her father.

"Who is your friend?" Robert asked. Ash resisted the urge to squirm under his scrutiny.

"This is Ash," Cat said. "She's a dreamwalker, new to town."

Ash cut a glance at Cat, surprised by the lie, but she kept her mouth shut. Cat must have her reasons, right? Like not wanting to put Ash under a microscope. If Robert knew she was a dreamwalker who had remained undiscovered for twenty-one years, his analytical brain might kick in.

"A new dreamwalker the Committee doesn't know about?" Robert said. "She should have contacted us already to make her presence known."

"That's why she's here," TJ said quickly. "Well, part of the reason."

"And what's the other part?"

Celia pursed her lips at her husband's tone. She picked up the pitcher and started pouring lemonade, passing out the glasses one at a time. First to Ash, then to Cat. Neither took a drink.

"We have some questions about eight years ago," Cat said. "About Griffin." Robert's expression shifted when Cat said the name, from annoyed to completely *blank*.

"And what happened to Sebastian," TJ added.

Celia's hands stilled halfway through pouring the last glass. Her eyes darted up at TJ, then she set both pitcher and half-filled glass back down on the tray. "Oh, honey. Why would you want to know about such awful things? Sometimes they're better left in the past."

"We've already told you all you need to know," Robert said coldly.

"Have you?" Cat said. "I feel like we're old enough to know the whole story."

"Celia, would you give us the room?" Robert said, his eyes trained on Cat. She stared back levelly, but her hands were clenched into fists by her legs.

Celia looked at him, then at the three on the couch. Silence gripped the room for a few seconds while she finished pouring TJ's glass and handed it over. Then she took the tray and wordlessly excused herself from the room.

"What happened eight years ago is none of your concern," Robert said the moment she was gone.

"Our brother *died* in the fight against Griffin," Cat said. "I think that makes it our concern."

"There are details you don't need to know."

"Who are you to decide what we *need* to know?"

"Cat," TJ said, a pleading note to his voice. Neither she nor Robert even looked at him.

"I am your *father*, Catalina," Robert snapped. "I say you didn't need to know back then, and you don't need to know now. These matters are for the Committee only. We decided to keep the details secret for the safety of the entire dreamwalker community. We didn't make that decision lightly."

"Please, sir," Ash said. She regretted it immediately when Robert turned his stare on her. She shrank back against the couch but pressed on anyway. "I'm the one who has been asking questions. I heard about Griffin and wanted to know that I will be safe here."

"I assure you, his prison is quite secure. We made sure of it."

"Forgive me if I don't take your word for it," Ash said.

"No, I don't think I will," Robert said. "You come into my city, to my *home*, and start making demands. Who do you think you are?"

TJ leaned forward slightly. "Dad, please—"

"I want you out of this house right now. All of you." He took Ash's untouched lemonade right out of her hands and slammed it down on the coffee table, so hard that some of the liquid sloshed out and rolled down the side of the glass. "You will register yourself officially with the Committee. And I'll deal with you two later."

"We just want to know what happened," TJ said meekly.

"Out," Robert said. "Now."

They rose in unison. TJ and Cat set their glasses down more gently beside Ash's, and they shuffled out of the living room. While they were putting their shoes back on, Ash heard the start of the argument between Robert and his wife.

"You shouldn't talk to them that way," she said in a hushed tone.

"They're my children. I'll talk to them how I see fit," he replied.

"Maybe she's right. Did you ever consider that? Maybe they ought to know the truth."

Ash wanted to hear the rest of it, but Cat grabbed her arm and dragged her out the front door.

No one spoke until they were seated inside the car. Cat slammed her door and barked out a laugh. "Well, *that* was a disaster."

"It's a sore subject," TJ said. "Bad things happened back then. He lost a son."

"And we lost a brother!" Cat fired back. He flinched and turned his gaze toward the steering wheel. "He still treats us like kids. We deserve to know."

"Maybe we can try again later. When he's in a better mood."

Cat snorted. "And when will that be?"

Ash was as eager to interrupt them as she had been to insert herself into the conversation with Robert, but as with then, she did it anyway. "Is there anyone else we can ask?"

"Maybe someone else on the Committee," TJ said. He still stared at the steering wheel, shoulders slumped. "Someone who was on it back then."

"We don't know everyone who was on it back then," Cat said. "And he sure as hell isn't going to tell us." She glared at the front door of the house. "No, we'll have to find the information ourselves."

"In Dad's dreams?" TJ finally looked at her again, his eyes wide. "That's a horrible idea. He'd see us coming."

"That's why we're not going into *his* dreams."

Ash caught on before TJ did. "You want to get the information out of your mother?"

"We're not exactly experts in memory extractions, Cat," TJ said. "We'd be stumbling around blindly looking for answers."

Cat nodded. "You're right. There's only one person who can help us."

Ash didn't think it was possible, but TJ looked even *more* nervous. "Are you sure? Last time you talked was..." He wrinkled his nose instead of finishing that sentence.

"She'll help us," Cat said, with the sort of feigned confidence that comes only from having no other choice. "She won't be able to resist."

"*Who?*" Ash asked. Neither answered nor even glanced at her, ignoring her so thoroughly she may as well not have spoken at all.

"We need to get some sleep," Cat said. "Ash looks like she's going to pass out from exhaustion. We'll rest today, then we'll go talk to her."

"Home?" TJ asked.

Cat looked from TJ to Ash, her expression turning pensive. "No... not home. To the Three Points cabin."

TJ sat up straighter. "Really?" Whatever that meant to him, it chased away the dejected demeanor that had taken him over since they'd left the house.

"Don't make me change my mind," Cat grumbled.

TJ bobbed his head and started the car. He backed out of the driveway and headed in the opposite direction from which they had come—north, out of the city.

"Where are we going?" Ash asked. "What's at the Three Points cabin?"

Cat twisted around in her seat so she could look at Ash squarely. "We have something to show you."

Chapter 12

A SH HAD NEVER HEARD of Three Points, but it turned out to be a community about an hour from Pasadena. It felt very much like the middle of nowhere to Ash, who had grown up in Los Angeles and rarely left the city, and she found herself staring at the mountains in the distance.

"So... why Three Points?" she asked after they parked. The word "cabin" accurately described the small house. Stonework lined the bottom half, with darkly stained wood above it. Wide, white-trimmed windows were set on either side of the front door.

"We used to come up here on vacation," TJ said. "There are a lot of hiking trails nearby, and Angeles National Forest is only a short drive."

"Hiking?" Ash wrinkled her nose at the thought of traipsing through nature surrounded by nothing but trees and rocks and *bugs*. Not to mention the amount of pollen in the air that would make her allergies go haywire.

Cat gave her a wry smile. "Yeah, city girl. Hiking." She sorted through a ring of keys until she found the right one and let them into the cabin.

The living room, dining room, and kitchen were mainly one open area. A brown couch and matching armchair were tucked into one corner with a round table with four chairs nearby. The kitchen had a small island in front of it, chairs lined up along the countertop. The furniture and decorations—photographs and paintings of snow-capped mountains and evergreen forests—made the place feel like a mountain cabin in the north where it actually snowed, not the Sierra Pelona foothills. The only thing that felt out of place was a simple dreamcatcher with white feathers that hung over one of the doors.

Cat opened the coat closet next to the front door and dragged out a shoe rack. "Sebastian was our older brother. When he died eight years ago, our parents did a complete purge." She straightened up and grabbed a handful of coats and their hangers. "TJ, help me?"

He hurried forward to take the coats from Cat, then brought them to the couch to lay over the back. "We had to get rid of all the pictures in the house. They even made us delete stuff off our *phones*." He remained by the couch, a haunted look crossing his face. "Dark day."

Cat huffed on her way over with the rest of the coats. "Ridiculous is what it was. TJ, move!"

TJ jumped a little and hurriedly stepped aside so Cat could drop her load of coats on top of the others.

Ash hovered by the door, trying to stay out of the way. "And his death is related to Griffin."

Cat returned to the closet and knelt inside it. "He was killed trying to bring Griffin down. I wasn't going to cut him out of my life just because he was gone, though. So TJ and I squirreled away some stuff of his here before they could get rid of it."

She felt along the back wall until she found a loose board and pulled it free. After fishing out a shoe box from the newly exposed cubby, she crawled back out of the closet. Cat brought the box to the coffee table and knelt in front of it. TJ and Ash took a seat on the couch while Cat began pulling things from the box with a certain reverence. A gold ring, a plastic dragon figurine, a Fall Out Boy CD with a signature scrawled over the front in black marker. Cat set an old copy of something called *How to Twist a Dragon's Tale* with worn pages and a faded cover on top of the CD and finally revealed a stack of photographs. She slid one out and handed it over to Ash.

Three teenagers stood with their arms around each other in front of a mountain backdrop. One of those hiking trips, Ash supposed, based on their clothing and the scenery. TJ and the other boy grinned at the camera, and even Cat was smiling.

"That's him," Ash murmured. "That's the man from my dreams." He looked younger in the picture, his dark hair tousled from the wind.

Cat and TJ glanced at each other. Cat looked wary, but TJ's eyes brightened with excitement. "He's not dead," he said. "Do you think Mom and Dad know? Would they really have lied to us about this?"

Cat put the rest of the photographs back in the box and shook her head. "Honestly? I don't know what lies they'd be willing to tell. But if Sebastian isn't dead, then maybe they've been lying to us about a lot more than that." She was trying to keep her voice level, but traces of TJ's hopeful energy crept in anyway.

Then Cat turned her gaze on Ash and narrowed her eyes. "Why would he come to *you*? He could have contacted either of us."

Ash had been wondering that from the very beginning. "He said I was the only one he could reach. I don't know why." She did feel a strange mix of confusion and exhilaration at the idea of being *chosen.* She had been searching for a purpose, and now she had one.

Cat scowled and snatched the photograph from Ash's hands so she could put it with the others, but Ash simply picked up the ring from the table instead. She turned it over in her fingers and paused when the letters engraved on the inside flashed in the light. "D&G? Does this mean anything to you two?"

TJ leaned closer and frowned at the ring. "He used to wear it all the time, but I didn't know there were letters on it. He stopped wearing it a few days before..."

Cat took the ring from Ash, with less aggression this time, and squinted at the letters. "Weird. I never noticed that. I found it when we were cleaning out his apartment, in one of those dictionaries that people cut out a hole in the middle to hide stuff." She dropped the ring into the box and replaced the rest of the items. "I suddenly have five hundred questions I want answers to," she muttered, but sometimes looking for answers was like chasing nightmares. People didn't always like what they found. "They'll have to wait for later. We all need some sleep. We're leaving after sunset."

There were two bedrooms, but neither sibling seemed inclined to sleep in their parents' room, so Ash didn't ask.

"I'm taking the couch. You two figure out what you want to do," Cat said. That left TJ and Ash with a bed and the floor.

"I'll just sleep on the floor. Guests should be comfortable," TJ said.

Ash wasn't in an argumentative mood, so she nodded and helped TJ get a makeshift bed together with a sleeping bag and blankets.

They had only settled down for a few minutes before TJ said, "It's really him, huh?"

"Yeah," Ash replied quietly. "It's really him."

"I don't understand why he wouldn't come see me."

Whereas Cat had sounded angry, TJ's words were riddled with hurt and... *guilt*, like it was somehow his fault Sebastian hadn't chosen him.

Ash rolled to the edge of the bed so she could look down at him. They had closed the curtains, but some daylight still leaked through. She could see him clearly, on his back staring up at the ceiling. "I'm sure there's an explanation," she said. "And I'm sure he still loves you."

"Yeah... yeah I know." TJ blinked a few times, trying to dispel unshed tears. "I just miss him, you know? When he died... when we *thought* he died, I—"

"It's hard to lose someone," Ash whispered.

He turned his head to look up at her. "Your parents?"

"And others." Ash knew it was different, that her friend hadn't *died*, but the loss had still left a gaping hole in her life. She didn't know which was worse—to lose someone to death or to have them force you out of their life because they hated you.

TJ fell silent. The seconds ticked by, but he didn't close his eyes, so Ash didn't either. "Did he seem... happy?" he asked finally.

"He seemed..." She didn't even know. "He was kind of annoying, honestly."

TJ let out a strangled laugh, and a single tear escaped. "But charming, right? He always had a way of making people like him."

"I guess so." Annoyingly charming. It was a gift.

Ash rolled onto her back and blew out a breath. "Would you just come up here? It's weird talking to you on the floor."

Blankets rustled as he sat up. "You sure?"

"Yeah, it's fine."

TJ wormed out of his sleeping bag and rounded the bed so he could climb under the covers on Ash's other side. "When Cat joined the family, Sebastian said he would take the couch so she could share the bed with me." He smiled faintly at the memory, though the sadness hadn't completely left his eyes. "We were already teenagers then. Cat was fifteen, a year younger than I was. She said she didn't want to sleep in a bed with a stranger and insisted on the floor instead."

Ash smiled. "That sounds like Cat." They certainly weren't strangers anymore, though. The way they acted with each other, you'd think they had grown up together.

"Yeah." He grasped the edge of the blanket and pulled it up to his chin. "He slept on the couch anyway. I think he was hoping she'd change her mind."

"Let me guess: she never did."

TJ shook his head. "She's not... *really* as mean as she seems. And she doesn't hate you."

"You sure about that?"

TJ frowned. "I think so."

"It's fine," Ash said, even though it wasn't. Every glare from Cat stung just as much as the last one, if not more. Ash kept thinking eventually Cat would stop being so prickly, but nothing had changed. "She has no reason to like me."

"*I* like you," TJ said. "For what it's worth, if it can't be one of us Sebastian chose, I'm glad it was you."

"Thanks, TJ," Ash said quietly. She turned onto her side, so she faced him. "What does it stand for?"

"What?"

"TJ."

His lips curled into a dry smile this time. "Tiberius Jerome. Very Filipino, right? I have no idea where my parents plucked those from."

"That's... that's something alright."

"Would you two stop yammering?" Cat called from the other room. "I'm trying to get some sleep here."

TJ and Ash both stifled their laughter with the blanket. They did go to sleep after that, though. Ash hoped she would see

Sebastian again—she had so many questions to ask—but her sleep was empty of dreamwalkers.

At least, it was until she got wrenched away.

Chapter 13

I T HAPPENED LIKE IT always did. One second Ash was in the pleasant embrace of her own dream world, the next she was sucked into somewhere *else*, like she had been pulled into a whirlpool intent on drowning her. A force tugged at her body—her dream trying to stop her from escaping—then released like a magnet pulled too far away from its counterpart.

When she became aware of her surroundings, she found herself in a nightmare. Maybe TJ's or Cat's or someone else's, though there wasn't much else around but trees and shrubs. Last time she checked, trees didn't dream.

All she knew for sure was she had zero desire to be here.

She stood in the center of a cemetery. Mist curled up from the grass like steam rising off water, emitting a faint luminescence that Ash realized provided the only light. Smooth headstones spread out in a neat grid around her, stretching into the distance until the thickening mist swallowed them.

The twisted silhouettes of gnarled trees stood among the headstones. They didn't look like they had grown from the ground but rather like something had dragged them, fighting every inch of the way, and the results were things so disfigured they hardly resembled trees.

Ash couldn't put her finger on it, but something about the cemetery felt distinctly *wrong*, in the way that dreams don't always make sense when you think about them too hard.

This was a bad place. Every instinct in Ash screamed to get *out*, but like every other nightmare, this one had her ensnared with no chance of escape. Maybe if she had shown any capacity to learn the lessons Cat and TJ had tried to teach. Maybe with more time. But here and now she was powerless, trapped in someone else's mind.

"What are you doing?"

Ash whirled to face the boy standing behind her. A younger version of TJ, maybe eight or nine years old, stared at her with wide, frightened eyes.

"I'm sorry," she said. "I didn't mean..."

"You shouldn't be here." TJ had never sounded so grave. But really, was there any other way to sound amidst the dozens of headstones?

"It's not like I came on purpose," Ash said, forever frustrated by her inability to choose when she entered someone's dream. If she could, she certainly wouldn't pay a visit to their nightmare. "Where exactly is *here*?" She looked around the cemetery. Something about it still tugged at her mind, but she couldn't explain what bothered her so much. "Is this a real place?"

"Real enough."

A flicker of movement caught Ash's eye. She turned sharply, but whatever she had seen was gone. "Is there someone else here?"

"Some*thing* else," TJ said.

Of course. Because why would she find herself trapped in a place with enemies so mundane as people?

"Should we run?" she asked.

TJ shrugged, the nonchalant gesture undermined by the way his eyes darted from side to side. He kept them trained on the ground, like he was trying not to look but couldn't help it. "Wouldn't do any good."

Ash's eyes drifted to one of the headstones nearby, and she read the name written there. Maria Rosario, with Adrian Rosario on the one beside it. This was TJ's dream, which meant the names should mean something to him. She glanced at the next headstone, the writing carved into the stone barely visible through the mist.

Ash finally realized the reason the dream felt so wrong. The graveyard was a pattern repeated endlessly, the same section laid out again and again and again. The same twisted tree, the same names on the headstones. This place was a figment of TJ's mind, perhaps a fragment of reality, but she could see the truth of it now. She also understood why he had said running wouldn't do any good. They could run as far and long as they wanted to, but the cemetery would never end. It was a cage.

Real enough, he had said. For her, real enough in the ways that mattered. Real enough to die in.

TJ flinched at something rustling, the only noise so far other than their own voices. There was no wind in the cemetery, no leaves on the trees, so what had made the sound? Something compelled Ash to keep her eyes on him, despite an underlying desire to search the mists for the source.

"TJ, what's—"

"Get down!" He grabbed the front of her shirt and yanked her down with him as he fell into a crouch behind one of the headstones. A moment later, something flew over their heads and shattered against the nearest tree. It sounded like breaking glass, high and sharp, but the patter of shards littering the grass didn't follow. When Ash looked toward the base of the trunk, she found no evidence of anything at all.

She turned her head to peer over the top of the headstone, but TJ caught her chin to stop her. "No! Don't look at them. If you look, they'll kill you."

His fingers dug into her skin so hard the pressure made Ash wince. "Okay," she whispered. "Okay, I won't look. You can let go."

He jerked his hand away and they crouched there, gazes locked, both of them breathless. Luminous mist swirled around them, casting strange shadows over TJ's younger face. Ash could feel the prickle on the back of her neck, that feeling that something was *watching.*

Movement flickered in the corner of her vision, disrupting the mist. Instinctively, she started to look, but TJ grabbing her wrist reminded her to keep her gaze focused on him. *If you look, they'll kill you.* Quiet sounds like footsteps and the rustling of grass behind her made her skin crawl. The urge to turn gnawed at Ash, like when someone tells you not to think about something and then it's impossible to do anything else. *Don't look, don't look, don't look,* she repeated to herself.

"Why don't they kill you if you don't look at them?" Ash asked, partly because she wanted to know and partly to distract herself from the sensation of something hovering at her back.

"Because they want to scare you," TJ whispered. They wanted to scare *him,* specifically, but TJ didn't say that part. This dream had been designed to frighten him.

"TJ, it's your dream. You can change it." She had seen him craft something beautiful from the remnants of a nightmare. Surely he could do the same in his own dreams.

But he squeezed his eyes shut and shook his head. "I can't. I never can."

Something was right behind her. She *knew* it. She could feel it in her bones, and Ash's imagination did her no favors. She saw a deformed hand stretching out slowly to grab her shoulder, a shadowy figure growing closer... closer...

A twig snapped right behind her. She instinctively spun on her toes to face the nightmare, but before she saw what lurked behind her, everything went completely black. It was a mercy, a blessing, but in that moment it didn't feel like one. The creature let out a rattling breath, and a smell like rotting corpses brushed over her face. Ash knew she was inches away from the thing that haunted TJ's dreams, even if she couldn't see it. She could reach out and touch it if she were foolish enough to do so.

She screeched when something grabbed her arm from the darkness, but the fingers weren't icy cold like she had imagined they might be. Claws didn't dig into her flesh.

"Ash, you need to get out of here."

The voice was wholly human and so familiar that Ash almost cried. The creature had gone, taking its stench with it. Instead, Cat crouched there, fingers wrapped tightly around Ash's arm.

"I can't... I don't know how," she said.

"A door. Picture a door. That door will take you back to the waking world."

Behind her, TJ let out a whimper. "Cat..."

"I know," Cat said. She didn't sound scared. She sounded *angry*, and Ash intuitively knew that anger was directed at her.

Ash tried desperately to do as she was told. She tried to picture her front door. The faded blue paint, peeling in places. The old brass knocker that never got used. But the image kept slipping away, her racing thoughts distorting it like a hand slapping a reflection in the water.

"I can't," she said again, the same way TJ had earlier. Apologetic, helpless, and terrified. "I'm sorry."

Cat let out a sound rife with frustration and annoyance, almost a growl. Then that rattling came from beside Ash again, like the distorted *tick tick tick* of a needle tapping against the pegs of a wheel. It brought with it the scent of rot so strong, it burned Ash's nose.

"I can't keep it dark forever," Cat said. "The dream is fighting me. You need to wake up."

A bare moment after she spoke, the first wisps of mist returned, seeping out of the earth. It illuminated the grass, then their shoes, rising and twisting and brightening the world until Ash could see the shadow of *something* out of the corner of her eye. A shifting darkness that might have been the flutter of a black cloak or the roiling of opaque water.

"*Shit.* Ash, you need to wake up right now! WAKE. UP!" Cat shoved Ash's chest *hard,* sending her sprawling directly toward the creature. She braced herself for impact but passed right through it. Instead of her back hitting the ground, she plunged into a dark hole that had opened in the earth. The sensation of falling catapulted Ash's mind back into her own body.

She sat up just as Cat burst into the room. In his sleep, TJ had managed to pull the blanket and sheets from Ash's side of the bed and was tangled up in them. Despite the nightmare, he was now still other than his eyes twitching beneath his eyelids. Cat looked at her brother, her face pained, but she made no move to rouse him.

"Shouldn't we wake him?" Ash asked.

"It won't work," Cat said. "He'll wake up soon." She sat at the foot of the bed with her knees pulled up to her chest, her arms wrapped around her legs. She had never looked so young as she did right then, the harsh lines of her face somehow softened by anguish. Cat always projected a confident, capable persona, but it was a lie. Oh, she was capable all right, when it came to fighting nightmares. Here in the real world, watching her brother battle his demons alone, she was helpless.

Finally, TJ's eyes snapped open. He bolted upright, gasping.

Cat grabbed his shoulder to steady him, and he turned his wild eyes on her. "It's okay!" she said. "You're at the cabin, with me and Ash. You're safe."

Instead of relaxing, TJ jerked away from her and scrambled to his feet, or at least tried to. He had to untangle his legs from the blanket first in an awkward and frustrated display.

When he finally managed, he yanked the offending blanket off the bed and threw it down in a heap at his feet. "Why were you in there?" he demanded. "You said you would never come in again!"

"I was trying to save this idiot who can't even control her own powers!" Cat snapped back. She shot Ash a glare that said *this is all your fault.* In that moment, Ash certainly agreed.

The anger that looked so out of place on TJ's face melted away. "I'm sorry... I'm so sorry." He fell to his knees on the floor, his head bowed, and Cat knelt to wrap her arms around him. "I didn't mean it. I just... I was so sure I was going to lose you, too."

"I know," Cat said, her voice uncharacteristically gentle. "I'm not angry. Everything's okay now."

Ash felt as much of an intruder on the moment as she had in his dreams. She rubbed her arm and looked away, her eyes lingering on the space above the door. The dreamcatcher hung on the other side of the wall, but it hadn't done TJ much good, had it?

Movement drew her attention back to TJ. He strode past the bed, out the back door to the patio. He didn't shut the door all the way, and a pleasantly cool breeze came through the crack.

"What was that?" Ash asked, keeping her voice low in hopes that TJ wouldn't hear.

Cat stared at the door, clearly torn between going after him and giving him space. "A nightmare," she said helpfully.

"Those graves... they were for his parents, right?"

Cat's eyes cut toward Ash. "His birth parents died when he was eight. The Knights brought him here from the Philippines."

"How did they die?"

"If you want to know that, you'll have to ask him."

Ash glanced through the cracked door to where TJ stood, then back at Cat. "What about your parents?"

Cat turned her face away, her expression disappearing into the shadows. "A story nowhere near as dramatic." She bent down to retrieve the blanket from the floor. "It's night. We should get ready to go."

Ash nodded, but instead of helping Cat make the bed, she slipped through the door to join TJ on the patio. He didn't look at her as she leaned against the railing beside him. She struggled between the desires to offer words of comfort and to ask about the nightmare. Asking felt intrusive, but she wanted to know.

TJ spoke before she could decide. "I love it here," he said softly. "Away from the city. You can actually see the stars."

Ash tilted her head up to follow his gaze to the night sky. It was just after sunset, the sky still a dark navy instead of midnight black, but she could see the faint pinpricks of stars scattered above. "It's beautiful."

"I like the stars. There are never stars in my nightmares, like they were taken away on purpose." His eyes darted over the sky, as if tracing some constellation. "I got an astronomy degree alongside the psychology one Dad insisted on. He said I shouldn't double major and should focus on the 'important courses,' but the universe is too interesting. He didn't approve when I went back for biology, either. But I juggled classes and working for him. Maybe just to prove I could."

"TJ... how many degrees do you have?" Ash asked.

"Just the three." He gave a feeble laugh. "Is it pathetic that going back to school was my version of acting out?"

"Not pathetic. Just really nerdy."

He gave a wry smile and looked back up at the stars. "Everyone either expected me to excel in school because of who my parents are or treated me like I was dumb because I was that foreign kid. It was a weird dichotomy. The Knights pushed us to be the best. They took me in, so I felt like I had to prove I was worthy. But I found I *did* actually like school. I have a good memory, and I like knowing how the world works. It felt good to be admired for something, instead of just being the orphan from the Philippines. I think maybe I leaned into it a little too hard."

"There are worse things you could have leaned into," Ash said.

"Like drugs?"

Ash laughed. "I didn't mean that exactly, but yeah that would be worse."

TJ grinned at her, but the expression didn't last long. "People have always treated me differently," he went on. "Because of where I'm from, who adopted me, or what I look like. I know most people think I don't look my age. I thought maybe when I proved how smart and capable I was, they would start treating me like an adult, but I have three degrees and people still think I'm in high school sometimes. It's... frustrating."

TJ paused for a long moment, then bent his head. He wrapped his arms around his body, as if trying to keep warm, even though the California night felt perfect to Ash. "My parents worked for a group similar to the Committee. Their job was finding people who were misusing their abilities. I used to call them the dream police."

His voice grew quieter, so quiet that Ash had to lean closer to hear his next words. "They went after the wrong people, though. Finally met their match. These people... they learned about me. Decided to use me against my parents. They knew they couldn't win in my parents' own dreams, so instead they crafted a nightmare that would lure my parents into mine, with monsters powerful enough to kill them. All I could do was cower and watch as those things tore my family apart."

He broke off, and Ash let the silence wrap around them. His words hung in the air, riddled with grief and regret. Even she couldn't imagine what it must have been like to be a helpless child watching his parents get slaughtered by a creature crafted to frighten him. She didn't want to know.

"I know a lot of people have probably told you this, but I'm going to say it anyway." She rested a hand on his arm. "It wasn't your fault. You were a kid. The people who made that nightmare... they're the ones to blame."

"I know that. *Rationally,* I'm well aware there's nothing I could have done." He let out a breathy laugh. "I'm supposed to be the logical one. But it doesn't stop me from feeling guilty. It doesn't keep those monsters out of my dreams. I haven't been able to get rid of them. I can create a masterpiece inside someone else's head, but I haven't been able to control my dreams since I was eight years old. Even the Knights had a hard time fighting the monsters off. One time Sebastian almost died, so I made them all promise they would never try again. I won't have anyone else die trying to save me."

"I'm so sorry, TJ," Ash whispered. Empty words, and she knew it. He'd spent his life helping other people with their nightmares, but no one could rescue him from his own. "That dreamcatcher is for you, isn't it?"

TJ nodded. "The Native Americans would hang them over their children's beds to protect them while they slept. I could use a little protection. The problem is, even if they do what people say... the dream is already inside me. You can't keep away something that's already burrowed in and latched onto your soul. Still... the dreamcatcher makes me feel safer, somehow. Like maybe it can keep the other bad dreams away, at least."

Ash slipped her hand into her pocket, where she had stashed the chalcedony Des had given her. She held it out to TJ on the palm of her hand. "It's not much, but someone once told me this would ward off bad dreams. I don't know. Maybe he was right, and it does hold some kind of power."

He took the supposedly mystical rock and studied it curiously. "Who knows. Sometimes there's truth to legends. At this point, I'll try anything." He looked up at her, his face open and vulnerable, and surprised her by throwing his arms around her. After a brief hesitation, she returned the hug. It felt strangely natural, like hugging an old friend, even though she had only known him for a short time.

The sliding door opened, and Cat poked her head out long enough to say, "If you two are done being sappy, it's time to go."

TJ gave an awkward laugh and pulled away. "We should go before she leaves without us."

"She wouldn't," Ash said, but she didn't sound convinced.

"Oh, she definitely would." Out front, there was the distant rumble of a car engine starting.

Chapter 14

ASH MIGHT NOT HAVE gotten much sleep, but she felt wide awake on the ride back to the city. Their destination was an apartment building down the street from Lady Sabri's Hospital. She was familiar with the place but hadn't visited in a long, long time.

"Hey, look. That's where my uncle used to work," she said. "Back before we moved to the other side of the city. He—" She broke off and squinted at the parking lot, which was still visible when TJ pulled over to park the car along the curb.

"Ash? What's wrong?" he asked.

"Nothing. That just looks like his car." It was the same model, parked at the back of the lot, but she couldn't read the license plate from that distance. When she got out of the backseat of TJ's car, though, she caught sight of the elephant beanie dangling from the rearview mirror that Ash had put there when she was thirteen. It was *definitely* his car.

"Why would he drive all the way over here?" she said quietly.

"Visiting old friends?" TJ suggested.

"Yeah... I guess so."

"It's not important right now." Cat shut the passenger door harder than necessary, which made Ash jump. Cat sounded even more irritable than usual, from lack of sleep or due to whoever it was they were about to visit.

Ash gave Tiernan's car one last frown before following Cat inside. They passed an elevator in the lobby, but Cat led the way up the stairs and down the hall to unit 203. She made no move to ring the doorbell, so TJ reached out to do it for her.

They waited a few seconds before a young woman opened the door. She looked like she was getting ready for a night on the town, with that glittering knee-length dress, bright purple against the warm chestnut of her skin. Her black curls, even more impressive than Ash's auburn ones, were loose and wild in a way that looked effortless but probably took ages to style. The amethysts dangling from her ears flashed in the light as her eyes went from Ash to TJ, then lingered on Cat, who gave her a sheepish smile.

"Hey, we—" Cat started. The woman shut the door in their faces.

Ash gave TJ an alarmed look, but he didn't appear surprised at all.

"Raisa, please!" he called. Silence came from the other side of the door. If the woman still stood there, she gave no sign. "We need your help. We have a job for a Dream Investigator."

A pause followed, then the rattle of the doorknob turning again. The door cracked open, revealing one brown eye beneath a skeptical eyebrow. "What do you need a DI for?"

TJ put those big brown eyes to work, giving her an imploring look. "Let us in, and we'll tell you." Raisa's visible eye narrowed, but she didn't shut the door again, which seemed like progress.

"Come on, Raisa," Cat said. "We wouldn't have come if you weren't the best DI in the city."

That earned Cat a raised eyebrow from Raisa. She opened the door the rest of the way and gave Cat a long, assessing look. "This had better be good," she said as she turned her back.

"Maybe I'll just wait out here," TJ said, a nervous hitch to his voice.

"TJ," Cat said darkly.

His shoulders slumped, and he trudged inside, followed by an apprehensive Ash.

The apartment was nicer than TJ and Cat's. One might go so far as to say swanky. Ash thought that whatever a DI was, the best one in the city must make a lot of money. A wall of windows with raised shades made up one side of the living room. At the moment, the windows showed a black sky and dark buildings, but during the day it would let the evening sunlight in, and Ash thought they would also give a clear view of the sunset.

Raisa settled down on the beige couch and crossed her legs. She rested an arm on one of the violet throw pillows, her other hand over her knee, like she was posing for a photograph. Cat stopped on the other side of the glass-topped coffee table and folded her arms, not out of annoyance but like she could use the gesture as a shield.

Ash paused in the doorway to the living room and buried a sneeze in her arm. Behind her, TJ murmured, "You did say you were allergic to cats."

She shot him a dry smile that he didn't see because he was edging along the side of the room to lurk in the corner, as far out of Raisa's eye-line as he could get.

The young woman fixed Cat with an expectant look. "All right, let's hear it," she said. "What's so important that it drove you back here after *two weeks?*"

Instead of answering, Cat eyed the shimmering dress. "Where are you off to?"

"Worried I might have a date?"

"Your girlfriend might dislike that."

"I don't *have* a girlfriend," Raisa replied primly. "I *had* a girlfriend. You don't leave your *girlfriend* on read for two weeks and then show up at her door asking for help. If she wants any piece of this, she'd better have a hell of an explanation."

Ash was putting the pieces together and suddenly understood why TJ had wanted to wait outside. This wasn't a fight any sane person wanted to get in the middle of, and she scooted after TJ as if staying out of Cat's general vicinity would protect her from the worst of Raisa's anger.

Cat stared at the floor. A faint sheen of sweat had formed on her forehead, probably the result of frustration or embarrassment or both. "I've been... busy," she said meekly. It obviously was not the explanation Raisa wanted.

"I suppose that has something to do with why you're here asking for help instead of apologizing," Raisa said.

Cat cleared her throat. "We need to access a memory."

"Whose?"

"My mother's." She still hadn't made eye contact with her girlfriend. Sorry, *former* girlfriend. "Really, we need information from my father, but his dreams would be impossible to infiltrate. We're hoping she might know something."

Raisa laughed. "You want me to help you invade your own mother's dreams? Honey, I knew you were bold, but that's a lot even for you."

"We *have* to! It's important." Cat had never seemed so desperate, never shown any kind of weakness at all.

"Why?"

"I... I can't tell you."

"Excuse me?" Raisa tapped her ear, causing one earring to sway. "I'm sorry. I thought you just said you need my help but *won't tell me why.*"

Cat folded her arms and scowled at the floor. "I just... need you to trust me, Rai."

Raisa looked her over, then turned her attention to Ash for the first time. "And who are you? The person who has been keeping Cat busy?"

That sentence could have sounded jealous, but Raisa didn't show even a hint of the ugly emotion. Oh, she was angry about Cat ghosting her, but she didn't think Ash was involved with Cat that way.

"I'm Ash," she said. "A new... friend, I guess. I'm not sure we're even that."

"She's a dreamwalker," TJ said. "We found her last week."

"I see. And I'm assuming this needed information involves you," Raisa said.

It involved a lot more than Ash, but she was the main driving force, so she nodded. "Please. I'm sorry we have to keep it secret, but it's really important."

"Clearly, if it got her ass back here." Raisa crossed her arms and glanced at Cat again. "Okay."

"Okay?" Cat said.

"On one condition." Raisa smiled in a way that made Ash feel as wary as Cat looked. "You come with me to Remington's shindig. It would be awkward to go alone."

"No. Absolutely not. Half of the dreamwalkers in LA will be there!"

Raisa waved a dismissive hand. "It's fine. Your parents won't. They never come."

"*Your* parents will be," Cat countered.

"Mmm. Yes, true. I'm sure they'll be ecstatic to hear you're not my girlfriend anymore."

Cat made an exasperated sound and turned toward TJ and Ash as if they could do anything to help.

"Good luck," Ash said helpfully.

"Oh, no," Raisa said. "You two are coming as well."

"*What?*" TJ said.

"The more, the merrier. Besides, if you want my help, you'll have to work for it."

"What's the problem with this party?" Ash asked TJ quietly.

Cat answered for him. "It's full of people we have no interest in talking to. And involves dressing up."

"And it's the only way you're getting my help," Raisa said. "What's it going to be, kitten?"

Kitten? Ash mouthed at TJ. He fought to keep a smile off his face.

Cat engaged in a futile staring contest with Raisa. Finally, she unfolded her arms and threw them back down at her sides. *"Fine.* We'll go. But I'm not staying the whole night."

"We'd have to go home to find something to wear," TJ said, still trying to get out of it.

"Nonsense. I still have one of Cat's dresses in my closet—she's lucky I didn't burn it—and you and Ash can borrow my things."

"I can do what now?" TJ said.

Raisa didn't answer. She swept out of the room and returned with several hangers of clothing that she passed out to each of them. "Now hurry up and change. Our window for being fashionably late is quickly closing."

Chapter 15

THE GARDEN PAVILION WAS like nothing Ash had ever seen before. The indoor event venue had been constructed to look like an outdoor garden. A wide cobblestone path ran from the entrance all the way to the double doors at the other end of the main hall. At least, the path *looked* like cobblestone. When Ash took her first steps onto the surface, she realized it was smooth but masterfully painted to appear 3D.

Sections broke away from the path into round patios with high tables in the middles. People in fine attire stood around most of them, chatting and smiling, glasses of varying shapes in their hands. Beds of flowers and other plants, species both familiar and exotic, lined the walls and the spaces between the patios. Ash picked out marigolds, lilacs, various kinds of lotus flowers, and others she didn't recognize.

Overhead, white lights were strung along the high ceiling like stars, surrounding a much larger light that could have been a full moon. They provided the only illumination, casting the entire atmosphere as a moonlit party beneath the open sky.

It was beautiful. Stunning, even. It left Ash feeling like she had stepped into a dream.

Cat moved past her and looked around the venue with an expression that said she would rather have been almost anywhere else. She kept tugging at the deep neckline of her floor-length navy dress, as if she could seal the V together. Raisa had said it was Cat's dress, and while it did fit her, it didn't seem like the type of thing she would voluntarily wear. Ash suspected she didn't wear dresses very often, based on the awkward way she wore one now.

Ash felt only marginally more comfortable than Cat looked. The black dress Raisa had given Ash was a touch too small and therefore too tight, the stretchy material clinging to her body. She had to resist the urge to tug at it as well.

TJ, unfairly, looked fabulous. He had been skeptical when Raisa had handed him the pair of loose black slacks and a lilac button-up shirt.

"I can't wear that," he had protested.

"Real men can wear women's clothes," Raisa had said in a *that settles it* voice.

They were about the same height and size, so the clothes fit him perfectly. Raisa had found him a black suit jacket to wear over the shirt, and with his normal boots that Raisa had deemed "acceptable," he almost looked like a runway model. Fashionable, rather than a man borrowing an outfit from his sister's former girlfriend.

Raisa wore her confidence like a second dress. She strode up to other party goers without hesitation, striking up conversation while the other three hovered nearby and avoided speaking unless spoken to.

"Would it kill you three to smile?" she said after disengaging from a small group. "You all look like you're in pain."

"That's because we are," Cat muttered.

"What is this party for, anyway?" Ash asked. She had been wondering but too afraid to ask, given that—once again—she was the only one out of the loop.

"Remington's annual fundraiser," Raisa said. "All of the people here are dreamwalkers or related to them. The money funds

Committee programs to help find and re-home dreamwalker orphans, like Cat and TJ. Most don't know how to control their powers, which can be dangerous."

Raisa didn't have to tell Ash that last part. She wondered how many kids had ended up dead because they'd accidentally gotten trapped inside a nightmare.

"Half of the money goes to the Committee here, half back to Egypt where Remington's wife is from," Cat said. "The Committee has been trying to forge connections with other parts of the world. Bring our people together as a whole or whatever." She clearly believed wholly and passionately in that mission.

Ash's eyes skimmed over the heads of the people packing the pavilion. There had to be at least two hundred. "All of these people are dreamwalkers?"

"Or their plus ones," TJ said.

"How many people have this ability?"

Raisa flashed her a smile. "Trying to determine how special you are?"

Ash's face flushed. "No, I—"

"About eighteen hundred in the LA area?" Raisa glanced at Cat for confirmation, but Cat was studiously not looking at her. "That's about 0.01%, but it's higher here than in other parts of the country."

"City of dreamers," Ash murmured. The number *eighteen hundred* made her head spin. She knew there were a lot of people in LA, but that many could enter others' dreams?

Only the most influential and wealthy graced the party that night, obviously. It was a high-profile fundraiser like any other. If you didn't have deep pockets, the invitation wouldn't fit.

"Raisa Sokolov, is that you?"

Their group turned as one to face the young woman who had spoken. She wore a sleek blue dress that fell almost to the floor and matched the color of her eyes. Her brown hair fell around her bare shoulders in perfect ringlets, and her broad smile seemed bright and genuine.

"Heather!" Raisa said with a matching smile. "I was hoping to see you here."

"You know I wouldn't miss it for the world." Heather's eyes wandered to the others in their group and widened when they fell on TJ, who stared at the floor like it was a very interesting textbook. "Hi, TJ." Something shy entered her voice, accompanied by a faint blush on her cheeks, and it had Ash glancing between them with growing interest.

"Hello, Heather," TJ said, his tone so formal that Heather winced. He didn't look up from the floor.

Raisa distracted Heather by resting a hand on her arm, which gave TJ an opportunity to slip away without another word. Ash spared a glance back at the other girls, who by then were talking about Raisa's dress. Cat looked like she wanted to fade into the bushes behind her, but her focus remained on Raisa and Heather. Ash decided Raisa could handle Heather on her own and followed TJ.

He had taken up studying the flowers in a nearby garden instead of the floor, and Ash didn't think the interest he showed in the bright pink lotus bloom was feigned.

She stopped a couple paces from him. "They're very pretty."

TJ jumped and tore his eyes away from the flower. "Yes. They're nice. Lotuses are often a symbol of purity. They're sacred in Hinduism and Buddhism."

"That's cool."

TJ nodded and took a breath, probably preparing to give her a history lesson on the lotus flower, but then his shoulders slumped. "I'm sorry I bailed. I had to get out of there."

"Not a fan of Heather?"

"She's fine."

"She's pretty. And she seems interested in you."

His staring at the flower intensified. "She's not my type."

"What is your type?"

TJ shrugged and folded his arms. He glanced toward where Raisa and Cat talked with Heather, then returned his eyes to the lotus in front of him. "I should say I'm not her type. She just doesn't know it yet."

Ash frowned. "You don't know that. You could at least give it a shot."

TJ made a quiet, frustrated sound. "I don't want what most people are looking for in relationships. Once she figured that out, she wouldn't be interested."

Ash still wasn't following his vague attempts at an explanation. "Like what?"

"Sex," TJ said flatly. "It's fine, I guess. I just... are you a sports fan? You like football?"

The sudden change in topic confused Ash even further, but she decided to go along with it. "Not really. I guess I can see why some people find it entertaining, but I don't understand why fans get so obsessed."

"Exactly. That's what sex is like for me," TJ said. "There's nothing *wrong* with it, but I don't get what everyone is so frenzied about. Imagine that *everyone* in the world is obsessed with football, and if you don't like watching football every night your relationship isn't going to work out."

"Oh." Ash joined him in staring at the flower garden. After a long pause, she asked, "Did you ever consider maybe she's not as obsessed with football as you think?"

TJ gave her a wry smile. "I tried to tell her once. Trust me, it didn't go well. I don't think I got my point across."

"Did you tell her like you told me?" She thought his analogy was rather eloquent.

TJ sighed and ran his fingers through his hair. "No. Maybe I should give it another try. Just... not tonight, okay?"

She nodded. TJ had the right to avoid Heather until the sun burned out if he wanted to. Ash couldn't imagine how hard it must be to explain something like that to a person you might want to date. He had to do what he felt comfortable with.

Raisa and Cat rejoined them, saving them from further discussing TJ's romantic problems. "Didn't anyone ever tell you it's rude to leave in the middle of a conversation?" Raisa said.

"Technically it was the beginning of the conversation," TJ replied.

"Because that makes it better." Raisa rolled her eyes and looped her arm through his. "Poor Heather is going to start thinking you hate her if you keep running away like that."

"I don't *hate* her." A touch of red tinged his cheeks. "I just don't want to talk to her. There's a difference."

"Sure, sure."

Inside the small purse Raisa had lent her, Ash's phone vibrated. She didn't have to take it out to know who had texted her, and she had no desire to respond. She could even guess the gist of the text, which probably went along the lines of "Where are you?" Ash, at twenty-one, wasn't obligated to share her every plan with Tiernan, but she had a habit of doing so anyway. The nights she spent with TJ and Cat, she always told him she was hanging out with friends. It was understandable, then, that he would worry when she stopped, especially after their fight.

"Ah, there's Byrne! Let's go say hi." Raisa released TJ so she could grab Cat's wrist and drag her down to the next patio. TJ and Ash trailed behind.

The woman smiled when she saw their little group. "Raisa! You look absolutely stunning tonight. And you managed to drag the Knights along."

"It wasn't an easy feat," Raisa said. "I paid a hefty price."

Cat snorted. "You did not."

"It's nice to see you again, Mrs. Byrne," TJ cut in.

"You too, dear," she said. "Where are you now... starting college?"

"I graduated already, ma'am."

"Of course, of course. You always were a smart boy. And Cat, do try to look a little less dour. There's free food and drinks. Enjoy it!"

"That is *exactly* what we need," Raisa said. "Four cocktails, coming right up. Come on, kitten, I'll get you a virgin daiquiri. Nice to see you, Mrs. Byrne!"

"Oh, Raisa? Tread lightly with your mother tonight," Byrne said before they could go. "She's in vote gathering mode again."

Raisa groaned. "Thanks for the heads up."

"Wait, vote gathering?" Ash asked.

"For the Committee," TJ said.

"Word is Aaron is thinking about retiring his position," Byrne said in the conspiratorial tone of someone spreading gossip she ought to keep to herself. "He says he wants to spend more time with his wife and children, but I'll believe it when I see it. That man is as attached to power as to his own right arm."

"Him and everyone else here," Cat muttered. She didn't look at Byrne, but it sounded like she included the woman in that statement.

"Yup, time for drinks," Raisa said. She took Cat's arm and pulled her away from Byrne before Cat could say anything else insulting. She set their path toward the bar at the back of the room.

Soon Ash held a frozen strawberry daiquiri in her hands. Raisa had ordered one for each of them, a virgin for Cat. Ash had never had one before, and she felt more like she was sipping a slushie from the gas station than an adult beverage.

"Here's to finally being twenty-one," Raisa said, holding up her adult slushie. It finally struck Ash that she and Raisa were the same age, something she hadn't even considered. The young woman had a nice apartment, a career, and a confidence that Ash could only associate with having found one's place in the world.

She hadn't thought anyone her age could honestly claim that confidence.

"I hope Winkler does retire. Our father would loooove that," Cat said. "Though I don't think anything could be worse in his view than Remington's getting elected."

Ash took a drink through her transparent blue straw, turned purple by the red cocktail. She was still trying to move on from the knowledge that Raisa was her age yet miles ahead of her in life goals. "So who is this Remington guy?" she asked.

"He's a business owner," TJ said. "As in, multiple of them. He owns a lot of shops and restaurants in LA, among other things."

Raisa stopped searching the room for some unknown thing—her mother, perhaps—and looked at Ash. "They hire mostly dreamwalkers. I think he sees himself as some sort of patron to the dreamwalker community. Providing jobs and raising money for good causes!" She rolled her eyes.

"He's the reason our parents aren't here," TJ said. "They never come to these things. Remington's on the Committee, but Dad avoids him as much as possible. They had some kind of falling out... around eight years ago, actually." He frowned. "You think it's related?"

"I would be shocked if it weren't," Cat said. "Robert *hates* Remington. He was furious when the man got elected to the Committee. I overheard him ranting to our mother about how they'll let anyone in these days."

"Well, then," Ash said. "I'm dying to meet him now."

She meant it sarcastically, but Raisa shot her a smile. "Here's your chance." She nodded toward an approaching couple.

"Raisa, don't—"

"The man and woman of the hour!" Raisa called. She waved a hand toward the couple to get their attention. It seemed Ash had no choice but to meet the man responsible for the lavish party.

Chapter 16

A SH DIDN'T MISS THE displeasure that flickered over Remington's face when he first saw them, but he drew out a polite smile and made his way over.

"Please, Raisa, you know this isn't about us," he said. "It's about those children across the world who need homes." The man held himself like a British aristocrat, and he had the accent to match it. His pale skin desperately needed the benefit of sunlight, and a spark of curiosity entered his brown eyes when they wandered to Ash. He held out his free hand, his other arm occupied by the woman beside him. "James Remington. A pleasure to meet you. This is my wife, Zahra."

The woman dipped her head. Everything about her was beautiful: her dark hair pulled back and held up in a jeweled net, her flawless light brown skin, her obsidian eyes adorned with golden eyeshadow and black liner. One might even go so far as to say exquisite, a sparkling serpent as venomous as her husband. Something about both of them made Ash uncomfortable.

She took Remington's offered hand with no small measure of reluctance. "Ash. I'm new to the area. Nice to meet you, too."

"And the Knight children. I didn't expect to see you here tonight. Does that mean Robert has graced us with his presence?"

"Not in a million years," Cat said.

Remington gave her a thin smile. "Blunt as always, Catalina."

A man with feathery wisps of platinum blond hair clinging to his balding scalp stepped up to Remington's shoulder. "Did you hear that Camila Sokolov is trying to garner votes so she can become my successor?" Too many drinks slurred his words together and had turned his cheeks red. "Who does she think she is? I might have to put off retirement long enough for her to give up this ridiculous notion." He blinked at the rest of the group, noticing them too late. "Oh. Hello, Raisa."

She gave him a stare that would have withered a whole forest, but intoxication or arrogance formed an impenetrable shield around the man. He didn't seem affected. Meanwhile, Ash was stunned on Raisa's behalf.

"If you ask me, the woman is chasing nightmares," Zahra said. "Even if she manages to get herself elected, the rest of the Committee won't welcome her with open arms."

"She works in a shop, for heaven's sake." Remington shook his head, as if perplexed by it all. "No offense, dear," he added to Raisa. "You've risen far beyond your roots."

"Camila is a nobody! Catalina here would make a better candidate." The man Ash deduced was Aaron Winkler waved a hand at her, carelessly enough that he almost knocked Remington's champagne flute out of his hand. "Her parents might be dead, but at least she has family connections here."

A moment before, Cat had looked like she'd wanted to hide behind Raisa, but the moment he spoke those words, her shoulders rolled back. Her spine straightened, bringing her up to her full, admittedly not very impressive height. Ash expected her to let loose some biting remark, a truly stunning string of insults, but instead she spun around and stalked through the crowd.

Ash turned on the so-called adults acting like bratty children gossiping about their classmates on the playground. "You know, for people who are supposedly raising money to help orphans across the world, you're pretty judgmental of those with 'nobodies' for parents. You should all be ashamed of yourselves."

She turned away, relieved to have an excuse to extract herself from the conversation, though she did feel guilty about leaving Raisa and TJ to fend for themselves. She hadn't seen Cat go out the side door, but it wasn't difficult to guess she would want fresh air, away from the people crowding the Pavilion.

It was strange, stepping outside into concrete and metal after the paradise garden indoors. Ash half-expected a balcony overlooking a moonlit hedge maze. Instead, she found herself in an alley. The ladder for an old fire escape had been pulled down, so Ash climbed it and followed the metal stairs to the roof of the building adjacent to the Garden Pavilion.

She found Cat there, standing by the wall that surrounded the roof. Ash approached cautiously, intentionally scuffing her shoe against the ground to alert the other girl to her presence. Cat didn't look at her or show any sign that she had heard.

Ash stopped a few paces away. "Are you okay?" she asked quietly.

Cat must have heard her arrival after all because she didn't seem surprised by Ash's voice. She huffed and leaned forward against the wall. "It's like they can't resist mentioning it, and I have no idea why. They don't do that to TJ. I know what happened. I don't need other people bringing it up constantly."

Ash copied Cat's position, keeping a few feet between them. Cat seemed like the type of person who might hit someone for invading her personal bubble. "My uncle raised me," Ash said. She looked up at the dark blanket of the real night sky. The crescent moon was partially covered by a cloud, and the stars were nowhere to be found. "My dad died of a heart attack when I was five. Mom three years later. She got hit by falling debris in an earthquake while trying to pull a stranger to safety."

Cat glanced over at her, but Ash kept her eyes forward, tracing the LA skyline. Some sort of spell had settled over them, and she thought if she looked at Cat, it might shatter. She still thought the conversation would die there, but after a long silence, Cat exhaled slowly and finally spoke.

"I was born in San Fransisco. My family and the Knights were old friends, so they took me in after my parents died." She picked at the edge of her neckline, no longer trying to pull it together but merely for something to do with her hands. "There was a car crash. Nothing special. Just... one of those things. The fog got really bad one night, and the other driver didn't see us.

"I hated being here. I hated everyone treating me like I was this fragile thing that might break. Everyone trying to get me to *talk* about what happened. Sebastian was the one who made me feel like maybe, just *maybe* there was any sort of hope. You have no idea what it's like, being adopted as a teenager. I felt like a pity project, not part of a family. TJ has a way of getting under your skin until you can't help but love him, but something was different about Sebastian. Something just... clicked. He made me feel wanted. But I only got to know him for a few months before Griffin took him away."

"But he's alive," Ash reminded her.

"Then why hasn't he come home?" Cat asked. "He abandoned us for *eight years*. I *needed* him. I didn't have any friends here. All I had was TJ, until I met Raisa. And I managed to screw that up, too."

Ash was hesitant to ask, but the question burned too hot in her mind, demanding to be set free. "So why *did* you ghost Raisa? She seems..."

"Amazing? Perfect? Out of my league?" Cat said. "Yeah, she is. There was just this one day when I didn't have the energy to talk to her. I was mad about something, I think, but I don't even remember what. Then every day I waited after that it got harder and harder to pick up the phone, let alone talk to her face-to-face. It got to the point where I figured it would be easier never to talk to her again, instead of..."

"Instead of her breaking up with you?"

Cat shrugged. "It was inevitable."

Ash mulled that over. She could understand Cat's fears and probably would have done the same thing in that position, even if she didn't want to admit it. "She said her parents would be thrilled you broke up. They don't like you?"

"The wonderful thing about having the name Knight attached to you is that people either respect you or hate you because of it. Usually the latter, and the ones who respect you are all asshats or suck-ups." Cat scowled. "Actually, the ones who hate you are asshats too."

"They can't all be terrible," Ash said. "Byrne seems okay."

"She's tolerable," Cat said, with an unspoken "barely" tacked on. "She still subscribes to the idea that she's somehow better than normal people because she's a dreamwalker. She's better than other dreamwalkers because her family goes back generations, and she's powerful enough to be elected to the Committee. You heard what they said about Raisa's mom. It's like they're racehorses or something. She doesn't come with a pedigree, so she's not worthy."

Cat turned her back on the city and sat on the wall. "It's more than that, though. The unspoken part of the reason they hate her. They can't say it because it means admitting that it worries them."

"Which is?"

"That Camila's parents aren't dreamwalkers," Cat said. "It runs in families, so I guess there's a genetic aspect to it. But sometimes dreamwalkers just... show up. TJ could probably tell you all about it, ramble at you about the potential origins of the ability. But the bottom line is the community here has turned dreamwalking into some kind of royalty system. You're supposed to inherit your position. It's a birthright. The idea that ordinary people can join the club? Unacceptable."

Ash hadn't even given thought to the source of this power. It was, after all, something she had mostly wanted to get rid of. It didn't matter where it had come from. TJ had said she'd gotten it from one of her parents, but now she realized she could be like Raisa's mother. "That's why you lied to your father about me," she said. "He wouldn't like it if he knew I might have this power without... a pedigree."

Cat nodded. "You're welcome."

"What about Raisa? People seem to respect her. More than they respect her mother, anyway." Though not enough to prevent them from trash-talking her family in front of her.

"Raisa has the benefit of being second generation. Not great, but better than a spontaneous anomaly. She's also very good at what she does and is a successful DI. They'd be idiots to treat her without *some* measure of civility." There was a note of pride in Cat's voice, along with satisfaction. She liked that someone had shaken their system. It was almost a rags to riches tale for Raisa, rising up from humble origins. *You've risen far beyond your roots*, Remington had told her.

Ash's anger at the way they had treated Raisa, as well as the things they had said about Camila, returned in full force. "They shouldn't be allowed to treat people like that. Raisa deserves better." And though she hadn't met her, Ash thought Camila probably did, too.

Cat shrugged. "Yeah. They shouldn't. And she does. But that doesn't stop them. It's why I don't deserve Raisa. She deserves someone with a family who will treat her better."

"That's not true," Ash said. "I mean, yeah, she deserves to be respected. But people fall in love with people whose families hate them all the time. If you love someone, you deal with that. For what it's worth, I do think she still loves you. And she's *not* out of your league. You should give yourself more credit."

Just when Ash had thought she was getting somewhere, Cat shut down again. "You don't know me, Ash. We're not friends. I have no idea why Sebastian picked *you*, and I'm still not sure he made the right choice." She pushed away from the wall and tugged at her dress to straighten it. "I'm going to find Raisa, and we're getting the hell out of here."

After Cat headed back to the fire escape, Ash's phone buzzed again, announcing another text from her uncle. Reluctantly, she took it out. She knew she should reply, lest he start calling hospitals trying to determine if something horrible had happened to her.

As she had suspected, the first text read, *Where are you tonight?*

The second asked, *When will you be home?*

What Ash hadn't realized was he had actually texted her three times. She had missed the second during the conversation with Remington and the others. His most recent text said, *Ash I'm getting worried. Please respond.*

She shoved down her guilt and typed out a message that she hoped would put his mind at ease. *I'm fine. Out with friends again. I'll be home late, don't wait up.* Then she slipped the phone back into the purse and hurried after Cat.

Chapter 17

SINCE WE HAD MET, it felt like I had spent all my time waiting for Ash to fall asleep so I could see her again. *Talking* to her for the first time had sadly been the highlight of my recent existence.

The dream took shape around me. The trees that formed the line of the forest, the open expanse of tall grass swaying in the mellow wind, and the cliff where we'd first met. It wasn't hard to guess this was her favorite place, even after that nightmare had tried to sully it.

She couldn't have closed her eyes more than ten minutes ago, which meant the dream shouldn't have looked as vivid as it did. I hadn't visited a lot of N-REM dreams, but everything in my training said they shouldn't look like this. It made me wonder if Ash were dreaming at all, or if she had conjured this in her waking imagination. A daydream. There was something special about her—about *us*.

Ash stood near the cliff, her back to the ocean, her eyes searching. "You're here," she said when she saw me standing in the middle of the field.

I started toward her, pleased to see that the wariness and suspicion she had shown me before had faded. "You've decided to trust me."

"I know who you are, Sebastian Knight," she said. "Why didn't you just tell me?"

I shrugged. "I knew you would figure it out."

"I think you just enjoyed tormenting me by being cryptic."

That made me laugh, a full, genuine sound that I hadn't heard in a long time. So, so many years since I had last laughed. "Maybe," I agreed. "I couldn't resist."

"But you're not going to tell me the rest of it, are you?" she said. "Where you are. Why you can't see me in person but can reach my dreams."

I shook my head, which she knew I would. She moved on surprisingly quickly.

"It's been an interesting week," Ash said. She looked at the ground, her lips pursed in concentration. I'm pretty sure she wasn't even aware of that adorable face she made when she tried to conjure something in her dreams. A green and brown quilt rippled into existence and settled over the grass at her feet. She sat down, her legs crossed beneath her, and gestured me over.

I approached and cautiously sat facing her. It was strange, being this close to her, even in a dream. It felt real enough. Even Ash looked real, though I thought there was something *off* about her. Some people change their appearances in dreams without even meaning to, taking away their flaws to create more perfect versions of themselves. Their eyebrows thinner. That beauty mark they never liked gone. Their hair a little straighter or curlier than in real life.

Ash did the opposite. The changes were subtle, but combined they had the effect of diminishing her appearance. Her auburn hair dulled from its natural color, and her eyes appeared less bright. It was an unintentional reflection of how she saw herself. Not necessarily her physical appearance, but something deeper than that, her inner insecurities brought to the surface.

She was still beautiful to me.

"Tell me about your interesting week?" I said.

"Well, first I met these two people in someone else's dream and learned that there's such things as dream therapists. Then this man who enjoys being mysterious far too much showed up in my dream..."

I rolled my eyes. "I already know this part. What happened after I last spoke with you?"

"I met your father." She wrinkled her nose—a very fair reaction to Robert Knight. I tried not to smile. Oh, the things I could tell her about that man. But they would have to wait. "Then Cat's girlfriend took us to a party where I met *way* too many dreamwalkers. Most of the Committee, I think."

"Was it a good party?" I asked. "Company aside."

She gave me a crooked smile. "Why do I get the feeling Griffin isn't the only one with a grudge against the Committee?"

I shrugged and got to my feet. "Can you show me?"

She glanced around, her expression softening into something pensive. Our surroundings wavered, like a glitch on a computer screen, then faded into something new. Suddenly, I stood in front of her in the lavish Garden Pavilion. It was blessedly empty.

Standing in the Pavilion once more dragged hundreds of memories to the surface, not all of them good. Not all of them bad, either. I didn't want to think about the past, so I focused on Ash instead.

She stood, and the blanket beneath her disappeared. Her casual outfit turned into a floor-length gown, not the slinky black dress she had worn to the actual party. The green dress glittered in the warm glow from the lights overhead. My own outfit changed as well, from my simple button-up shirt and jeans to a tux. I brushed my fingers against the black bow tie and grimaced. The cursed thing disappeared.

Ash frowned up at the ceiling, with its strings of small lights and fake moon. The covering shimmered and vanished, revealing the night sky beyond. Real moonlight—or as real as anything in a dream can be—streamed down into the room. It was brighter than in real life, I thought, but sometimes it got hard to remember.

"Much better," I said. "Leave it to you to improve on my work."

Confusion furrowed her forehead. "Your work?"

"Well, partly my work. I helped design this place." Not that anyone would give me the credit I deserved for that. "I always loved designing spaces like this. Bringing something unique and beautiful to life. I wanted to be an architect, back before... everything."

The moonlight perfectly illuminated Ash's face, highlighting the sad lines and tired angles. Someone like her shouldn't look so worn down. "I know what it's like to watch a dream slip out of reach," she said.

"Oh, Ash... no dream is out of reach for you." I stepped back and held out a hand to her. I smiled, and I swear the moonlight brightened. "Did you save me a dance?"

The skin beneath her freckles flushed red, and she lowered her eyes to the fake cobblestone floor. "I can't actually dance."

"Sure you can." I kept my arm outstretched. "If you can fly in your dreams, what makes you think you can't dance?"

"That's different." She clasped her hands together, her shoulders curling forward. She still avoided my eyes.

"How?"

"I don't... I don't know. It just *is*." She finally looked up, her expression almost panicked.

"All you have to do is believe you can," I said. "The rest will come."

She held my gaze, her green eyes still uncertain, but she hesitantly stepped forward to slide her hand into mine. I pulled her closer and rested my hand on her hip while she awkwardly placed one hand on my shoulder. She smelled like autumn, like cinnamon with subtle traces of vanilla and crisp fallen leaves. This amused me because I was pretty sure she had never worn perfume in her life.

"You're tense," I murmured. I could feel it beneath my fingertips and in the way her hand clutched mine. "Relax."

Music swelled to life around us, and I led us into a waltz. The first steps were awkward and resistant, but then she stopped thinking about the dancing and simply let it happen. The tension slid away, and she let me guide her around the room.

"See? Not so hard," I said. "You're an excellent dancer."

"No, I'm not," she said, but an almost giddy smile spread on her face. She squeaked in surprise when I spun her around. After I pulled her back in, she let out a laugh. "*You* are an excellent dancer."

"Would you believe that in reality I'm terrible? Can't keep a rhythm to save my life."

"I can't imagine you're terrible at anything."

I raised an eyebrow at her, which caused her to blush again.

"Just shut up and dance," she muttered.

I wrapped my arm around her waist and spun us both, lifting her feet off the ground for a second, which had her laughing once more. We waltzed around the dance floor like two professionals, even though what I had told her was true. I was terrible at dancing. In a dream, it didn't matter.

With her in my arms, it was easy to forget everything else going on. Easy to forget that all we had was this dream. *For now*, I reminded myself. Soon everything would change, but until then I would have to settle for gliding around the empty Pavilion inside her dreams.

I caught the moment her expression changed, her mind wandering as doubts crept back in. "What's wrong?" I asked. My feet kept moving, hers following my lead, even though our focus shifted elsewhere.

"We're going into Celia's... your mother's dreams," she said. "And I don't know if I can. Cat and TJ have tried to teach me, but I've never been able to do it. Not on purpose."

I let the music fill the gap between her words and my answer while I pondered what to say to her. I needed the right words to convince her that she *could* do it. She was holding herself back. That much was certain. I didn't know if I could fix that, but I could make the next step a little easier.

"Maybe you need to look at it from another angle." To demonstrate my point, I sent her into a dip that turned the world upside down. "Dreamwalking is a connection, like two cellphones communicating. All you need is the right number. We form a connection with everyone we meet. The more we get to know them, the more time we spend around them, the stronger that connection gets. Your thoughts on that person, your memories... that's the right number. Does that make sense?"

We changed direction when we reached the edge of the room and lapsed back into silence while Ash turned what I'd said over in her mind. "Maybe," she said finally.

We fell into the comfortable rhythm of the dance after that. I lost myself in her smile, in the way the moonlight turned Ash's eyes a mottled forest green. I reveled in her infectious joy, letting the sound of her laughter envelope me when I spun her around or surprised her with a dip.

Why couldn't life be this? Only this.

The song slowed—Ash's doing—and I wasn't sure if it were intentional or a subconscious change. Our steps adjusted accordingly, until our movements became less a dance and more swaying from side to side. Ash leaned closer, her face tilted up. Her eyes drew me in, her lips inviting. I should have shown more self-restraint, but her eyes asked for me to kiss her.

I was a breath away from surrendering when static cut through the music. I froze, my hand still holding her close, but I knew we were out of time. I turned my face away to survey the shimmering walls. "You must be back at Raisa's," I said. "Until next time, dreamer."

"Wait, I wanted to ask you—"

Whatever she wanted to ask, it would have to wait. The dream fell apart as Ash's mind was pulled back to the real world.

Chapter 18

ASH HAD CHANGED BACK into her normal clothes, glad to be rid of the small black dress. She had liked the one from her dream much better. She had liked the way blue eyes had lingered on her and made her skin prickle. She felt something she couldn't shake, a *pull* she couldn't explain. She had never felt that way before.

She sat on Raisa's couch, along with Cat and TJ, waiting for the DI to emerge from her bedroom. *You must be back at Raisa's*, he'd said. Except Ash had never mentioned Raisa's name, which left her wondering how he knew.

It left her thinking that Sebastian knew far too much for someone who had been missing for nearly a decade.

"What's taking her so long?" TJ whispered. "I thought girls were supposed to take forever to *get* ready, not... un-get ready."

"Oh, trust me, she took this long to get ready, too," Cat muttered back.

Just then, the door down the hall opened, and Raisa swept into the living room. She looked like a completely different person. Her dark curls were pulled back into a ponytail, and her dress had been exchanged for loose purple sweatpants and a black t-shirt that said "in your dreams" in looping cursive letters. Her make-up was gone, too, but Ash couldn't help thinking that she didn't need it.

No offense to Cat, but she had definitely been dating out of her league.

"Ahh, that's better," Raisa said. "Let's get down to business." She rolled a white board out from behind the TV and situated it squarely in front of the couch where the others sat. It was currently blank, but evidence of repeated use lingered, faded lines that wouldn't completely come off no matter how many times Raisa cleaned it.

"So... can someone tell me what exactly a Dream Investigator is?" Ash asked. They kept throwing that term around, and while she had a guess, she didn't know for sure.

"She can search for answers in people's dreams, uncover secrets," Cat said. "Usually for the same types of cases private investigators take on, but she has helped the cops in the past too."

"Although most of them see me the way they see psychics trying to aid police investigations." Raisa rolled her eyes. "Doesn't stop them from taking my information when it helps close cases."

It was pretty much exactly what Ash had expected. "My dad was a private investigator, before he died." She didn't know why she added that last part. TJ and Cat already knew her parents were dead, but she thought she would get it out of the way with Raisa too, lest it come up in a more awkward moment. "He never helped the police, though."

"It's not as glamorous as TV makes it look." Raisa hopped in front of the white board and clapped her hands together. "Now, the easiest way to get answers from a dreamer is to recreate a memory that holds the answer you want. The key is in the details. You take every scrap of what you know and put it into the dream, then let the dreamer fill in the rest." She turned toward the board and grabbed a marker. "The first thing is to determine exactly what we want to know."

"Who was on the Committee eight years ago," Ash said.

Raisa glanced at Ash with eyebrows raised, but she wrote the goal across the top of the board in neat red letters. She set the marker in the tray that ran along the board's bottom and grabbed another, blue this time. "Next, what do we know already?"

"Dad was on it back then. So was Winkler," TJ said.

"And Remington wasn't," Cat said. "I think he took the post... what, six years ago?"

"Remington replaced Brown when she died," Raisa said. "And Rossi took over after Moreau's death. That leaves three more. No one knows when Byrne and Schultz took office? What about Dotson?"

Cat and TJ both shook their heads. Ash, of course, struggled to keep up with the onslaught of new names. She had met several of the current members at the party, at least.

"Elena Garcia died around that time. Actually, I think she was one of Griffin's causalities," Cat said. "But whoever replaced her might know something."

"Dad sometimes hosts dinner parties with the others," TJ said. "Maybe he did back then, too."

Raisa nodded and made a list of bullet points:

- Who's coming for dinner?

- Robert Knight, Aaron Winkler

- Hugo Moreau, Charlotte Brown, Elena Garcia (deceased; not useful)

- Byrne, Schultz, or Dotson?

"We can work with that," she said as she capped the marker. "Set up a dinner party eight years ago, tell her it's the Committee, and let her brain invite the guests. Maybe we can figure out the others, then decide where to go from there."

"I don't think Schultz or Winkler will be at all interested in talking to us," Cat said. "Byrne maybe. If she even knows anything."

"You guys were in the same house back then, right? You two can recreate it. Down to every last detail. Your mother isn't a dreamwalker, so she'll be less likely to notice discrepancies, but the more realistic the better."

Ash got the feeling that last part was more for her benefit than anything else. "Okay... now what?" she said.

"Now we go in," Raisa replied.

"Aren't we kind of far away to reach the house from here?" Ash asked. "I thought proximity mattered."

"TJ and I have a stronger connection with her. We've been inside her dreams before, so we can reach her over a greater distance," Cat said. "I can pull you and Raisa with me. Unfortunately, that means Ash will have to go into Raisa's dreams, since I can't get into Ash's."

"You can't get into her dreams?" Raisa studied Ash with a newfound fascination that made Ash fidget with the hem of her shirt. "Interesting."

"Right, interesting. And *annoying*," Cat said. "Inconvenient. Unhelpful."

"Okay, we get the point," Ash muttered.

"Anyway, either you come to Raisa's dream and I take you both, or you get left behind. I'm not waiting around all night for you to try."

"I can do it." Ash was surprised to find that her confidence wasn't faked. Her recent conversation with a certain dream man had helped her see entering someone's dreams in another way.

Cat didn't look convinced, but Raisa clapped her hands together. "Wonderful. Ash can take the couch. Cat and I will just use my bed. TJ, you okay with the floor?"

TJ gave a sigh but nodded. Meanwhile, Cat looked alarmed. "Are you sure?"

"Don't be silly. It's not like we haven't shared a bed before."

"I know, but you said—"

"I'll get you two some blankets so you can get comfortable. We don't know how long we'll be in there."

Raisa disappeared down the hallway, leaving Cat staring helplessly after her. Down the hall, Ash could hear her pulling stuff out of a closet.

"So now we just have to wait for Raisa to fall asleep," TJ said. "Ash apparently dreams pretty reliably in N1, which is cool, but—"

"So do I, actually," Raisa interrupted as she walked back into the room with a stack of blankets in her arms. Probably way more than Ash and TJ needed between the two of them.

Cat frowned as Raisa dropped the blankets on the floor. "You do? Why didn't you tell me?"

Raisa shrugged. "You never asked. Now hurry up. The real problem will be the timing of getting into your mother's dreams."

"She's almost obsessive with her routine, so that shouldn't be too hard," TJ said.

"Wait, what if Raisa falls into a deeper sleep?" Ash asked.

"Won't be a problem," Cat said. "You get locked in whatever stage you were in when you left your body."

There was still so much about dreamwalking that Ash didn't understand, but she had to trust these people. She was surprised to find how much she *did* trust Cat and TJ, after such a short time knowing them. Even Raisa, whom she had only met that night. You could say Ash had found her people.

Cat stood to follow Raisa to the bedroom, but she paused and fixed Ash with an icy stare. "Just stay out of the way and try not to die, okay?"

Ash might have found her people, but she didn't think Cat was quite on board yet.

She grabbed two blankets and settled down on Raisa's remarkably comfortable couch, which was heaven compared to the cots at the dream therapy office. She snuggled into the plush cushions, her body warm under the weight of the soft blankets, and closed her eyes.

There are connections between everyone. It would have been easier to get into TJ's dreams, since she had known him longer, though not by much. That wasn't an option for reasons Ash now understood, thanks to the trip to Three Points and her encounter with his nightmare.

Ash held an image of Raisa's face in her mind. She thought about her quick wit and self-assuredness, and the way she looked at Cat while Cat wasn't watching. Ash followed an invisible string from her own mind, down the hallway to Raisa's room. There was something *there*, intangible and elusive but there nonetheless. Ash latched onto it. Instead of the force that yanked her into someone's dream involuntarily, Ash seized that invisible string and pulled herself in.

The dream formed around her like a watercolor painting, vague splotches of green and blue and brown that slowly sharpened like a camera coming into focus, transforming into a lakeside scene. Waves stirred by a gentle wind lapped at the sandy beach, the water a brilliant blue beneath a cloud-dotted sky.

The dream might have come into focus, but there was still something not quite right about it. Not quite reality. It had the feeling of a realistic digital painting, beautifully rendered but still slightly fake. Patches faded in and out of detail, colors dulling before brightening again, and the landscape in the distance grew fuzzy. It could have been merely Raisa's dream style or maybe a side-effect of the N1 dream.

"I knew you could do it."

Ash whirled away from the water to find Raisa sitting on a boulder behind her. The young woman's feet were bare, and a ridiculously wide-brimmed lavender hat shaded her face. When she tilted her chin up, her grin flashed white in the sun. Like the landscape, Raisa looked different than in real life. Her brown skin was perfectly smooth, its warm undertones more pronounced in the daylight.

"Make sure you rub it in when Cat gets here," Raisa said. "If you don't, I will."

Ash's face grew hot, and she questioned how it was fair she could still blush so easily in a dream. "Where are we?"

"Lake Tahoe. My family used to come here when I was a kid."

Raisa turned her head when a new form appeared nearby. Like the dream itself, Cat's figure started as a vague dark shape, gradually coming into focus. Her eyes lingered on Ash with undisguised displeasure. She had probably hoped they would get to leave Ash behind.

"Would you look at that, Cat," Raisa said in a chipper tone. "Ash is here, too. Isn't that exciting? Are you proud of her?"

Cat scowled and waved her hand impatiently at them. "Come on. We don't have time to waste."

Ash and Raisa exchanged a look, Ash trying to fight back a smile, but she broke when Raisa grinned at her.

Raisa popped up from her boulder and jumped into the sand, which tugged at Ash's shoes as she walked toward Cat. Grains slid through the cracks between her shoes and ankles.

Cat turned her back, and a door started to form in front of her. The wood was painted a reddish brown, and a Christmas wreath hung at eye-level, complete with clumps of holly berries and mistletoe. Raisa's eyes ran over it, a faint smile on her lips, but the wreath disappeared from sight when Cat opened the door.

Cat held out her hands, and Raisa and Ash each took one. Together, the three of them walked through the door and out of Raisa's dream world.

They stepped into the foyer of the Knights' house, as if they'd come through the front door. TJ was still working on constructing it, his forehead scrunched in concentration as he moved around the room, details shimmering to life one by one. The painting on the side wall. A vase of flowers on the entryway table.

"That painting wasn't there," Cat said as she let go of Raisa's and Ash's hands. "Mom got it like three years ago."

"Oh. Right." TJ frowned at the desert landscape piece, and it vanished. "Uh... do you remember what was there before?"

Cat grimaced at the conspicuously blank wall space. "I think it was some kind of forest picture... with a deer, maybe?"

"Oh! No, it was an elk." A new frame appeared when TJ snapped his fingers. The photograph showed a bull elk among the white trunks of aspens bearing the yellow leaves of autumn. Ash wondered how closely the details aligned with the original picture.

Raisa walked past them into the kitchen. Ash trailed after her, curious about what she had planned. The dream investigator looked around the room thoughtfully, then stepped up to the kitchen counter. A newspaper appeared in front of her, placed in a casual but obvious way.

"There's no way you know what the headlines were on...." Ash peered over Raisa's shoulder. "August 4th, 2016."

Raisa grinned. "That's what's great about dreams, though. I don't have to. I can make the details I want, then encourage the dreamer's mind to fill in the rest. She probably doesn't know what the stories were that day either, but our minds know that newspapers have headlines. Since her own subconscious filled in those details, she won't question them."

Ash frowned at the big letters that said MAN FOUND WITH A HOARD OF TWENTY-THREE CATS and wondered how someone would accept that as front-page news, but she got distracted when the date in the top corner flickered. It changed from August 4th to June 15th.

"That's weird," Raisa murmured. "Did you do that?"

Ash shook her head. "Not intentionally. It *is* weird, though... That's my uncle's birthday."

Raisa eyed the newspaper suspiciously but didn't change it back. They rejoined TJ and Cat, who had moved from the foyer to the dining room.

"Almost done?" Raisa asked.

Cat looked up from where she'd been squinting at a dent in the dining room table. "Yeah... It's hard, remembering what was different back then."

"Those are the details that matter most."

Cat nodded and refocused on the dent. After a couple more seconds of consideration, she brushed her fingertips over it, causing the dent to vanish.

"Where is your mom now?" Ash asked. "Shouldn't she... be here? It's her dream."

"Upstairs," TJ said. "I started with their bedroom and built the rest of the house around it. She hasn't come out yet."

"Now we need to nudge her toward the idea of the dinner party," Raisa said. "What were you two usually doing when these gatherings were happening?"

"Back then? We were told to stay in our rooms, out of the way," Cat said.

"Good. We can all stay out of sight, then." Raisa looked up at the ceiling at the sound of someone moving around upstairs. "Let's do this, shall we? Cat, your father, please."

Cat shifted her weight. "TJ has a better eye for detail."

The two Knights exchanged one of their glances with an unspoken message, and TJ nodded. He concentrated again, and a man began to appear, starting with his feet and moving upward like a 3D printing. Soon Robert Knight stood in front of them, dressed in what Ash would call too formal for a friendly dinner but which he would probably call "business casual." TJ really did have an eye for detail, because Robert looked eight years younger. Less gray at his temples, less pronounced lines on his face, but nothing too drastic.

"Beautiful work," Raisa said, and TJ flushed at the praise. "All right, Robert. Tell your wife it's almost time for your guests to come over. Don't want to keep the Committee waiting."

After meeting the man, Ash half-expected the dream crafted version of him to demand why she thought she could give him orders, but Robert turned away and called up the stairs to his wife. He repeated the words Raisa had given them, then walked to the kitchen of his own volition as far as Ash could tell. A few seconds later, footsteps sounded on the stairs.

Raisa waved a hand at the rest of them. "Okay, against the wall. I'll cloak us."

They followed Raisa's orders and backed against the wall by the windows. When Ash glanced past the half-drawn curtains, she elbowed TJ lightly in the side. He gave a surprised yelp, then followed her gaze.

"Oops," he said quietly. The landscape around the house was plain and out of focus, a field of golden grass and splotches of color that were probably wildflowers. The scene melted away like paint running off the canvas and was replaced by the manicured lawn, palm trees, and beds of lilacs and morning glories that surrounded the Knight house.

The last details sharpened a moment before Celia Knight reached the bottom of the stairs. She joined her husband in the kitchen, and the sounds and smells of them preparing food drifted in from the other room. Ash started fidgeting with the hem of her shirt, growing more agitated the longer they had to wait. Being a fly on the wall in an empty room was anything but interesting, believe you me.

Finally, a deep bonging like that of a bell tower sounded through the house when someone rang the doorbell. Celia hurried out of the kitchen to answer it, while Robert carried dishes of appetizers to the dining room. Ash knew full well this was a dream, but the sight and smell of bacon-wrapped jalapeños and crab cakes made her mouth water.

Celia guided a woman Ash didn't recognize into the dining room. Robert paused in setting up the table to shake the woman's hand. "Thank you for coming, Elena. Please, help yourself."

She gave him a smile, but there was something cold behind it that made Ash actually shudder. This was Elena Garcia, one of the Committee members who had been killed eight years ago.

One by one, the rest of the guests arrived. None of them brought along a plus one, which made Ash wonder whether their significant others hadn't been invited, or if none of them had one. Eventually, seven people loitered around the dining room, chatting and smiling: six Committee members plus Celia. Ash recognized Aaron Winkler, and TJ pointed out Charlotte Brown when she arrived. Raisa identified the fifth as Hugo Moreau. No one knew the name of the final member, a plump man with a perpetually flushed face.

"Robert! Our honored guest has arrived!" Celia called from the foyer.

"Elena, do you mind?" Robert said.

Garcia gave him a long look that said she *did* mind, but she set down her drink and disappeared through the doorway to the kitchen. She returned a few seconds later with a small, round cake covered in what was probably chocolate frosting, a single birthday candle stuck in the middle. At the same time, Celia entered the room with the final member of the Committee.

Tiernan O'Shea, Ash's uncle. The guest of honor and the birthday boy.

Chapter 19

A SH STARED AS HER uncle walked farther into the dining room. Of all the insane things she had seen inside a dream, this was the worst. Tiernan was a dreamwalker. And he used to be on the *Committee*. She kept learning new secrets that made her wonder how much she really knew about him.

He grinned at Garcia when he saw the cake in her hands, and she returned a much colder smile as she set it on the table.

"Happy birthday to the newest member of our Committee," Charlotte Brown said warmly. "Here's to many more years to come."

Moreau raised his glass of wine. "To Tiernan O'Shea."

"To Tiernan!" the others echoed with varying degrees of enthusiasm.

"We got what we came for. Can we go now?" Ash said quietly, without considering that maybe she shouldn't speak. They might be hidden from sight, but she didn't know if anyone had bothered to hide their voices. Luckily, no one in the dream looked at her. They started cutting the cake, evidently opting for dessert before dinner.

Raisa frowned at her. "What's wrong?"

"O'Shea," Cat said. "Is that your uncle?"

Ash nodded wordlessly. She avoided looking at Tiernan, but she could still see him out of the corner of her eye as he got a piece of cake from Garcia.

"Yeah, I think it's time to go," Cat said. "We—"

"Did you really think I wouldn't see this coming?" a voice said from the doorway to the kitchen.

The four of them spun to face a second Robert Knight. The dream version of him still sat at the table, conversing with the others and oblivious to the presence of the uninvited guests, but this one was eight years older and supremely pissed off.

"It's not what it looks like," Cat said.

"It's *exactly* what it looks like," Robert snapped. He scowled at Raisa, who for the first time since Ash had met her looked intimidated. "I told you not to go digging, but you just couldn't listen, could you? And using your mother to do it! That's a new low, even for you, Catalina."

Even for you? That was harsh, and yet not surprising. Cat stared at the floor with her jaw clenched.

"It wasn't Cat's idea!" TJ said.

"You don't have to lie to protect your sister," Robert said sternly. "I'm assuming you all are somewhere nearby. It won't take long for my people to find you."

"Get out. Now," Cat said. A door appeared a few steps away, standing free in the middle of the room. It looked exactly like the front door of the house. She reached for Ash, but before she could make contact, the ground split between them like an earthquake tearing the house in half. Within only a few seconds, they stood on opposite sides of a gaping black chasm, too wide for them to jump. Raisa and Ash on one side, TJ and Cat on the other.

"Time to wake up." Robert grabbed each of his children by an arm and shoved them through the door Cat had created. Ash could see the rest of the room on the other side, but the moment the two passed the threshold, they vanished.

Raisa and Ash were on their own.

Robert turned toward them. A chasm still separated him from them, but Ash doubted that meant they were safe.

Raisa grabbed her wrist. "Run, Ash."

"Why? What happens if he catches us?"

"I really don't want to find out."

The house around them vanished, everything but the dining room. Celia and the dream Committee continued on with their birthday party like nothing strange had happened.

Raisa tugged Ash into motion, and the two fled through the space that had been a window moments before. They crossed the garden TJ had crafted, without care for the delicate flowers they trampled as they cut down to the street. Rather than sticking to the sidewalk, they opted for sprinting down the middle of the road, their shoes thudding against the asphalt. Cars lined the curb, but none were in motion.

Raisa and Ash turned the corner at the end of the block, but instead of stepping onto another side street, they found themselves in the middle of downtown Los Angeles. Skyscrapers rose around them, windows glinting in the sunlight, and people bustled along the sidewalks. Cars now drove on the streets, if it could be called driving during downtown rush hour traffic.

At first, Ash didn't notice anything wrong with the people. She and Raisa darted between them, doing their best not to get separated, and Ash never looked too closely at their faces. She had passed several dozen before she realized there was nothing to look *at*.

The people who hurried on their ways had no faces.

Ash was stunned so badly that she forgot to keep running and found herself staring at a man in a business suit who stepped by her. Then a woman in a green dress whose hair fell around her face in brown waves. Her face itself was blank, a canvas of pale skin with faint indentations where eyes should have been and the hint of a small lump that could have been a nose.

Raisa was several paces ahead by the time she realized Ash was no longer with her. She backtracked and grabbed Ash's arm, tugging her forward again. "Come *on*. What the hell are you doing?"

Ash staggered along behind her, still staring at the people they passed. "Why are they like that?"

Raisa followed Ash's gaze to a man with graying hair but didn't show any of the alarm that Ash felt. "Her mind filled in the people because that's how LA should be, but sometimes the mind doesn't bother with all the details the dreamer isn't likely to notice anyway. Are you done freaking out now, or do I have to give you a little longer to gawk while Robert catches up?"

"I'm fine," Ash said defensively. Both Raisa and Cat had a way of making her feel like an idiot.

"Good. This way." Raisa turned and yanked Ash toward the entrance of what looked like a hotel. The sudden change in direction almost pulled Ash's arm out of its socket.

They pushed past the revolving door and ran through the lobby populated with faceless people. Ash missed a step when the patterned carpet beneath her feet changed from ugly purple swirls to equally ugly paisleys. Raisa didn't bother with the elevators, instead following a sign that pointed toward the stairs. She slammed into the metal crash bar and flung open the door. The sound of it colliding against the wall echoed up the stairwell.

Raisa finally released Ash's hand and started up the steps. She moved faster than Ash would have thought possible, and Ash struggled to keep up, already half a flight behind by the time they reached the second floor.

"Do you have a plan... or are we just going to keep... running forever?" Ash panted.

"The plan is to not get caught," Raisa replied. "Our bodies are too far away for us to get out of the dream without Cat's help, which means we need to buy ourselves time for her to get back in and find us. I'm hoping she's clever enough to know I'll come here."

"Why? What's here?"

They both jumped when the door banged open below, and Ash made the mistake of pausing to glance down at the same time Robert looked up. He locked eyes with Ash for a moment before sprinting up the stairs. The sound of his heavy footsteps spurred Ash back into motion, and she hurried to the third-floor landing where Raisa waited. She pushed Ash behind her and stared downward while Robert grew closer.

The stairwell between the second and third floors *stretched*, as if the fabric of reality were rubber being pulled taut until it snapped apart and split into two separate sets of stairs. Robert paused, now three floors below them instead of two, and glared up at Raisa. She flashed him a smile before spinning to push through the door into the third—now fourth—floor hallway.

Once the door closed behind them, the crash bar flattened against the surface, though it retained the illusion of being 3D. The cracks between the door and the frame melted together, until they stood in front of what looked like a door painted onto the wall.

"That should stall him for a bit," Raisa said with satisfaction.

"Can't he just change it back?"

"He's a powerful dreamwalker, but a lot of people are bad at undoing what others have done. Plus, it's no secret that the man has *no* imagination." Raisa turned and ran down the hallway lined with doors. They had plaques on their surfaces that should have shown room numbers, but the metal was as blank as the faces of the people.

Nearly to the far end of the hallway, Raisa came to an abrupt stop, like she had hit an invisible wall.

"Shit. We hit the dreamline," she said.

"The dreamline?"

"The edge of the dreamscape. You can only go so far away from the dreamer. She's probably still back at the house enjoying her dinner party." The dream continued ahead of them, but it was a part of the dream they couldn't reach, so she turned her back on the dead end.

The fake door to the stairwell remained the same, but Ash winced when something slammed against the other side.

"Pick a room, any room," Raisa said. She tried the door to one, but the handle didn't turn.

Ash turned to another on the opposite side of the hall, expecting the same result, but a moment before she touched the handle, a light on the card sensor flashed green. "This way!" She slipped through the door, leaving it open for Raisa.

Once they were both inside, Ash latched the deadbolt and turned to face an unremarkable hotel room with two beds, a nightstand between them, and a small desk in the corner.

"Now what?" Ash asked.

"Now I'm really hoping Cat shows up."

Ash looked at the room door, willing it to open and for Cat to step through. They had reached a dead end, trapped in this dream with nowhere else to go, the distance to their bodies as insurmountable as the chasm that had split the house.

The whole building trembled when a sound like an explosion rattled through the walls.

"Well, that's one way to get through," Raisa muttered. "Typical manly brute force move. Time to go."

She threw apart the curtains and opened the window, exposing the screen on the other side. A knife appeared in Raisa's hand, and she used it to slash through the flimsy mesh. She leaned out, first looking down at the street and then up toward the sky.

"Grab the sheets from one of the beds," Raisa said.

Ash did as ordered. She threw aside one comforter so she could yank both sheets underneath free. She handed them to Raisa, who tied them together and started knotting the sheets every several feet to form a rope.

"You girls think you can hide from me?" The voice came from the hallway, but it filtered through the walls far more clearly than it should have. His footsteps, too, were not necessarily loud but starkly obvious as they moved down the hallway. "Your new friend doesn't know how to get out, does she? Tiernan must be so ashamed of his niece."

Ash's face flushed. She kept her eyes trained on Raisa, but her mind raced. *Was* he ashamed of her? Was that why he had never told her about the dreamwalkers? Everyone else showed their powers as a child, but Ash had only developed the ability recently. She could imagine how disappointed he must have been when she never showed a lick of talent.

"That's who you are, right?" Robert said, his voice closer now. "I recognized you when they brought you to the house, asking questions that should remain unanswered. I had to pretend I didn't know. He was so insistent on your not learning about the dreamwalkers. He thought you had no power. Apparently he was wrong, and you're just weak."

"Don't listen to him," Raisa whispered. She finished knotting their makeshift rope, only to pause and frown at it. She grabbed it in the middle, and when she pulled her fists apart, the sheets lengthened the same way a whole flight of stairs had stretched into existence. She did it again, until the rope had grown several feet.

She tied one end of her newly extended rope to the bedpost, then threw the rest of it out the window. Instead of dropping toward the street, the makeshift rope fell *up*, toward the roof of the building.

Ash gaped. "How...?"

"No time. Up you go." Raisa shoved her toward the window.

Ash stuck her head out and craned her neck to look upward, where the sheet reached toward the sky like an impossible magic beanstalk.

Ash awkwardly pulled herself through the window, her fingers wrapped tightly around the rope. Her legs swung free for a moment when she stepped off the window sill, until her feet found one of the knots. The rope swayed, its other end dangling high above her, and Ash had the surreal sensation of clinging to the rope upside down, even though gravity still pulled her toward the street below.

"Take your time!" Raisa said from inside. "Not like we have my girlfriend's dad chasing us like I broke her heart on prom night."

Ash tore her gaze away from the sky and focused on the section of sheet directly above her hands. "I thought you broke up with her."

"Only until she admits she was wrong and begs for my forgiveness."

Despite the fact that she hung four stories in the air, Ash smiled. She started inching upward, using the knots Raisa had tied as footholds. The rope swayed again when Raisa pulled herself nimbly out the window. Back inside, the footsteps stopped outside the room.

Ash was almost to the roof when Robert finally forced his way in. His broad shoulders barely fit through the window when he leaned out to call up at them. "This is ridiculous! You can't run forever."

"Maybe *you* can't, old man," Raisa said. "I can do this all day."

The rope ended about a foot from the top of the wall that surrounded the roof. Ash had to stretch her arm upward and just managed to hook her fingertips over the edge. She pulled herself closer and made a desperate leap from the rope to get her other hand on the wall. Her feet scrabbled against the side of the building before her shoes found purchase. She still mostly had to use her arms to haul herself up, and by then her muscles were already screaming.

She tumbled ungracefully over the top of the wall and spun around to peer over it. Raisa was halfway up, and Robert was in the process of climbing out after her.

"Hurry up!" Ash shouted.

"Thanks, I was going to break for a little sightseeing down here," Raisa called back.

"Joke all you want, Sokolov," Robert said. "Waste your breath. It'll make you easier to catch."

Back inside the hotel room, the knot holding the sheets to the bed frame started to slip. First an inch, then it unraveled completely. The moment it did, the rope started to fall. Not up toward the sky but down, like it had suddenly remembered it ought to obey gravity.

Ash threw out her arm and managed to catch the end of the sheet. She got both hands on it and leaned back, her feet braced against the wall. The weight of two people should have sent her tumbling over the edge, but something kept her rooted to the spot.

Raisa's head appeared above the wall, and she pulled herself over to join Ash. "You can let go now," she said.

"What about Robert?" Ash asked. "He'll die."

"I doubt it."

Ash met Raisa's eyes for a moment, then decided to trust her. She let go, and the end of the rope slithered over the edge of the wall. They both leaned forward to look down at Robert, who had managed to catch the window sill as he fell. He pulled himself up so he crouched in the open window and glared up at them.

Robert turned his attention toward the brick wall above him, and one by one bricks started to slide outward, forming hand and footholds at evenly spaced intervals.

"Ope. Maybe he's not as dumb as he looks," Raisa said. She stepped away from the wall, her eyes sweeping over the roof. "So... I can't actually do this all day. I'll wear myself out eventually. You got anything in you?"

"I... I don't know. I've never changed something on purpose. It just happens." Like the force that had held her to the roof when she should have gone tumbling to her death.

"I don't want to pressure you, but now would be an excellent time for it to *just happen.*"

Ash glanced around, searching for their next move, anything that could help. There wasn't much to look at. A metal door that would take them back inside seemed like their best option. She looked back at the wall, where she expected Robert to appear any second, and shook her head helplessly.

"Raisa! Ash!"

Ash turned to find Cat standing in front of the door that had been closed a moment before. It still appeared to lead to a stairwell, but it had changed from plain metal to the Knights' front door.

"Hurry up!" Cat said, holding out both hands.

They ran across the roof to join her, and Cat yanked them through the door. Ash's vision went black.

Chapter 20

A s Ash's awareness returned, the first thing she noticed was the pressure on her chest. Not the comforting weight of blankets but something more like someone had placed a sack of flour on top of her. The second thing she noticed was the rumble that vibrated through her whole body.

The urge to sneeze tickled her nose, then thankfully receded. When she opened her eyes, she found herself staring into a massive orange-striped face with amber irises and slitted pupils. A Maine Coon blinked its eyes slowly and released another wave of purring.

Another sneeze threatened to escape, but Ash held it back, as if worried the creature might attack her face if she moved. She had thought TJ was echoing her joke about his sister earlier, but apparently there was a cat in the apartment, the kind with fur that made Ash's allergies go wild.

She saw movement out of the corner of her eye as someone entered the room from the hallway. "Uh, a little help here?"

"Rascal. Be a good boy and get off." Raisa stepped over and nudged the cat, who gave an irritable meow and didn't budge. It wasn't until an involuntary sneeze ripped free from Ash that Rascal sprang from her chest, startled, and squirmed his way behind the couch to hide. He didn't even look like he should be able to fit through the crack, but he managed.

"Sorry about that," Raisa said. "He either hates strangers or loves them and won't leave them alone. I guess you're one of the lucky ones." She spoke in her usual light tone, but signs of fatigue crept in around the edges. A dullness in her eyes, her posture not quite straight. She had expended a lot of energy in that dream to keep them ahead of Robert.

"Yeah, lucky me," Ash said. The person who was allergic got the stamp of approval. From the way the human Cat scowled at her, she could guess which group Raisa's temporary ex-girlfriend belonged to.

"We need to go," Cat said. She held out a hand to help TJ to his feet. "When they figure out we're not actually anywhere near the house, they'll check here next."

Ash sat up and brushed a stray curl out of her face. Raisa pulled on a pair of slipper boots while Cat retrieved the rest of their shoes. She handed TJ's boots to him, then chucked Ash's flats at her head. Ash barely managed to catch them before they could smack her in the face.

"What will he do if he finds us?" she asked while she shoved her feet into the shoes.

"Lock us in the basement and never let us out again," TJ said.

Cat gave him her signature *TJ stop it* look, but it was less forceful than normal, which made Ash think Robert might actually lock them in the basement. "He'll make sure we never find what we're looking for," Cat said. She finished tying her sneakers and grabbed the car keys from where TJ had left them on the coffee table.

"Cat, wait..." Raisa grabbed Cat's arm before she could stalk out the door. "I need you to tell me the truth. You're looking for Griffin, aren't you?"

Cat's eyes widened. "Why would you—"

"Come on. The Committee eight years ago? What else could this be about?"

Cat looked like she was considering denying it, but then her shoulders slumped. "Are you going to tell me not to?"

"That depends on why you're looking."

"We think he's going to escape the prison the Committee put him in."

To her credit, Raisa didn't look immediately skeptical. She had an open mind, this one. "And what makes you think that?"

Cat hesitated and cast a glance at TJ, who shrugged. "Because Sebastian told us so," she said quietly. "He's alive, Raisa. He came to Ash in her dreams."

Raisa's eyes widened. Ash waited for her to say, "Are you sure?" or that it was impossible. But Raisa slid her hand down from Cat's wrist to lace their fingers together instead and asked, "Are you okay?"

Cat looked down at their joined hands, and her confident exterior cracked. Even when she had been confessing truths to Ash on that rooftop, she hadn't looked so vulnerable. "Not really," she said in a choked voice. Tears glinted in her eyes, but she blinked several times to chase them away and pulled her hand from Raisa's. "If Sebastian thinks Griffin is about to escape, then I believe him. We need to stop it before it happens, but to do that we need to figure out where the Committee imprisoned him in the first place."

"We tried asking Dad, but he seems to think Griffin escaping is impossible," TJ said. "Which is why we needed to know who else was on the Committee back then."

"And now we know who to target." Cat looked straight at Ash.

"Wait, Tiernan?" Ash should have seen it coming, but a part of her was still in denial about what she had seen.

"It's perfect. He doesn't even know *we* know he's a dreamwalker. We can go into his dreams and find out what he knows about the prison."

Ash shook her head. "No. I can't do that." Invading Celia's dream was one thing, but her uncle's was another matter entirely. "I'll talk to him. Get him to tell us."

"*No*, you won't. Because his answer is going to be the same as our father's. Sebastian clearly knows something they don't, and they're not going to listen to us. Our best hope is to sneak into his dreams and extract a useful memory before he realizes we're there."

"You think we can?" TJ asked. "I mean... Tiernan was on the Committee. If he's as powerful as the rest of them, he might see us coming anyway."

"The element of surprise," Cat said. "But if we ask him first, he'll know we're coming."

Ash bowed her head and slid her fingers into her hair. The agitation inside her was building, until it took all her will to sit still instead of pulling her hair out. "I can't do this. I can't go into the dreams of someone I love uninvited again." It had broken one of the most important relationships in her life. Even after the secrets and the lying, she cared about Tiernan too much for that.

Cat raised an eyebrow, probably curious about the word *again*. "You want to stop Griffin from escaping, don't you? Well, this is the way forward. The *only* way."

"What about Aaron Winkler? We could go after him."

"Dad has probably already told him that we were asking about Griffin," TJ said. "It sounds like Tiernan removed himself from the dreamwalker community, though. If he's not in contact with anyone on the Committee, they might not have warned him yet."

"Which means we have to act fast," Cat said.

Ash hated how right they both were. Her uncle wouldn't give them answers willingly, and he was the best person to try to steal the memory from. They were chasing nightmares again, going into the dreams of someone as powerful as Tiernan O'Shea, but she didn't think they had another choice.

"I hate this," Ash said. "I hate all of this. I just want that on the record."

"Noted," Cat replied. "Can we go now?" She tossed the keys to TJ, who caught them awkwardly.

"Can someone else maybe drive?" he asked. "I could really use some reprieve."

"Don't look at me," Ash said. No one wanted her driving.

"We'll take my car. I just need the address," Raisa said, despite her clear exhaustion, which made Ash wonder why Cat never volunteered to sit behind the wheel. And why no one else expected her to.

Like her apartment, Raisa's car was nicer than what Ash would've expected from someone her own age. Ash didn't even *have* her own car. She had been determined to buy her own car, rather than let her uncle get one for her, but she had never managed to save up enough money. If she had, it would have been something used that barely ran and had a bunch of junk in the back seat, not a sleek and pristine SUV with leather seats that smelled like pine needles thanks to the Christmas tree air freshener hanging from the rearview mirror.

After they got their destination into Raisa's phone, Ash settled back and tried not to squirm. TJ curled up in the seat beside her, fidgeting with the chalcedony Ash had given him. He promptly passed out, the gem still clutched in his hand. For someone who suffered from recurring nightmares, he sure had an easy time falling asleep.

"Oh, turn here," Cat said suddenly.

"Why?" Raisa asked.

"We need to take a quick detour to the office."

"For your sleeping drug?" Ash didn't know how they were going to slip Tiernan pills, but it was a decent idea.

"We have some in serum form too. It'll work a lot faster. Lasts less time, but we only need it to work long enough to get in, find what we need, and get out."

Raisa nodded and ignored the directions to Ash's house telling them to go straight. They headed toward downtown and the dream therapy office instead.

Ash leaned her head against the window and watched the buildings flash by as they drew closer to what felt very much like a betrayal. She closed her eyes, trying to chase away her worries long enough to fall asleep. Enough to dream. She was surprised to find there was only one person who might be able to comfort her at the moment. His showing up was a long shot, but she had to try.

Chapter 21

A SH LOOKED AGITATED WHEN I joined her in the dream. She radiated a mix of anger and hurt that only betrayal could bring. I knew the feeling.

"What happened?" I asked. "Did you find what you were looking for?"

"Sort of." She grimaced. "Let's just say I found answers I didn't know I was looking for. And now I have to figure out what to do about them." She sat down on the ground and wrapped her arms around her knees. "Someone I thought I knew has been lying to me my whole life. About who he is, about my own history. He *raised* me... You'd think I would know him better than anyone."

I sat down beside her and hesitated for a brief moment before putting my arm around her. She leaned into me, and I rested my chin against the top of her head.

"Now they expect me to craft a dream to get answers from him," she said. "I don't know if I can do that."

"You're really planning to go into Tiernan's dreams?" I still had this shred of hope I could talk her out of it.

I realized my mistake the moment his name left my lips.

She jerked away from me and narrowed her eyes, suddenly guarded again. "How do you know my uncle? How do you know so much about my life in general?" She got to her feet and took a step back, putting even more distance between us. "Did you know all along that he was a dreamwalker?"

Reluctantly, I nodded.

"And you didn't *tell* me? Why the hell not?"

"I was hoping you would find answers without having to involve him." As badly as I wanted them to find the prison, going into Tiernan's dreams wasn't the answer. He would spot them coming from a mile away. "Please, Ash. There has to be another way. You were right—you think you know him, but you don't. You can't go into his dreams. You don't know what he's capable of."

"You're right, I don't, because no one ever tells me anything. You're going to tell me right now how you know my uncle and what your involvement in all of this is. I'm tired of the secrets! What happened to you? Why does everyone think you're dead, and *why* can't you come see me outside my dreams?"

I stared up at her, and she glared back, her arms crossed. There were so many things I wished I could tell her, but how would she react if she knew the whole truth? It was too soon for her to understand. Some secrets were necessary, even if I wished they weren't.

"I swear, I will walk away right now if you don't tell me the truth," she said. "I'll walk away from all of it." I believed her.

I bowed my head and took a deep breath. I had spent a lot of time thinking about what I would tell her if it came to this. Now it was time to see how it went over. I looked back up and met her fierce stare levelly. "The fight wasn't Griffin against everyone else. He had friends. Some stood with him."

She watched me, and I knew the uneasy feeling that prickled at her. She didn't want to ask, but she had to. "And which side were you on?"

"The side you don't want."

I kept my face carefully blank while I waited for her to process that. TJ and Cat had painted their brother as some kind of perfect hero who had stood against the evil Griffin, but they had been lied to. Their parents didn't want them to know what had really happened.

I could see the questions churning in her mind. She had so many, but she had to sort through them and pick one to ask first.

"And why do you want me to find the prison now?" she said finally.

I looked away. Talking about what happened eight years ago stirred a cold ache inside me. Heavy guilt, festering anger, and above all grief. I had lost so much back then. "Mistakes were made," I said. So, so many mistakes. "I'm trying to set things right."

I knew I didn't really have to breathe in this place, but my chest tightened, and I found it hard to take in the nonexistent air anyway. "He wasn't all bad, Ash. He was... special. And certain people took advantage of that. Things didn't go the way we planned. But that's why I need you to find him. Anyone else might decide to kill him without giving him a chance."

"Maybe he doesn't deserve a second chance," she said. "Maybe they should have killed him instead of locking him away."

"You don't mean that," I said softly. I got to my feet and stepped toward her, but she countered with another step back. She watched me like I was a venomous snake that might strike at any second. That look stung; I had no desire to hurt her.

"*Please.*" I put everything I could behind that word. I wished I knew how TJ did that thing with his eyes that made people cave. I could have used some of his magic right then. "I know I've kept things from you, but I need you to trust me for a little bit longer."

"Why should I?" she demanded. "You've been lying to me since we met."

I shook my head. "I might have withheld information, but I've never lied to you."

"It's the same thing! If you're deluded enough to think there's a difference, you're really not who I thought you were."

I gritted my teeth and fought back a swell of anger. I wasn't angry at Ash. Frustrated, maybe, but if ever there was a time to keep my temper, it was now. "You're right, okay? I shouldn't have kept things from you, but I didn't tell you which side I was on because I was trying to avoid this exact reaction. I needed you to trust me, and admitting I tried to destroy the Committee didn't seem like the way to do it."

She eyed me, still suspicious, but I could see her walls cracking. She *wanted* to believe me, as desperately as I wanted her to. "And Tiernan?" she said. "Why didn't you tell me about him?"

"Tiernan is dangerous."

"He's my uncle! He would never hurt me."

I really wished I could be certain of that. I took a deep breath and let it out slowly. If I had learned anything about Ash, it was that the more I told her not to enter Tiernan's dreams, the more determined she would be to do it. The best I could do was make sure she didn't get hurt in the process.

"If you're determined to extract memories from him, then I'm going to help you." I hated saying those words, but I did see her relax a little bit more. I could feel her coming around, her resistance slipping away. "Do you have a plan?"

"Not really," she said. "They want me to figure out how to get to the memory, but I haven't been able to change *anything* in someone's dream, not on purpose. I can't create some masterfully detailed dream to trick him into reliving what happened back then."

"You can, though." I stepped closer again, and this time she didn't back away. That seemed like progress. "I'm going to let you in on a secret, something the Committee wouldn't want you to know. They wouldn't want anyone to know, maybe not even each other." I gave a knowing smile that I'm sure she loved as much as my cryptic introduction. "Why do we die if we die in someone else's dream? Why don't we wake up like we do from our own? Better yet, why *can* we die in a dream, if we can control it? Why aren't we just invincible?"

Ash shrugged. "I don't know. Because that's how it works?"

"Because that's how they *believe* it works," I said. "It's all about belief. Limitations don't exist in dreams. If you believe you can do it, then you can. The only thing holding you back is you. Something happened, and it's blocking you. Am I right?"

Her eyes flickered away as she recalled a memory she didn't want to remember, one that still caused her nightmares.

"Part of you doesn't want this power," I went on. "You've convinced yourself that you can't control it, so of course you can't. You have to let go of whatever happened. It wasn't your fault. Accidents happen, and sometimes there's nothing we can do to fix the fallout, but you shouldn't let that constrain you now. You're capable of so much more than you're letting yourself achieve."

She glared at me, then spun on the ball of her foot and stalked to the edge of the cliff. I joined her and marveled at the way the wind off the ocean caught her hair, the light from the perpetual sunset setting it aflame.

She stared at the horizon until her anger faded, replaced by the glistening of frustrated tears in her eyes. "I *know*, okay?" she said finally. "I know that. But it doesn't change the fact that dreamwalking cost me the most important thing in my life, and I can't *fix* it because he would never believe me."

"You don't know that. Some people have very open minds."

She shook her head, and when she blinked, a few tears escaped and rolled down her cheeks.

"Hey," I said gently. I nudged her arm so she turned toward me, and I brushed my thumb against her cheek to wipe away a tear. "It's okay."

"It's not." She stepped closer, and I wrapped my arms around her. She felt so small and fragile, even though I knew she was anything but, especially here. "I learned something I shouldn't know in a dream. I invaded my friend's privacy."

"You didn't mean to."

"But it *happened*. And I didn't tell him about it because what on earth would I say?" She tucked her forehead into the crook of my neck, and her next words came out muffled. "I tried to keep it secret, but I let something slip and it just... went downhill from there." She pulled away and wiped her face dry with the cuffs of her sleeves. "Maybe I could go to his dreams. I could find out if he still hates me, or if there's any hope at all."

"Whatever you find there, it won't make you feel better," I said. "You would only be chasing nightmares. If you want to know if there's hope, you need to go to him. *In person.* Come here." I took her hand and led her back a step, to where the couch from her house appeared a couple yards from the edge of the cliff. I sat down, and she curled up beside me, her head resting on my chest.

I could have stayed there forever in the warm glow of the sunset with my arm wrapped around her. I would have loved to forget about the outside world and let this dream become my reality.

"I wish I could stay here. With you," Ash murmured.

I let out a slow breath. "It's easy to get lost in a dream. A world you can bend to your will, where you can do whatever you want and change monsters into butterflies. But waking up isn't a curse. It's a gift. Trust me."

"Sometimes it feels like the real world is the dream." Ash snuggled closer and closed her eyes. "Sometimes I hate it there. After everything I lost, I just... I didn't know who I was anymore. What I was meant to do with my life. I was just trying to get by, day to day. Then you showed up and suddenly I felt... special. Important."

"You *are* special. You're one of a kind. And I don't mean that in a 'everyone is unique' sort of way." I gently lifted her chin. "You have no idea how special you are, dreamer."

She stared into my eyes, and I knew we both flashed back to our dance. That moment when I'd been so tempted to kiss her. Now Ash shifted closer, an invitation, but I turned my face away. Her disappointment was palpable.

"And what about you?" she said after a beat. "I feel like I still know so little about you. Who are you, Sebastian Knight?"

"I... Honestly, I don't know anymore." I thought I had known, once, but the person I had been was long gone.

"Tell me something," she said. "Something real."

I mulled over her request. Something *real.* It had been so long since someone had asked me that, I didn't even know where to start. I guessed the easiest thing was to go all the way back.

"I was never good enough for my father," I said. "It didn't matter what I did. Perfect grades. Excelled at my dreamwalking lessons. It was like with each expectation I met, he decided to raise the bar a little higher. I think he wanted me to take after him. Continue the family legacy. He didn't give a damn what *I* wanted."

"And what did you want?"

I thought back to the plans I'd had in high school, before my life had veered off course. "I wanted to go to college to become an architect. I always liked buildings. Designing things. I thought maybe I could learn to create something beautiful. Everyone would look upon it and think... *wow,* what a beautiful building. A work of art. My dreams never mattered, though. It was always about what others wanted from me, what *they* envisioned."

"I wanted to be a photographer," Ash said. "I still do, I guess. I just don't know if I'm cut out for it. I don't know if I'm cut out for *anything.* I went to college because I thought it would make my uncle happy. The thing is, he never asked me to. He's always been supportive of my dreams, but I still feel like I'm letting him down by not becoming a doctor or something. Even now, after learning he's been lying to me, all I want to do is make him proud of me." She closed her eyes, but a tear escaped from one corner and rolled down her cheek. "All I've done is fail, though. I dropped out of college. I can't keep a job for more than a few months. I can't bring myself to even *apply* to the company I want to work for, because I don't think I could handle it if they rejected me."

I wished there were some advice I could give her, something I could say to make her feel better, but who was I to be giving advice? If someone looked at my life, where I had ended up, they would probably do the opposite of anything I suggested.

But I couldn't stand to watch her cry and say *nothing.*

"Rejection is part of life," I said after a long struggle to find words. "People aren't always going to like or accept us. What they think says more about them than it does about you, though. *You* are brilliant and beautiful and talented, and if they don't see that, it's their loss."

Ash opened her eyes and let out a strangled laugh. When she looked up at me, the orange light of the sunset reflected off the unshed tears that still glistened in her eyes. "You have a way with words sometimes, you know that?"

I shrugged. "I have a lot of time alone with my own thoughts." Too much time.

"Well, you're not alone anymore. You have me and TJ and Cat. You don't have to hide."

I gave her a sad smile that harbored my every wistful thought, every lost opportunity, every regret. Oh, the things I would do differently if I could go back and change them.

I didn't know what to say to her after that, but I was saved by the wavering of the dream as Ash's consciousness drifted back to the waking world. We both stood, and the couch behind us vanished.

"Go find your answers," I said. "And remember, dreamer. The only limits are the ones you place on yourself. You can do this." She reached for me as I stepped away, but I vanished before her outstretched fingers could touch me.

Chapter 22

A SH DIDN'T KNOW WHAT to expect when they reached her house. During the last ten minutes of the drive, her mind had conjured all sorts of scenarios. Robert might already be there, waiting for them. It wasn't hard to guess their next move. But maybe Robert didn't have their new address. Or maybe he'd called Tiernan to warn him, and the element of surprise would be lost.

She didn't know if Robert and Tiernan were still in contact. She didn't know *anything*.

But when Raisa pulled the car into the driveway, the house was silent, the lights off. Ash unlocked the front door, and they tiptoed through the entryway and up the stairs. They left Raisa by the door to stand guard in case someone showed up. Cat might have had other reasons for asking Raisa to stay out of this mission, but she was also right. They didn't want to leave their bodies unguarded while they poked around in Tiernan's head.

They found him sleeping soundly in his bed. While Cat pulled the syringe with the sleeping serum from her pocket, Ash stepped up to Tiernan's nightstand and tapped her finger against his phone screen. No missed calls or texts. She picked up the phone and unplugged it, then held it over Tiernan. The screen light illuminated his sleeping face, growing a bit brighter when it unlocked.

She checked his texts and calls, but his most recent text had been from her, and the last call from the hospital where he worked. She moved her finger toward the button to relock the phone but paused, frowning at another contact on the list of recent calls: Lady Sabri's Hospital. First his car parked outside it, and now they were calling him? He hadn't worked there for years.

"We're ready," Cat said.

Ash winced at how loud her voice sounded in the dark room. Cat held an empty syringe, which meant Tiernan should be fast asleep for the next several hours, but the atmosphere still encouraged whispering.

Ash replaced the phone on the nightstand and plugged it back in. Then she looked across the dark room at Cat and TJ. "We're really doing this?" She still didn't want to, but she also knew there wasn't a better way.

When they were certain Tiernan was out cold, the drug having taken effect, they moved down the hall to Ash's room to get comfortable. It had been a long time since Ash had invited anyone into her room, and she found herself growing self-conscious about it.

Cat peered at the drawings and photographs above Ash's desk, her eyes lingering on the sketch of Sebastian's face, while TJ studied Ash's collection of stuffed animals. She had four different types, grouped in separate parts of her room, from the different years when young Ash couldn't decide what her favorite animal was. First elephants, then bats. She had become obsessed with octopuses in the fifth grade when she learned they had no bones. She had finally settled on foxes, with their pointed noses and bushy tails, or at least her uncle thought she had. In truth, once she turned fifteen, she had stopped sharing her current favorite animal so he would stop buying her plushies.

"We shouldn't waste time," she said, sounding remarkably like Cat. The other girl must have picked up on that too, because she gave Ash a wry smile.

Ash grabbed one of a dozen throw blankets she had stashed in her closet. Another collection she had accumulated over the years. She liked the softness of them, and the weight of multiple blankets over her while she slept. She tended to get too hot most nights, though, hence why she slept with her window open. She took a pillow from the bed and handed both it and the blanket to Cat, who would have to make do with the floor, while Ash and TJ shared the bed again.

Getting into Tiernan's dream was infinitely easier than finding Raisa's. Ash didn't have to grab hold of that imaginary string and drag herself in. A little tug was all it took, and she was tumbling in without resistance.

Unlike Raisa's dream, which had formed gradually, Tiernan's dream simply *began.* One second Ash was guiding herself to his mind, and the next she stood at the edge of an operating room. Tiernan was leaning over the table, his hands moving above a body covered in a surgical drape with blood seeping into the edges of the hole in the middle.

Ash found the setting odd, since Tiernan was a pediatrician, not a surgeon, but then dreams didn't always reflect reality.

The room was also empty, aside from the two of them, no nurses or other doctors holding clamps or offering instruments or whatever it was surgical assistants did in operating rooms. Tiernan didn't acknowledge Ash, too absorbed in his own work to notice the new person in the room. She had never seen him look so distraught.

Behind him, Cat and TJ winked into existence and looked around with oddly identical expressions of curiosity. Cat's face was fuzzy, the way it had been when Ash first met her. When TJ glanced over at her, the shifting features solidified into Cat's familiar face.

The blood from Tiernan's patient continued to spread across the drape. Ash wasn't an expert, but it didn't look like a good thing, and Tiernan's expression confirmed it. His forehead furrowed, his eyes tense above his blue surgical mask. He reached awkwardly for a tool from a tray nearby, no one there to hand it to him at his request.

Ash stepped forward cautiously. With Celia, they had constructed the dream unnoticed, but instinct drove Ash to reveal herself. "Can I help?" she asked.

Tiernan froze and lifted his eyes slowly. Confusion replaced the distress on his face. "Ash?" he said, his voice slightly muffled by the mask. "What are you doing here?"

The heart rate monitor hooked up to the patient flat-lined. The steady beep filled the room while Ash and her uncle stared at each other.

"I think you lost them," Ash said gently.

Tiernan blinked and looked down at the body on the table. The sheet covered the person's face, as if they had already been dead, a cadaver waiting to be autopsied. "I failed him," he said. "Is that what this is about? Is that why you're here?" He rested his blood-coated gloved hands on the edge of the table, and his shoulders slumped. "How often does my subconscious need to rub in that I failed you, too?"

"How have you failed me?" It seemed Ash had somehow forgotten about the way he had kept secrets from her. He had let her flounder alone with her powers. *In his defense,* Ash thought, *he didn't know I had any.*

"I..." Tiernan looked at the heart rate monitor, which still blared the patient's demise, and reached out to turn it off. Silence fell in the room, though the sound still rang in Ash's ears. "I made mistakes," he said finally. "So many mistakes, Ash."

She glanced around the room and focused. She thought about what she wanted and about the advice she'd been given. *It's all about belief.* She could do this. She did it in her own dreams as easily as breathing. Why not here?

The operating room faded smoothly into a new scene: their living room, the place Ash had always felt safest, even when everything else felt like it was falling apart. Tiernan glanced around and relaxed as well, the tension leaving his shoulders and his expression softening into something more familiar.

"Were some of these mistakes eight years ago?" Ash asked. It was bold, direct, and could have tipped their hand, but they had the advantage. Tiernan still didn't know she could dreamwalk. From his perspective, this was his guilt plaguing him.

The scene around them changed again, not Ash's doing this time. Suddenly, they stood in the circular driveway of a spectacularly pompous house. One might go so far as to call it a mansion.

White stone pillars held up the broad, gabled roof over the portico. The sprawling two-story house spread out behind it, multiple peaks of the gray-shingled roof making it look like an unnaturally symmetrical mountain range. The only break from the blindingly white facade was the pale gray trim around the wide windows. Closed curtains behind the glass shut the inhabitants off from the view of the cobbled driveway. A fountain near Ash gurgled happily, spewing sparkling water into the air.

Ash looked over the house, her lips parting in surprise. "I've seen this before." The words slipped out unintentionally. One of the sketches Cat had been perusing earlier showed this exact house.

"Me, too," Tiernan murmured. His sad eyes ran over the facade. "It haunts me."

His face glazed over, and he started toward the door. He ascended the white marble stairs, one slow step at a time, and stopped when he reached the top. He didn't ring the doorbell, didn't knock. He just stared.

"What are you doing here?"

Tiernan and Ash both spun to face the young man who sat on the wall that surrounded the fountain. His dark eyes watched Tiernan like a hawk eyeing its prey. And Ash recognized him.

She had drawn his face before, this man with short black hair and light brown skin. Like the house, he lived in her mind, like a memory she couldn't shake. He always looked sad in her drawings, but now his face was twisted with rage.

Ash now knew who he was, with the same certainty she knew her own name.

He rose from his place on the fountain wall and stalked across the driveway, his black shoes clicking on the cobblestones.

Tiernan held up his hands and took a step back. "Please, give me five minutes. That's all I ask."

"No!" the dream Griffin snapped. He stopped at the bottom of the stairs and glared up at Tiernan. Though Tiernan had the higher ground, he still looked intimidated. "I have no interest in listening to *anything* you have to say. Did you think I wouldn't find out it was you who told them? This is all your fault. He's *dead* because of you!"

The anguish on Tiernan's face stirred only more anger. How could he pretend to care when he was so full of lies? "Zain—"

"Don't call me that! My parents gave me that name, and I want nothing to do with them."

Tiernan glanced briefly over his shoulder at the door behind him. When he looked back, Griffin stood on the first step. "Are you going to kill them?" Tiernan asked.

Griffin's eyes flicked past him. "Yes. But not today. It started with them, and it will end with them. Which is why I'm not going to kill you yet, either."

Tiernan let out a shuddering breath. "This isn't you."

Griffin's grin was wildfire sparked by grief and fueled by rage. It was cold and dangerous and maybe a little insane. "I am the monster you made me."

"Not me," Tiernan said quietly.

"Yes, you. *All* of you." Another step up. Tiernan was backed against the door with nowhere to run. "You think you can separate yourself from what they did? You're a part of this, too."

"I didn't want this for you!" Tiernan protested. "They didn't tell me what they had planned."

"You think that matters?"

Tiernan squeezed his eyes shut and the dream stopped. Griffin's foot froze in the process of taking another step. Ash hadn't noticed the breeze in the air until it was gone.

"It's a dream," he whispered to himself. But it had happened. He could never escape that one simple fact. That was the thing about reliving memories in the embrace of sleep. Even if you know it's a dream, on some level it's still *real.*

Their surroundings dissolved into a new scene. Instead of standing outside the mansion, Tiernan sat on the couch in a room Ash remembered. It was the living room of their old house, before they had moved across the city. By now, Ash was pretty sure what had caused the move. Tiernan had run from what had happened back then, fleeing from what he had done.

Too much of a coward to face the fallout.

The dream version of Griffin remained, but he looked younger by a few years. His hair was shaved on the sides but longer on top, revealing tight curls. He sat on the floor across the coffee table from Tiernan, and he had a scowl on his face.

"Try it one more time," Tiernan said, his voice gentle.

"We've tried like six times!" Griffin said. Back then he hadn't really been Griffin, though, not yet. He was still Zain, a boy who trusted the adults in his life, who had faith in the Committee that was supposed to protect him and others like him. Except there had never been anyone else like him.

"Lucky seven, then," Tiernan said.

Zain snorted. "I know you're angry that I can't do it on purpose."

"I'm not angry."

"Disappointed, then."

"Worried." Tiernan leaned forward and rested his hands on his knees, centering Zain in a somber stare. "If you can't learn to control this, it will control you. You don't want another incident like last week, do you?"

"It won't happen again," Zain said. "I lost my temper, that's all."

Tiernan raised his eyebrows. "And you'll never lose your temper again?"

Zain's scowl was answer enough. "She deserved it."

"Zain," Tiernan said disapprovingly. "Whatever people do or say to us, it is not an excuse to hurt them. Understand?"

"I didn't *hurt* her. She's fine."

Tiernan dragged a hand over his face. "Listen to me... Just because something isn't real doesn't mean it can't hurt someone. Images and feelings can hurt us. So can words. Those kids were trying to hurt you with their words, but you have to be better than they are. You have power they don't, so you have *responsibility* they don't."

"With great power comes great responsibility?" Zain said sarcastically.

"You mock it, but it's true." Tiernan got up from the couch and rounded the table so he could sit on the floor beside Zain. "I need you to promise me, Zain. Whatever happens, you won't use this power to hurt people. You have the potential to be something great... or something terrible."

Zain eyed the man who had been his mentor, more of a father to him than his real father. There was a glimmer of fear in his eyes when Tiernan's warning sank in. *Or something terrible.* "I promise," Zain said softly.

The living room vanished along with Zain, leaving only Ash and Tiernan standing in a vast blank nothingness, surrounded by white so bright it hurt Ash's eyes. Cat and TJ were still around somewhere, hidden from sight.

Tiernan's eyes settled on Ash. "I did what I had to do," he said, like he was pleading with her to understand.

He turned his back on her, and the dream shifted once more. They stood in the Knights' kitchen, Tiernan and Robert on opposite sides of the island.

"It will work," Tiernan said.

"It's insanity," Robert countered. "You're one of the most powerful dreamwalkers I've ever met, but Griffin is stronger than you and I put together."

It was a shock to hear Robert admit someone could best him, let alone him plus someone else.

"How will you even get close enough to enter his dreams?" Robert asked.

"I don't need to. Closeness is a balance. He's like a son to me." Tiernan laid his hands on the countertop. "Don't you see?

It's the perfect prison. A place he won't be able to escape back to his own body. He won't even be able to dreamwalk. He'll be trapped there forever."

"And I suppose you have someone in mind?"

Tiernan hesitated, then nodded.

"Who?"

"I can't tell you that."

"You damn well can and will!"

"This works best if no one but me knows whose mind he's trapped in," Tiernan said, with the resolve of someone who would sooner die than change his mind. "The more people who know a secret, the more likely it is to get out. This is one secret I'll take to my grave."

It all came together as Ash listened to the conversation, until she had a mostly formed picture.

"The prison is someone's mind," TJ said at her shoulder. Ash jumped, having forgotten she wasn't the only one eavesdropping on the memory.

"A passenger in someone else's body," Cat said. She sounded awed. "It's... it's *genius.*"

Genius and cruel. To be locked away in someone else's life, watching the world move and change around you, with no ability to participate. It would become a torture chamber as well as a prison.

Ash's head spun with the implications. "We should get out of here before—"

"Before someone notices you?" Tiernan said.

Ash's eyes snapped back to where he and Robert stood, only Robert was gone. Tiernan stood alone in the kitchen, watching them with anger laced with confusion. He knew now that Ash was more than simply part of his dream. He could see Cat and TJ, too. Their ruse was up.

"You shouldn't be here," Tiernan said. "It shouldn't be possible." He shook his head and took a step toward them. "But it doesn't matter how, not right now. You've learned something no one was ever supposed to know."

He flung out his hands, still several paces away, but he didn't need to touch them to send them flying backward. Ash found herself falling, like she had when Cat had shoved her out of TJ's dream, and her eyes flew open to find herself back in her bedroom.

She blinked, more disoriented than she had ever felt waking up from a dream. When her mind refocused, Tiernan stood in the doorway of her bedroom, looking at her with a mix of disappointment and fury. Cat and TJ jumped up from their spots on the floor and inched toward Ash, like she could shield them from Tiernan's anger.

"Why are you looking for Griffin?" he asked, his voice low and dangerous in a way Ash had never heard before. This wasn't her uncle, supportive and loving and full of really bad puns. This was the Committee member, the man who had designed a prison for someone who, as he had put it, was like a son to him.

"Why did you keep secrets from me?" Ash countered. "You never told me about your being a dreamwalker. There was this whole other world I knew nothing about! I had to figure it all out on my own."

"I never told you because I thought you didn't have the power," Tiernan said in a flat, lifeless tone. "Why are you looking for Griffin?"

"Was my father a dreamwalker too?" Ash asked. "He didn't die of a heart attack, did he?"

"Ash—"

"Did he?"

"No," Tiernan said. "He was a very special kind of investigator who found answers in people's dreams. He went into one and never came out." He held her gaze, and his silence asked his question a third time.

Ash glanced from Cat to TJ, but for once neither seemed willing to speak. "We have reason to believe he's close to escaping," she said. "Whoever's mind you trapped him in—"

"And what reason is so good that you invaded my dream, digging for answers, instead of talking to me?"

"We tried talking," Ash said quietly. "We talked to Robert Knight. He told us to get the hell out of his house. We expected the same result with you."

Tiernan's eyes flickered over the Knights on either side of Ash. "I see. I'm guessing your new friends are Robert's children?" He didn't wait for an answer. "Griffin is secure. And even if he weren't, you three wouldn't be the ones to handle it. You're not going anywhere until I sort this out."

He took a step backward into the hallway and slammed the door shut so hard that Ash winced.

Cat raced for the door and tried to open it, but the knob wouldn't turn. They were locked in. "Raisa!" she shouted. "Raisa, we need your help!"

"Your friend won't be able to help you," Tiernan said from the other side.

"Why? What are you going to do to her?" Cat demanded.

But Tiernan didn't answer. His footsteps retreated down the hallway, and he was gone.

"Damn it!" Cat slammed her foot against the door, but it didn't budge.

"The window?" TJ suggested.

"It doesn't open all the way." Ash demonstrated by sliding the window open until it hit the point where it always got stuck. It left a gap maybe five inches high, not even enough room for TJ to squirm through. At one point in time, Ash had liked the quirkiness of the old house. Now it felt like everything about it was designed to thwart her. "It's useless. We're trapped."

Chapter 23

C AT SPENT THE NEXT five minutes pacing in front of the locked door. Then about thirty seconds trying to kick it down, which proved harder than they made it look in movies. The frame held firm, Cat's attempts accomplishing nothing but giving Ash a headache.

Ash sat on the foot of the bed, picking at a snag in the comforter, while TJ stared intently through the cracked window at the world outside. The warm breeze ruffled his dark hair.

"What do you think he did to Raisa?" Cat asked. She paused long enough to glance at Ash before resuming her pacing.

"He wouldn't *do* anything to her," Ash said. "He's not a bad person. He just..." He'd just locked them all in Ash's room and walked away to do who knew what. "He's a doctor. He wouldn't hurt anyone. He thinks he's doing the right thing by keeping us here."

"The right thing!" Cat scoffed. "Griffin could be on the verge of escaping, and all these arrogant Committee members are so confident in their fancy prison that they're doing *nothing.*"

"I actually have an idea about that, at least," Ash said. "And would you stop that? You're going to wear a hole in my carpet."

Cat let out a scream of frustration and grabbed Ash's desk chair. TJ barely got out of the way before she swung it at the window, which only snapped the wheels off the bottom of the chair.

"What the hell is this window made of!" Cat shouted. She threw the chair aside and returned to the door, which allowed TJ to resume staring out the window. After a few more seconds of pacing, she stopped and leaned against the door, her arms crossed. "What idea?"

Ash had watched all of this calmly, though she wasn't happy about the broken desk chair. "Tiernan said they were going to trap Griffin inside someone's head. That means his body is still out there somewhere, in a coma."

"Right."

"And where do they bring people in comas?"

"To hospitals," TJ said without taking his eyes away from the window.

"Exactly. Remember when I saw his car parked outside Lady Sabri's? He used to work there, back when we lived in Glendale. We moved when I was thirteen—*eight years ago.*"

Cat's posture straightened. "You think his body is being kept there." The gleam of excitement only lasted a second before her back curled again, her shoulders slumping. "That's great. But it doesn't do us any good if we're stuck here."

"I know." Ash glanced miserably at her phone, where she had her texts to Tiernan open. She had sent him about a dozen messages, begging him to come back so she could explain. She was even ready to tell him about Sebastian. The texts went unanswered on read.

She sighed and flopped backward. "We pushed too hard. If I had been more subtle, if we had been more careful, maybe he wouldn't have realized what we were doing and shoved us out."

"That's the weird thing," Cat said. "He shouldn't have even been able to wake up. That was a heck of a dose we gave him. And TJ, *what* the hell are you doing?"

TJ's head snapped around, his eyes going wide as he finally put it together. "*That's it.* You're right." He looked around the room, searching for something while Cat and Ash watched him curiously. He finally grabbed a book from Ash's motley collection of classics, childhood stories, and fantasy novels. He flipped it around to show her the cover. "You've read this?"

"Only six times," she answered. "Why? What's going on?"

"Has Tiernan read it?"

She frowned. "No, I don't think so."

He opened the book and gave a triumphant smile that Ash still didn't understand until he tossed the book to her and she opened it to a random page.

The book was blank.

"Tiernan shouldn't have been able to wake up," TJ said. "Which means...."

"We're still dreaming," Ash whispered.

"That clever bastard," Cat said quietly. Ash didn't know whether it was meant as an insult or a compliment. Ultimately, Tiernan deserved both.

"I was staring out the window because something is wrong. There's stuff going on out there, but it's too... *measured.* People walking their dog or couples going on strolls. Someone passes the house every two minutes. And the breeze is too regular. Tiernan crafted this to keep us here until he wakes up."

"And if that's the case..." Ash turned to the door and focused. At first, nothing happened, probably because Tiernan was keeping an eye on them and resisting. Eventually, she heard the lock click.

Cat stepped away from it and spun around. She twisted the knob to throw it open, revealing Tiernan still standing on the other side.

"Well, it almost worked," he said. "Ash, you don't understand—"

Ash didn't hear the rest of whatever he had to say. She didn't need one of Cat's doors to escape the room. She exited as easily as she had entered, snapping back to her own body. The throw blanket fell away as she sat up, for *real* this time, and TJ stirred beside her.

When they checked in on Tiernan's room, he was still fast asleep in his bed.

Ash hurried down the stairs at a reckless pace to where Raisa waited in the entryway, staring out the window with a bored expression. Her head snapped up when she heard them coming.

"Well?" she asked. "What did you find?"

Ash filled her in on what they had seen in Tiernan's dream. "We don't know whose mind they trapped him in, but we think we know where Griffin's body is," she finished.

"And you're not coming," Cat interrupted before Ash could say more.

"Excuse me?" Raisa stared at Cat like she'd announced she was moving to Canada.

"We've already put you in enough danger. Who knows what we'll find there? He could already be awake."

"You dragged me into this. You're not booting me now."

Ash glanced between the two girls locked in a staring contest that would probably go on until one of them collapsed from exhaustion. "Actually, we need you to do something else," she said. "Someone needs to look after Tiernan."

"I'm not a watch dog!" Raisa said. "I'm not babysitting your uncle while you go save the world."

"I don't think Griffin's going to destroy the world," TJ murmured.

The way Robert and Tiernan acted, it seemed like that's exactly what they thought. Ash didn't understand how they could fear one man so much.

"Raisa, please. He's my uncle," Ash said. "He's the only family I have left. I can't leave him alone after drugging him."

Raisa's mouth opened, preparing to deliver another protest, but then she closed it and pursed her lips. Family meant something to some people.

"I hate you right now," Raisa said. "I *really* hate you."

"Noted," Ash said. After a brief hesitation, she stepped forward and threw her arms around Raisa. *"Thank you.* You don't know what it means to me."

Raisa returned the hug and gave Ash's back a somewhat awkward pat. "Yeah, yeah. Whatever. Just don't have too much fun without me." When Ash released her, Raisa turned to Cat and jabbed a finger at her. "And you..."

Cat eyed her warily. "Yeah?"

"Come here." She grabbed the front of Cat's shirt and pulled her in for a kiss. TJ averted his eyes, but Ash only grinned. When the kiss ended, Raisa smoothed out Cat's rumpled shirt and gave a dazzling smile. "Just to remind you what you have to live for, in case Griffin tries to kill you."

"Hey, what about me?" TJ said.

"I'm not kissing you." But when TJ spread his arms, Raisa stepped over to give him a hug as well. "Watch her back, okay?"

"Always."

"Ready?" Ash said.

Cat still stared at Raisa like the other girl had hit her with a stun gun but snapped out of it when Ash gave her arm a nudge. She nodded, but TJ looked hesitant. "Should we... be doing this?" he asked. "We could try talking to Byrne. She might help us. Or someone else. We don't know what we're getting into."

"We don't have time for anyone else to tell us no," Cat said. "If you want something done, sometimes you have to do it yourself."

"If Sebastian is right, we need to do something about this *now*," Ash agreed.

TJ's soft face hardened with determination. "Let's go, then."

Ash grabbed the car keys off the counter on the way to the garage. Once in the driver's seat, she checked the car's GPS history. Tiernan had been visiting Lady Sabri's Hospital at least once a week for as far back as Ash scrolled. She was right. She *had* to be.

"TJ, you're driving." She tossed him the keys, then went to the backseat.

Normally, she wouldn't hear the end of it for letting someone else drive Tiernan's car, but considering everything else, she figured it would be at the bottom of the lecture agenda. She had drugged him and invaded his dreams. Taking his car seemed like a minor offense. Besides, TJ had proven himself to be a good driver. Better than Ash, certainly. But then, most people were better drivers than Ash.

She had something more important to do than trying not to get them into an accident. As soon as she got comfortable in the backseat, she closed her eyes and slipped easily into her dreams.

Chapter 24

"**S**EBASTIAN!"

Ash's voice carried a lot farther than it should have. And really, she didn't need to shout.

"I'm here," I said.

I shouldn't have loved the way relief broke out over her face when she saw me. I had forgotten what it felt like to have someone look at me like that. It's like you see someone and nothing else matters for a few seconds because you're that happy to be back in their presence. It should have felt good.

So why did I feel so guilty?

Because I don't deserve her. I knew it, and she would know it soon enough. I had to focus on the mission, not her.

I approached her across the same cliffside field where we always met. "I take it you found something."

"The prison is someone's mind." Her green eyes were bright with excitement. She looked more real, less like a faded dream version of herself. "I don't know whose, but I think I know where Griffin's body is. Lady Sabri's Hospital. My uncle visits every week. Can you meet us there?"

The hope in her eyes made my stomach sink. This was what I had been waiting for, so why did dread settle into my chest?

"Yes," I said quietly. On a real cliff, the wind would have stolen the word, but the air was still.

"Great! We'll figure out what to do once we're all together."

My eyes darted over her face. "Ash, I need to tell you something...." My ominous tone killed some of her glow, and I wished I could take it back. What was the point, anyway? What could I say?

"What is it?" she asked cautiously.

"There are still things you don't know about me. Things I should have told you."

"I know you had your reasons for keeping secrets," Ash said, with so much faith in her smile. "You can tell me everything when we meet, okay? Cat and TJ, too."

Yes, Cat and TJ. That only made the dread grow.

She took my hand and gave it a squeeze. "I don't know why, but I feel closer to you than I have to anyone else in my life. We met and it was like... This is going to sound stupid and maybe a little crazy, but I felt like I'd known you in another life. Like we were meant to find each other. And now we finally get to."

"Ash..." Before I could think better of it—and there were so many reasons I shouldn't have done it—I drew her in and pressed my lips against hers. She responded instantly, leaning into the kiss and even deepening it. There was a desperation in that kiss, at least on my side.

I knew it might be the last time. The only time.

I could have stayed there. Ash in my arms, with my hands on her back, pressing her closer. Wrapped in the smell of cinnamon and vanilla and fall leaves. My mind started to stray. I started to think it wouldn't be so bad to stay in this dream forever.

Waking up is a gift. I had to remember that. I had to remember what was at stake.

I broke the kiss first, reluctantly. Ash leaned forward as I pulled away, her eyes still closed, her lips begging for more. I almost let myself kiss her again, but instead I slid my hands away and took a step back.

"I should go." She sounded like she didn't want to. "I'll see you soon."

"See you soon, dreamer," I murmured.

Chapter 25

T HEY WERE ONLY HALFWAY to the hospital when Ash roused herself from her light sleep. She sat up in the backseat and peered over Cat's shoulder, searching for a street sign. So late at night, there was less traffic, though *less* traffic didn't mean no traffic, not in the heart of LA.

The feel of the kiss lingered on her lips, even though it had only happened in a dream. She still felt breathless, her face flushing at the thought of hands sliding across her back. The excitement lingered as well, due to the knowledge that she would see him soon. For *real.*

"Sebastian is going to meet us at the hospital," she said. Cat's shoulders stiffened, and TJ's eyes darted to the rearview mirror to look at her.

"He's really alive," TJ said quietly. Ash almost couldn't hear him over the hum of the engine. "I thought I would never see him again."

"We haven't yet," Cat said. Always keeping her expectations low. It was hard to blame her for that. "Hopefully he can help us more once he stops skulking around in Ash's dreams."

"He wasn't *skulking,*" Ash said, although the insistence that they couldn't meet in person had been shady. Again, she assumed he had his reasons. She still thought maybe he just enjoyed being enigmatic.

"What exactly are we going to do when we find him?" TJ asked. "Griffin. We can't just... We can't *kill* him." He flipped on his blinker to turn right. They were getting closer. Every stoplight they passed beneath, every turn, every *second* brought them closer.

"Move him to somewhere more secure in case he wakes up, I guess," Ash said. She hadn't thought that far ahead. She'd been so focused on finding whatever answers she could, she hadn't considered yet what they would do after.

"If we can find somewhere secure," Cat said. "There's a reason the Committee decided to do what they did. If Griffin is as powerful as they say, no normal prison could hold him."

"You don't really think he can mind control people, do you?" Ash asked skeptically. She had seen what was possible in dreams, but that seemed ridiculous to her still.

Cat shrugged. "Maybe not. But it could be possible to plant the idea of releasing him inside the dream of a guard. People are suggestible when they're asleep. There could be some truth to the legend."

Ash leaned back in her seat to ruminate on that troubling thought, though not for long before she brushed it away. "Sebastian will know what to do."

"I hope you're right," Cat murmured.

When they finally reached the hospital, it only took them a minute to find a parking spot, but even that was too long. Ash was practically bouncing in the backseat, eager to get out of the car and see if she was right. Eager to see Sebastian.

She tried to open the door the moment the car stopped moving, but it didn't unlock until TJ put the car in park.

"Calm down!" Cat snapped. "You're like a child on the way to the zoo."

Ash wanted to say it wasn't anything like the zoo, but she kept the words to herself. Her excitement was laced with a healthy dose of apprehension and the knowledge that she was seeking out a dangerous man who might already be awake. For all they knew, they were too late.

"How exactly are we going to figure out where to go?" TJ asked. "It's a big hospital."

"Yeah, I bet Remington's proud of this one," Cat said.

"We're going to ask— Wait, Remington?" Ash said.

TJ nodded. "It's one of Remington's 'businesses.' Renamed after his wife's maiden name when he took it over."

"I guess it makes sense that my uncle worked at a place owned by a dreamwalker." The community of dreamwalkers in LA was a fairly close-knit group, and most of them seemed concentrated in the northern part of the city, which explained why he had moved them all the way to Torrence when trying to sever ties. "I used to visit here a lot when I was a kid. I might still know some of the staff."

They got lucky when they stepped into the lobby, because Ash did indeed recognize the receptionist working the night shift. She gave the woman a hesitant smile as they stepped up to the counter. "Hey, Cindy. You probably don't remember me but—"

"Oh, my goodness! Ash O'Shea, is that you?" The woman stood and looked her over, a huge grin on her face. "Well, I'll be damned. You're all grown up."

"It's been a while, hasn't it?" Ash's face grew hot, and she hoped Cindy would interpret the blush as embarrassment rather than anxiety over potentially getting caught in her lie. "Listen, Tiernan asked me to stop by to check on the patient he's been visiting. Only thing is, I forgot the room number and I'd hate to bother him. Would you be able to look it up?"

"Oh, I don't have to look it up! He's been visiting that John Doe in room 217, in the long-term care ward. Bless his heart. He was the one who brought that boy in... gosh, nearly a decade ago. Pays for his care and everything. No one here is optimistic he'll ever wake from his coma, though."

Ash glanced at TJ and Cat and found her own excitement reflected in their faces. "Great. Thank you so much."

"Oh, but honey... I'm afraid I can't let you back there tonight. You're about four hours too late for visiting. Tiernan should have known better than to ask you to come so late."

Ash's face fell. "You sure I can't just pop up there for a few minutes?"

"Sorry, Ash. I really am. But rules are rules."

"Right... Okay. Thanks anyway. I guess I'll try again in the morning."

Cindy gave an apologetic smile. "It was nice to see you. You should stop by more often."

"I'll try. Thanks again."

They hurried away from the counter. Ash felt like an idiot for thinking she could talk her way past reception. They had the room number, at least, but that didn't do them any good if they couldn't get in to see him.

"We're not waiting until morning, right?" Cat asked once they were outside.

"I don't want to, but I don't have another plan," Ash said.

"Actually..." TJ raised his hand like a student in class. "I might have an idea."

Cat seemed extremely reluctant to carry out TJ's plan, but Ash thought it was brilliant. She did think TJ looked a little too excited about it, though.

They rounded the building to the ER entrance. Ash supported a wheezing TJ while Cat rushed up to the desk.

"It's my brother! He started having this chest pain, and I think it's gotten worse. He's having a lot of trouble breathing. Please help!"

A nurse hurried over to assess his condition and how long they would have to wait for actual treatment. The ER wasn't too crowded that night, considering how bad Ash had seen it sometimes. Tiernan had told her to stay away from the ER when she visited, but Ash had never been good at listening. No one should have let a kid roam the halls while she waited for her uncle to get off work, but they had.

She felt a little bad for stealing attention from the people in the waiting room who actually needed medical care, but this *was* an emergency, even if it wasn't a medical one.

"Are you experiencing any nausea or light-headedness?" the nurse asked.

TJ nodded, managing to look like he might pass out. If Ash had known he was so good at acting, she would have suggested he consider that as a career.

"Any pain in your arm or shoulder?"

Ash recognized the symptoms of a heart attack, which would definitely get them in for an X-ray or EKG. "He was complaining about his shoulder on the way over. You think it's related?"

"We need to get him an EKG to check for a heart attack," the nurse said. "You two will have to wait here."

"They can't come?" TJ said, the pitch of his voice spiking with feigned panic. Tears welled in his eyes. "No, I need them with me. I'm scared." His breathing grew more labored, to the point where Ash worried he might actually make himself pass out.

"Okay, okay. Calm down, kid." The nurse looked annoyed when he glanced over at Ash and Cat. "Keep him calm, or he's going to make it worse."

Someone brought over a wheelchair for TJ, and then they all headed down the hallway to an exam room. The nurse started prepping TJ for the EKG, but the moment he had his back turned, Cat stabbed him in the neck with a needle. He looked confused for a moment, but the special drug kicked in almost immediately, and he collapsed backward. Cat caught him as he fell and lowered him the rest of the way to the ground.

"Cat!" Ash said, horrified.

"What? It's a tiny dose. He'll wake up in like ten minutes." She grabbed the pillow from the exam table and tucked it under the nurse's head. "How did you think we were going to slip away?"

"I don't know! I just... feel like we shouldn't go around knocking out ER nurses."

TJ hopped off the exam table. "It's done now. We should get going before he wakes up. And, you know, before the evil dreamwalker wakes up."

Ash had to shake off her guilt *again* and focused on the reason they were there. She opened the door and poked her head into the hallway to check that the coast was clear. This late at night, they wouldn't have to deal with a lot of staff. The hallway was empty, so she gestured for TJ and Cat to follow her out.

It had been years, but Ash still knew the layout of the hospital, burned into her memory like an afterimage. She knew every room number, every nook, every hiding spot. She found her way easily to the long-term care ward and room 217. She paused for a moment with her fingers wrapped around the knob of the closed door, steeling herself before she entered.

Ash stopped in the doorway, her eyes trained on the limp body on the bed. The heart rate monitor beeped, reassuring anyone nearby that the patient was still in a coma and not experiencing cardiac arrest.

She had seen my face before, in her mind, her drawings, and in Tiernan's dream, but even I hardly recognized myself. My skin had turned a pallid tan from lack of sun. My hair was shorter, too, shaved close to my head.

For eight years I had been trapped in that bed, my mind disconnected from my body. Now, with Ash standing so close, something changed. I could feel a *pull*, the sensation of two long-separated parts of a whole calling to each other, then the satisfying click of two magnetized puzzle pieces finally fitting back together. I had been watching the world through her eyes for *eight years*, but it was time to wake up.

I opened my eyes.

Part III

Awake

Chapter 26

T HE LIGHT BURNED MY unused eyes. Every muscle in my emaciated body ached from lack of movement, and I knew if I tried to stand, I wouldn't have the strength to. I could barely muster the energy to give Ash a smile. Sweet Ashlin. My prison and now my savior. And she was *beautiful,* so beautiful, now that I was seeing her for the first time with my own eyes. She was even more lovely than in her dreams.

"Hey, dreamer." My voice broke, the words scraping out of my dry throat like they were made of sandpaper. Everything hurt—everything hurt *so much*—but I was alive. I was *awake*.

Waking up is a gift, I had told Ash. I had meant it.

She shook her head slowly as TJ slipped past her, his small body able to fit between her and the door frame. Cat wasn't so courteous and simply grabbed Ash's shoulder to push her to the side. I watched them warily, unsure what they would do now that I was awake. I didn't want to hurt them. I would prefer them on my side, but their heads had been filled with lies, and people did foolish things when they were afraid.

"Griffin," Cat said with an impressive amount of anger packed behind my name.

I tried to lift my arm and reach for the bed controls that would let me sit up, but my muscles didn't respond. Eight years, mind absent from body, and body hadn't reacted well to that. "You don't understand. Give me a chance to explain." I sounded so incredibly weak. How pathetic I must look, skeletal and hardly able to move.

Ash still looked stunned, struggling to process this turn of events. A part of her knew, but she didn't want to believe it yet. "Where is Sebastian?" she said. "He said he would meet us here." I could still sense her thoughts and emotions without even trying, our connection dulled but not gone. She still clung to the shred of hope that Sebastian would miraculously appear and sweep her into his arms.

"I'm sorry. Sebastian isn't coming." I met her eyes. I could feel the pieces falling into place in Ash's head. *Good.* She never had been the type to deny the obvious when it flashed in front of her like a neon sign.

Cat stepped forward, murder in her eyes, even though she carried no weapon. In my current state, all she needed was her bare hands, or maybe a pillow to smother me with. I didn't know if she was capable of such a thing, and I didn't care to find out.

I reached out with my mind, picturing what I wanted. I conjured fire, bursting into life around her, the sting of heat against her skin. I held it inside my head and *pushed.*

Cat gasped as the flames licked her skin, but instead of backing away from the wall of fire, she looked at her arms in confusion. Could she not see it? Maybe I was more out of practice than I thought.

"Cat? What's wrong?" TJ said, his voice thin and frightened.

"I don't..." Cat took a step back and the burning receded, though she could still feel the heat of the fire in front of her. "It was like my skin was on fire." She looked dazed, the way people often did when someone started messing with their reality.

I let the flames vanish. "Not another step or I'll do much worse." It sounded less threatening than I'd wanted, but Cat remained still, watching me warily.

"TJ, please get a wheelchair or I will hurt your sister," I said softly. I had been conscious for all of three minutes and already I felt like I had expended all the energy I had to give.

"TJ, don't listen—" Cat said, but TJ scurried out of the room before she could finish.

"Follow my orders and no one gets hurt," I said. "I don't want to hurt any of you, but I will."

Cat glowered at me, but I only had eyes for Ash. She watched me with a blank expression, but I didn't need her face to tell me what was going on inside her head. I could feel the disgust, the anguish at realizing the man in her dreams had lied to her. I had warned her, hadn't I?

"Give me a chance, Ash," I said. "That's all I'm asking."

"You threaten me and my friends, and now you're asking for a chance? Not a great start, buddy."

"It was necessary. I can't have you doing anything rash."

TJ returned, pushing a wheelchair ahead of him. He stayed by the door, his hands gripping the handles so tightly it had to hurt. I could see the tension in his arms and his shoulders. I could feel his fear, swirling around inside him. Practically bled his emotions, this one.

"How did you do that?" she asked. "How did you burn Cat?"

"You can tell a mind what to think while it's dreaming. I just take it one step further and do it while the person is awake."

"So the legends are true," TJ said quietly. "You *can* mind control people."

I snorted. "Mind control? Hardly. What I do requires more finesse than that. It takes creativity, knowing what to make a person see and feel and hear."

"You can't actually hurt us," Ash said. "It's just a trick." I knew she didn't wholly believe it. She tried to sound confident, but she couldn't hide anything from me.

"Is it?" I met her eyes. "Do you think that just because something is inside your head, it can't hurt?" Tiernan had been right, all those years ago. Just because something wasn't real didn't mean it couldn't hurt you.

Cat and TJ believed, but they had spent eight years with the legends, some true and some myths fabricated by fear. The surviving Committee members had kept the details secret, but their attempts to keep the dreamwalker community from learning the truth had only fueled the rumors. When people didn't know the whole story, they tended to fill in the blanks for themselves.

I finally found the strength to lift my arm and gestured Ash forward. "Come here." When she continued to stare at me, I let out a slow breath. "Ash, please. I don't want to continue to manipulate you. I only want the opportunity to explain."

She took a small step forward, then another, hesitantly approaching the bed. "I'm listening," she said. "This had better be a very good explanation."

"The Committee betrayed me. They tried to harness what I can do, turning me into a tool. When they realized they couldn't control me, they turned against me. I was too dangerous to walk free, so they built a prison to contain me. Then they lied to everyone about what happened."

"All right. Let's separate the truth from the lies, then," she said. "True or false: you killed people."

I looked down at my hands, bony fingers folded together on my lap. "True." One had been an accident, but I doubted that detail would make much difference to her.

"You pretended to be Sebastian so you could manipulate me into freeing you. You made me think that he... That you..."

"Liked you?" I said. That was what really had her so twisted up inside. Not that I had deceived her, but that I had made her fall for me. That I had kissed her. "I used Sebastian's face to get you to trust me, yes. But everything I said to you was the truth. Everything that happened was real. What I *feel* is real. I love you, Ash."

Her lip curled in disgust. "You honestly expect me to buy that? Every second we spent together has been a lie. You hardly even know me!"

"Oh, Ash..." I murmured. "I've known you for eight years. I've been with you every step of the way, privy to your every thought and feeling. I know you better than anyone, maybe better than you know yourself." A sort of affection had grown over the years. Every struggle I'd watched her overcome, every tear she'd shed, every smile. I hadn't realized it until we actually spoke, though. The first time she'd looked at me, the first time she'd acknowledged my existence, something had unfolded inside me. It grew with every annoyed look she gave me when I wouldn't answer her questions and every laugh when we danced.

Are you real? she had asked. Honestly, for a while I had started to believe I wasn't. I had become a ghost, a fragment of what I once was. I had been so close to losing myself, until I'd realized I could change things. At first, little things here and there. I got pulled with her when she dreamwalked and could alter the dreams she found herself in, even if she couldn't. Then I tried changing small details in her own dreams. Eventually, I was confident I could appear to her, even as someone else.

I waited for her next question, but Ash only shook her head, trying to reconcile her own feelings with the repulsion she knew she *should* feel, now that she knew the truth. At least she understood now why she had felt so close to me. That pull she couldn't explain. She had been as close to me as two people can get.

And now she used that knowledge to convince herself what she felt wasn't real.

When she still didn't speak, Cat jumped in instead. "True or false: you killed our brother."

I stared at her for a second, then barked a laugh full of pain and anger rather than amusement.

She scowled at me, and somehow her fury made her look her age, a girl of twenty-three rather than a confident, mature woman. "Is something funny?"

"Your parents really didn't tell you anything, did they?" I said. "But then, they're not really your parents, are they?"

Despite my sincerity when I'd said I wished them no harm, I felt a twinge of satisfaction at the way she winced. She wasn't so strong now, was she? With her anger and judging eyes.

"I didn't kill Sebastian." I tried to sit up straighter, but I only got an inch from the mattress before my strength gave out and I fell back again. "He fought against the Committee with me."

"You're lying," Cat said, but the conviction had left her voice. Her eyes no longer judged. No, now they were afraid. The truth was always more frightening than a pretty lie.

"He was my friend," I said. More than that. "I loved your brother, and he loved me."

"If he loved you, why did he never mention you?" Cat said, as skeptical as ever.

"Because we had to keep our relationship a secret. Our families didn't get along. He was the most important person in my life. And the Committee took him away from me." It was my turn to scowl as a familiar rage bubbled up inside me. I had lived with that rage for years, letting it fester while I was trapped in a prison. A prison built by someone I once trusted.

Now it was time for all of them to finally pay for their sins.

Maybe Ash could sense my thoughts the way I could hers, because she said, "And now you're planning to go after the remaining Committee members."

I quelled my anger, tucking it into the back of my mind to summon later, when the time was right. It wouldn't serve me here. "Yes," I said levelly.

"And if I asked you not to? If you truly love me, that should make a difference."

I considered that. If I walked away, did I actually have a chance with her? Could I really do that? I looked into her green eyes and thought about the way she had smiled at me. The way her kiss had felt in the dream. How badly I wanted to kiss her in the real world.

But the Committee had taken everything from me. "No," I murmured. "I'm sorry. They need to pay for what they have done."

That was the moment I lost her. I saw the change in her face, felt her resolve settle. I'd made my choice, and it wasn't her. Would I come to regret that?

"The man I thought I knew... the one I was falling for wouldn't do this." She backed away, so she stood shoulder-to-shoulder with Cat again. "You're a killer. A monster."

I am the monster you made me. My words to Tiernan rang through my head. Maybe she was right. Maybe they had all been right about me.

I closed my eyes briefly. I pictured Ash's smile again. I held onto it for a moment, savoring it one last time, before I let it fade away like the last traces of a dream. That was all she had ever been for me. A dream, a fantasy, forever out of reach.

"TJ. The wheelchair," I said. When he didn't move, I forced my way into his mind and made the floor beneath his feet glow red. The heat burned its way through his shoes and stung the soles of his feet. He yelped and jumped away from the glowing tile.

He kept his eyes downcast as he approached with the wheelchair.

"Cat, some assistance," I ordered.

Unlike TJ, she glared at me as she crossed the room. Together, they lifted me from the bed and settled me into the chair. I couldn't have weighed all that much.

"Check the cabinet over there to see if they left me anything," I said, nodding toward it. Would the clothes I had been wearing when they'd brought me in still be there?

Cat produced a plastic bag from the cabinet and tossed it onto my lap with more force than necessary. I ripped it open and dug through the contents until I found the pocket of my jeans. I could change later, though I doubted the clothes would fit me well anymore. For now, there was something else I needed. I curled my hand around the little gift from Sebastian and gestured for TJ to turn me around.

TJ complied, and soon I faced where Ash stood blocking the door.

"Show us to the morgue, Ashlin." She didn't move, so I said, "Don't make me ask again," in the most dangerous tone I could muster. She spun on the ball of her foot and led the way into the hall.

The moment TJ rolled me out of the room, the elevator at the end of the hall opened, and four people dressed in security uniforms ran out. Their eyes found us immediately. They closed in, but they dropped one by one as I tunneled into their minds and convinced them that they were very, very sleepy. Finally, only one remained. His boots squeaked on the tiles when he stopped suddenly, bewildered.

He pressed his hand against the wall that had appeared in front of him, and the wall pressed back. It looked and felt real to him, but if he accepted the fact that it wasn't and continued forward, he could have pushed right through it. He didn't.

"I have a message for my father." I let my voice filter through the wall loud and clear, stronger and more imposing than it was in current reality. "Tell him I'm coming. There's nowhere he can hide from me. His worst nightmares are all about to come true."

I waited until I was sure the guard had heard my message, then put him to sleep as well. The guard crumpled to the floor. Unconscious bodies lined the hall like fallen dominoes. I waved a hand at TJ, signaling it was time to go.

We left the cursed room 217 behind, and I vowed to myself I would never set foot in this place again.

The morgue was on the ground floor and had its own exit from the building. It would be the easiest way to leave unnoticed, and I had something I wanted to drop off on the way out. We passed a few nurses and orderlies, but none of them even glanced at us. All they saw was an empty hallway. Ash eyed the first nurse as they walked by, then glanced back at me with a spark of understanding in her eyes. I mustered a weak smile for her.

We took the elevator to the first floor, then continued down a long hallway that led to a place few entered unless they were on a gurney or pushing one. The morgue was deserted by the living this late at night, the door locked, but with the picks Sebastian had given me, that didn't pose much of an obstacle. I was out of practice, with neglected muscles and shaking hands, but eventually the lock clicked in concession.

Once we were inside, I held up a hand to signal TJ to stop. "End of the road for you, Ash."

The panicked look she gave me almost made me change my mind, but I shut out the memory of Ash's laugh and hardened my heart. She was my weakness, in more ways than one. As much as I longed to, I couldn't bring her with me. I couldn't afford any weakness.

"You're not... You're not going to kill me, are you?" she said.

That stung a little. I knew she didn't believe me when I said I loved her, but kill her? "Only the Committee needs to die today." My voice was calm and cold, growing more level with every word I spoke, like my mind and body were remembering how to form words properly. "Cat, put her in one of the drawers."

"*What?*" Ash took a step away, horrified, at the same time Cat said, "I'm not doing that."

"Yes, you are," I said. "She'll only be there until morning. The medical examiner will find her, and by then we'll be long gone. I can't have her getting in the way. Now, put her in a drawer before I lose my patience."

"You're insane," Ash whispered.

"Quite possibly." And I was getting tired of their fighting my every request. Did I need to prove how serious I was?

Cat cried out and clutched her head in her hands. I imagined blood vessels bursting inside, a dozen little aneurysms. Not real, of course, but the mind was such a fragile, impressionable thing.

"Stop!" Ash shouted. Her voice echoed around the empty morgue. "Just stop. I'll do it, okay? You don't have to hurt her."

I released Cat's mind. The pain vanished, and she lifted her head, her eyes blazing in anger. "Ash, don't," she said through gritted teeth.

"It's okay. I'll be fine." Ash opened a drawer, only to find it already occupied, so she shut it and tried another. She pulled out the empty drawer and climbed onto the table. Before lying down, she met my eyes. "I'm going to find you. I'll find you, and I'll stop you. No one else is dying."

I didn't respond. I could tell she believed it, and I admired that, but in this case her confidence was baseless. She didn't stand a chance against me. None of them did.

"Take her phone," I said to Cat. "And close the drawer."

She glared at me the whole way, but she stepped forward to take Ash's readily offered phone. Then she slid the drawer in and shut the door. While she did, I had TJ push my chair over to the temperature controls for the drawers. I didn't want Ash dying from hypothermia before someone found her, so I increased the temperature setting to something survivable, if still chilly.

After I'd finished, I held out my hand for Cat to give me the phone, which she did.

"Good girls," I murmured. They were learning. Maybe I wouldn't be forced to do anything distasteful anymore. If they followed my orders, this would all be over before the sun rose.

Chapter 27

I HAD CAT SHOVE the wheelchair into the back of the car once they got me into the passenger seat, and then we were on the road. I would have preferred to strike immediately, but my strength was waning. I needed rest before I tried to go after the remaining Committee members. *Real* rest, not the light dream state I had existed in for years. As far as I knew, no one had ever been trapped for that long in someone else's mind. At least, no one who had come back from it. It was perhaps a mystery of dreamwalking that I hadn't gone insane from the sleep deprivation. People weren't meant to go eight years without the deeper stages of sleep.

Or maybe Ash was right, and I had gone insane.

We passed dozens of landmarks I recalled from before my imprisonment. Some were gone or had changed. A night club had become a diner. That one place was still a Chinese restaurant but had a different name, a new serpentine dragon curled around the sign.

All of it was linked to memories of Sebastian, but the dragon especially. A memory floated to the surface: Sebastian in his bedroom, trying to decide where to put the new dragon figurine I had bought him.

I had picked up a black dragon plushie with a wide face and big green eyes from the bed beside me. "What's with your obsession with dragons?" I had asked.

"They look cool," he'd replied. "And they breathe fire. If I were a mythical creature, I'd be a dragon."

I tossed the fire-breathing lizard back down on the mattress and sat up. "Can I be one too?"

"You're more like a griffin."

I wrinkled my nose. "What, that horse bird thing?"

He set the plastic dragon on a shelf beside a very similar porcelain one and gave me a wry smile over his shoulder. "That's a hippogriff, silly. Griffins are half bird, half lion. That's what you are. Fierce like a lion but free like a bird."

I wasn't free, though. I might have escaped from the prison Tiernan had concocted for me, but I was still a prisoner to my memories and everything that had happened eight years ago. I would never be free.

We found a motel on the northern outskirts of Pasadena, but only after making a few stops along the way. A department store to pick up some supplies, and a late-night tavern I knew would still be serving food for a desperately needed grilled cheese sandwich. I only got three bites in before my neglected stomach decided it couldn't take any more. I tossed the rest of the sandwich into the to-go container and leaned my head back, fighting down a wave of nausea.

I felt marginally better by the time we pulled into the parking lot of the dingy Paradise Inn. A lovely place to find some bed bugs, I was sure.

That sounds like something my mother would say, I thought. I pushed down the revulsion that was likely the product of growing up in a mansion and told myself it could be worse.

Once we had a room—I specifically requested anything *except* 217—I used the zip ties from the store to tie my hostages to the legs of the desk that was bolted to the floor.

Content that my new helpers weren't going anywhere, I pushed my wheelchair over to the bed. It was a struggle to get myself out of the chair, my legs unwilling to hold my weight. I got myself upright and simply fell forward onto the waiting bed. I passed out immediately.

I was running faster than I had ever run in my life. My lungs had started aching a long time ago, my heart struggling to keep up, but I had to keep going. I had to.

It wasn't so much a dream as a memory. After eight years asleep but not really sleeping, I would have preferred a dreamless oblivion, or at least dreams that didn't feel like I was still awake. The curse of being a dreamwalker, of being *me*—I was always aware.

I probably could have changed the dream if I'd wanted to. Instead, I let myself fall into it. I knew where it was going, and as little as I wanted to relive it, I also knew where I was running to. *Who* I was running to.

And I would give anything to see him again.

I took the steps up to his apartment two at a time, stumbling on the last one when my legs threatened to give out. The door was unlocked, and I threw it open hard enough that the hinges rattled when it slammed into the doorstop.

Sebastian looked up from his spot on the couch, a book open on his knee. "Griffin?" he said, alarmed. The real me, not past me, melted at the sound of him saying my name, the one he had given me himself. "What's wrong?"

"It was... an accident." I could hardly get the words out between my ragged breaths. I clutched the handle of the door and leaned against it. Now that I had stopped running, I felt ready to collapse on the floor and pass out.

He slid his bookmark into place and set the book aside, gentle with it even in his haste. He met me at the door and pulled me away so he could close it. With me no longer able to use the door for support, Sebastian had to hold me upright. He was taller than me and strong enough to handle my weight, but he still struggled a little getting me to the couch.

Once we were seated, he took my hands in his. "Tell me what happened."

I shook my head. I had come because Sebastian was the only place I felt safe, but I didn't know what he would think if I told him. Would he look at me like I was a monster, too?

"Please, Griff," he said softly. "Whatever happened, you can trust me with it."

I met his worried blue eyes, and the dread writhing in my stomach only increased. This is *Sebastian,* I told myself. He had always stood by me, never judged me, never feared me. He loved me. If I couldn't confide in him, then I really was a lost cause.

"Edgeworth is dead." If Sebastian weren't sitting so close, he wouldn't have been able to hear the words that barely left my lips. I lowered my eyes to our joined hands, unable to look at him when I said the next part. "I killed him."

"What?" Sebastian said. He sounded shocked, but it was concern not horror that laced his voice. "Did he hurt you?"

I gave a weak laugh. Of course he would assume it had been self-defense. His faith in me had never wavered. "No. Not today, anyway." The man had never laid a hand on me, but that wasn't the only way to hurt someone, was it? I had certainly proved it that day. "I didn't mean to. I didn't know.... I didn't know what it would do. I promise, I didn't mean to."

"Hey, I know." He cupped my cheek in his hand and brushed a kiss against my forehead. "It'll be okay."

I jerked back, anger unfolding in my chest. "How? How is it going to be okay? I *killed* someone. They're going to come after me. Who knows what they'll do to me now?" I was angry at myself, at Edgeworth and the rest of them, not Sebastian. Never him. He probably knew that, but he still looked hurt by my reaction.

"Then we'll leave." He tucked his hands in his lap and looked at me steadily. "We'll go so far away they'll never find us. Start over. That's what you've always wanted, right?"

"What about your siblings?" They had always been his excuse for not going before. He didn't want to leave them behind, with that monster who called himself a father.

Sebastian glanced away, and I knew I had hit a sore spot, the one thing that might keep him from running away with me. Maybe it had been stupid to bring it up, but I didn't want him living with that regret. He would resent me for it someday.

"They're tough," he said finally. "They'll be okay. You're the one who needs me now." He looked back at me, his eyes pleading, though I didn't know why. I should have been the one pleading. I should have been begging him to stay with me. I'd never deserved him, and we both knew it. "I would do anything for you. You know that."

I took a deep breath and nodded. Did I feel guilty about his abandoning TJ and Cat? Maybe a little. Not enough to stop him from doing it. Because in the end, that was who I was. Selfish. I needed to go and I needed Sebastian with me, everyone else be damned.

We both jumped when the door flew open, sending splinters of the frame flying across the room. In the dream, they moved in slow motion, cutting through the scene like shards of glass.

They left dark gashes across Sebastian's living room, until the dream fell apart like shredded canvas.

For a few seconds, I was drifting through darkness. Or falling. It was hard to say for sure. Then I found myself seated in a chair, still in darkness, a thick bag covering my head. I felt woozy, like I had been drugged, and I found it difficult to keep my eyes open.

"What are we going to do with him?" asked a quiet voice. It sounded strange, distorted, though I could still tell who was speaking. I could name everyone in that room.

"Kill him." The second voice was gruffer, but nearly identical to the first. That would be Aaron Winkler. "He's more trouble than he's worth."

"We can still use him," said a cold and crisp version of the voice. Garcia. "We'll just have to be more careful now that we know what he's capable of."

"Walter is *dead.* We're playing with fire, and when it gets out of hand, we're going to burn the whole damn city down." Robert had said that, but like the others, his voice wasn't his own. In my mind, they all blurred together into one entity intent on ruining my life.

A chorus of voices—the *same* voice—rose in the room. Snippets of arguments filtered through, though I lost track of who was speaking. Some supported killing me. Someone advocated for locking me away in prison. One person still insisted I could be controlled. That was Garcia, of course. She would hold to that foolish belief until it got her killed.

The clamor could have lasted for hours or for all of ten seconds. It was cut off abruptly by a series of pops. Someone shouted, then a body bumped into my chair and sent me toppling sideways. I winced when my shoulder slammed into the ground.

I can change it this time, I thought. This was a dream. This was *my* world.

The ropes binding my wrists to the chair slithered away. I ripped the bag off my head and rolled to my feet with speed that left the Committee members gaping at me. One of them was already sprawled on the ground, unconscious but unfortunately not dead. That should have left only three standing, but four surrounded me. Unlike the first time, they all wore the same long black robes, hoods up to hide their faces, which made them look like a secret order of assholes who thought far too highly of themselves.

Which, really, was exactly what they were.

The sight gave me pause, until one of them threw back their hood and stepped forward. Garcia drew the gun I knew she had hidden. She pointed it at me, not at my chest but at my leg. She still didn't want me dead.

The bullet ricocheted off thin air, deflected by my mind. Splinters flew when it hit a support beam overhead. I spun and kicked the awful thing out of her hand, sending it flying across the room. It clattered against the concrete floor and skidded a few more feet before it hit the wall.

"You—" she started, her face a furious red.

I thrust my palms at her. I didn't touch her, but an invisible force lifted her off her feet and launched her over the heads of the other Committee members. Her ridiculous black robes fluttered in languid slow motion, then her back hit the wall hard enough to crack the plaster. She crumpled to the floor below a Garcia-shaped dent.

The rest of the Committee rushed me. I jumped over a fallen body with a dart in his neck and grabbed the chair they'd tied me to. I swung it in a high arc into someone's head, and the chair shattered like glass rather than wood, pieces flashing in the light that came through the dirty windows. The man staggered backward, dazed.

I could have taken them all out in seconds if I'd wanted to, but I savored every punch, every crack as bones snapped. Every drop of blood that spattered the concrete. They fought like trained assassins rather than the pampered cowards they were.

None of their attacks landed. I wasn't a helpless boy bound to a chair who didn't understand how to control the full extent of his abilities. I was a blur, a force of nature, an avenging angel come to bring their deserved destruction.

Eventually, only one remained standing. A kick to his chest sent him staggering backward, and his hood fell away to reveal his face. Tiernan's face, even though I knew he hadn't been there that day.

"This isn't you," he said to me.

I held out my arm and Garcia's fallen gun flipped through the air into my waiting hand. "Yes, it is," I said, and I shot him in the chest. Scarlet bloomed over black robes that should have hidden the color of blood. He fell to his knees, mouth open in shock. Then he toppled forward, his hood covering his face so he was just another black-robed Committee member.

"Wow, that was incredible!"

His voice brought me back to myself, the way it always did. The gun fell from my hand, and I turned to find Sebastian working his way down the ladder from the catwalk that ran around the warehouse. He had a hunting rifle slung around his shoulder, loaded with tranquilizer darts instead of bullets.

His feet hit the floor with a quiet thud, and he turned to grin at me. "I didn't know you could do that."

"I can't." I looked down at my bloody knuckles. Not my own blood. The skin underneath was intact.

In the dream, I could do anything. I could fell armies. I could save myself and Sebastian, and we could run away together like we'd planned. But this wasn't how it had happened. It hadn't been in a dream, and it hadn't ended with black-robed bodies littering the ground. Only two bodies that day, and one of them had been my everything.

I woke to a world without Sebastian in it. I would have given anything to go back to sleep, even to relive that horrible day again and again. I would suffer through any nightmare if it meant he were there with me.

Waking up is a gift. I pried my eyes open. Sebastian was gone, and no amount of dreaming could change the past. All I could do was go on and finish what I had started.

Chapter 28

IT FELT STRANGE HAVING to find Ash's dreams instead of simply appearing there. Even though I had escaped my prison, I still felt a connection between us, a tether I could probably follow to the other side of the city. I wanted another chance to talk to her, to explain my side of the story. I shouldn't have clung so doggedly to the hope that I could reach her, but what was life without hope?

When I sought out Ash's mind, though, it wasn't *her* dreams I ended up in.

I kept myself out of sight, as usual, a formless entity tethered to Ash, but I needn't have bothered hiding. All that surrounded us was darkness. *True* darkness, the kind that made Ash realize she had never been completely without light. This was absolute nothingness, a void that had her questioning which way was up, even though she could feel her feet firmly planted on... something. Not ground. It was too hard for that. The darkness seemed to press against her ears as well, creating a hum that faded in and out.

All Ash could think was that something had gone horribly wrong and she had found herself in some kind of limbo that existed between dreams.

Then a voice came from the darkness. "You really make a habit of invading other people's dreams, don't you?"

Cat. "Your voice has a habit of coming from the dark," Ash replied.

Surprisingly, Cat laughed at that. Ash had never heard her laugh before. It was quiet, breathy, and filled the darkness despite the softness. "Is it dark? I suppose it would be."

"What do you mean? It's pitch black. Absolutely nothing here. Where are we?"

"My dream." Cat's voice was closer now, though she hadn't made a sound as she moved. "Just because you can't see it doesn't mean there's nothing there."

Ash reached out with her other senses, forcing the blackness that covered her eyes out of her mind. She stretched out a hand until her fingers brushed sunbaked metal, warm enough to sting a little but not burn her. She curled her fingers around it and slid her hand over the top of what felt like a railing. Then she realized that the hum wasn't some auditory illusion created by the darkness, but rather the sound of passing vehicles. She could feel the whoosh of air as the cars zipped by.

She could also feel Cat's presence as the other girl stepped closer. "Do you know where you are?" Cat asked.

"The Golden Gate Bridge," Ash said. She didn't know why she was so certain. The *concept* of it hung in the air, even if she couldn't see it.

"You should keep your hand on that railing. People sometimes lose their sense of balance in here."

"Why is it so dark?" Ash asked.

"Because it can't be any other way."

That made absolutely zero sense to Ash, but Cat said it so matter-of-factly that Ash wondered if maybe it should.

For me, though, it all started to make sense. The darkness of the dream and why my first attempt at manipulating Cat's perception had failed. I wasn't out of practice. She simply couldn't see what I had been trying to show her. It didn't bode well for my staying hidden. With other people, it was easy for me to stay out of sight, but I worried Cat might have the ability to *feel* my presence. I didn't know how to prevent that.

"Have you heard of aphantasia?" Cat asked. Ash shook her head before remembering that Cat wouldn't be able to see it, but Cat continued anyway. "It's a... condition, if you want to see it that way, where a person can't voluntarily visualize things. When you change your dreams, you conjure an image to your mind and then make it real, right?"

"Right." It was exactly what she had always done in her own dreams and what she had finally accepted she could do in others' just as easily.

"Well... I can't," Cat said. "You might say my mind's eye is blind. Not everyone with aphantasia dreams without images. Maybe about half. I'm one of them."

"But I've seen you change dreams." It had always seemed so effortless, too. TJ's face scrunched up when he concentrated, but Cat always looked calm. Focused.

"I found a different way to do it. And not easily." Clothing rustled as she leaned against the railing. "When you change someone's dream, you're not conjuring what you want yourself. Other dreamwalkers never think about what's really happening, but I had to understand it to be able to do it."

"Okay, what's really happening then?"

"You're telling the dreamer what to dream about. Pushing your will on them, in a way. Dreaming minds are susceptible to suggestion. You can tell the dreamer *exactly* what you want by visualizing it and showing it to them. For me... I deal in concepts, not images. I can hold the *idea* of something in my mind, even if I can't see it. Sometimes I don't get exactly what I want, because concepts can be interpreted differently, but it's usually close enough."

"Like the doors," Ash said quietly. "They're always different. You ask for a door, and you get whatever the dreamer conjures."

"Exactly."

It explained so much, and I wondered if Sebastian had known. He had mentioned TJ's nightmares, but never this. Robert did have a way of collecting abnormal children.

A hand wrapped around Ash's wrist, and Cat guided her away from the railing. They took a step, me tagging along with them, and suddenly we were somewhere else, somewhere familiar. Ash looked around at her own dreamscape, then at Cat, who stood beside her. A cracked blue door, conjured by Cat from Ash's memories, closed behind them.

I was relieved to find myself out of the darkness. I knew I relied too heavily on what I could see in my mind and what I could make other people see. Sure, I could and did manipulate the other senses, but I felt at a disadvantage without sight as a weapon.

Ash frowned and brushed her fingers against the peeling paint. "I thought you couldn't get into my dreams."

Cat glanced away. "I have a confession... I've been trying to find a way in since I learned I couldn't."

Ash cracked a smile. "Of course you have. Couldn't stand there being something you can't do, right?"

"Shut up," Cat said. "So should I assume you actually managed to intrude on my dreams because you have a purpose, or did you just want to have a friendly chat?"

"Right." Ash had been so caught off-guard by the darkness that she had forgotten about her reason for seeking out Cat in the first place.

I was very curious about the answer, too. Though I could still sense Ash's thoughts, the details of her intentions had slipped through the cracks, like she was avoiding actively thinking about them. That itself was quite impressive. Most people who try not to think about something only manage the opposite.

"How much do you remember about what happened at the hospital?" Ash asked. It was a fair question. Messing around with waking minds often left behind fuzzy memories.

"Enough. Griffin is free. His prison was in your mind. He manipulated me and TJ somehow."

"How is TJ?"

"He's... coping," Cat said. "I think he's dazed still. Learning you've been duped and then getting mind controlled will do that."

"I have a plan to stop Griffin, but I can't tell you about it yet," Ash said. "I think he's watching."

"Here?" Cat glanced around, her eyes passing right over me. I was part of the air, a consciousness without form.

"Everywhere," Ash said. "I think he can still see inside my mind. There's something I need to do before anything else. Otherwise he'll see my plan."

"Why are you telling me?"

"So you and TJ know I'm coming. Griffin won't get away with this."

"He's going to kill them. You know that, right? Robert, Aaron Winkler, probably your uncle, too."

"I know."

"He's in bad shape, but I don't think that's going to stop him from going after them." Cat walked to the edge of the cliff, first looking toward the horizon, then down at the crashing waves. She grimaced and took two steps back.

Ash ventured closer to the cliff, fearless in her own dreams. Her eyes lingered on the sunset, and her thoughts wandered back to the times we had stood on this cliff together. When I had held her on that couch and offered words of comfort. When I had kissed her. She longed to have those moments back, before they had been tainted by the exposure of a lie, and promptly felt guilty for wanting it.

Again, I thought back to what my father had always said. *The truth is always more frightening than a pretty lie.* But it's better, too, in the end. Ash was still having a hard time coming to terms with that. She had two versions of me in her head—the version she had met at the hospital and the version who wore Sebastian's face in her dreams. She was having a hard time accepting both were versions of the same person. Even harder was the fact that most of what I had told her hadn't been a lie. Deep down, she knew our conversations had been real.

Denial still didn't suit her, but she did her very best to pull it off.

She tried to distract herself from her conflicted feelings by focusing on Cat. "You were everything I wanted to be, you know," she said. "Confident, capable, independent. You didn't care about what anyone thought. You were a badass... and you *hated* me."

"You're right." Cat dug a small rock out of the ground and chucked it over the cliff. Far below, it disappeared into the water with an almost imperceptible splash. "I did hate you."

Ash gave her a wry smile. "Thanks."

"What? Were you hoping I would contradict that?"

"Maybe."

Cat shrugged. "I hated that you accidentally did what had taken me years to learn. I never even got pulled into nightmares the way most dreamwalkers do. For a while, I thought I didn't have the power. I had to work my ass off to enter someone's dream, and there you were falling into them without meaning to." She laced her fingers together and finally looked over at Ash. "Then I found out how completely useless you were. It was easier to like you after that."

Ash couldn't help but laugh. She would've thought being called useless would sting more, but the way Cat said it somehow made it not sound like an insult. "Thanks," she said again.

"I guess we were both wrong, though," Cat said. "I'm not as confident as you thought, and I *do* care what people think. I just learned not to show it."

"You're still a badass."

"Damn straight."

Ash grinned at her. "You'll need to be for what comes next. Be ready."

"Whatever you're planning... be careful," Cat said. "He's unstable. I can't tell if he thinks what he's doing is right or if he doesn't care anymore."

Even I couldn't answer that for her.

"You be careful, too," Ash said. "Try not to provoke him into killing you before I can get there, okay?"

"No promises." With that, Cat summoned Ash's front door and left the dream.

Chapter 29

A SH HAD TO WAKE up before she could do what she planned
next, though when she opened her eyes to reality, she
wished she could move between dreams like Cat could. She
couldn't see anything inside the drawer, which made her hy-
per-aware of the cold metal against her back. After having been
in Cat's dream, she realized it wasn't the darkness itself that
made her feel so trapped. No, it was the knowledge that six
metal walls surrounded her, one of which was a door that only
opened from the other side.

She had never been claustrophobic. She didn't have nightmares about being trapped or crammed into small spaces. But
there was something about being shut into a corpse cubby that
would make anyone feel like the walls were closing in.

She closed her eyes and tried to redirect her focus from the
feeling of cold metal beneath her back. She thought of Des
instead, conjuring every detail she could. Not only his face, but
his laugh and the way she felt around him. He had made her feel
like she belonged in a place she really didn't.

Why Des? I wondered. The thought came with a spark of
jealousy that I quickly stifled. She had a fondness for him, but
not exactly romantic. Beyond that, Ash wasn't mine. She would
never be mine.

The mission. All I had was the mission. *Destroy them all.*

I didn't think Ash would be able to reach Des. After all, finding one person in a city of eighteen million wasn't an easy feat. But Ash remembered something I had forgotten. Des had said he lived in Westlake, which happened to be not terribly far away.

Still, what Ash accomplished remained impressive. A week ago, she hadn't been able to enter the dream of someone in the next room. Now she managed to find someone she hadn't known for that long who was miles away.

She thought of it like shooting an arrow with a rope attached. When the arrow struck its target, all she had to do was follow the rope to her destination. I had never considered that analogy before, but it worked.

The dream we found ourselves in had a surreal quality to it. A wide range of dreams existed, and Ash had only seen a fraction of the possibilities. Even I had probably only seen a somewhat larger fraction. Some dreams were startlingly realistic, like Tiernan's or Celia's. Then there were dreams like Raisa's painted landscape, some with unnaturally vibrant colors and some black and white. They weren't always consistent with the same dreamer, though most did tend toward a certain style.

The style of Des's dreams surprised me, but not Ash. She didn't know what to expect exactly, but what she found made an incredible amount of sense to her. It looked like she had stepped into an anime, or some mix of anime and Disney.

Inside the dream, her curls were a brilliant scarlet rather than their natural auburn, and her eyes actually glittered like emeralds. She looked around in wonder at the animated world. Colored lights moved over the floor of the dimly lit bowling alley. A neon sign that said "Get Shoes Here!" flashed over the front desk. Unlike in Celia's dream, the people were detailed, though not realistic. They had faces, unique outfits, and varying expressions. The cartoon characters occupied every lane, throwing glowing balls at brightly colored pins. Music that sounded like it belonged in a video game played in the background. The synthetic notes played a repetitive, cheerful tune that I hoped wouldn't get stuck in my head later.

The dreamer himself looked like a punk version of Naruto. His platinum blond hair was a more golden color, spiky and impossibly upright. He stood facing the pins on his own lane with a neon green ball in his hands. He had his back to Ash, but from my vantage point I could see the look of concentration on his face, his tongue sticking slightly out the side of his mouth. The rest of the world froze for a moment, everything except Des going from vibrant color to a washed out gray with a bluish tinge. Then he took his first step, and the bowling alley resumed its normal flurry of activity.

He did his approach like a true pro and released the ball from his left hand. It hooked to the right and crashed into the spot right between the headpin and the pin beside it, sending the rest flying in a multi-colored starburst. He whispered, "Yes!" with a fist pump and spun on the balls of his bowling shoes.

The screen above his lane showed a bowling ball chucking a stick of dynamite into the center of lined up pins. The explosion blasted the pins away, and the smoke turned into a big X with lines above and below it, like a roman numeral. The words "TEN IN A ROW!" solidified beneath it. The screen went back to showing his score, which was a series of X's all the way to the current tenth frame.

So, what Desmond dreamed about was a perfect game. He needed two more strikes, but I had no doubt where this would go, unless it turned into a nightmare and he missed the last one.

"Des?" Ash walked up to him as he stepped down from the lane. Behind him, the lane reset the pins for his next ball.

He squinted at her, confused to find his coworker in his dream, then broke into a grin that came along with actual sparkles around his head. "Ash! You come to see me finish out this shit?"

"Uh... I guess," she said.

"You should join me for the next game!"

"I don't think that's a very good idea." Her eyes darted up at the screen. "I'm not very good at bowling."

What had I been telling her about dreams? It didn't matter what she was good at in the real world. For all we knew, Des wasn't any good at bowling, either.

"That's okay!" he said. "I won't judge. Hey, I'll even bowl with my right hand. I love a challenge."

She glanced down the alley at the various other bowlers, her worried expression exaggerated and oddly cute on her animated face. "Sure. Okay. Just one game."

"*Yes.* Great. Hold on a sec." He grabbed his ball and bounced back up to the approach area. Two more strikes finished out the game, and the screen played a Perfect Game animation of twelve dominoes toppling each other. The rest of the characters in the place stopped what they were doing, and a wave of clapping and cheering went through the alley. The applause lasted for a few seconds before everyone went back to their own games.

Des rejoined Ash by the ball return and gestured at the line of balls already there. "Pick your weapon, m'lady."

Ash's eyes scanned the options, none of which called to her. She reached out and grabbed a random one, which changed colors the moment she touched it, from a navy blue to powder pink swirled with magenta. Des exchanged his green one for a ball of an identical color. The only difference, if I had to guess, was the second was designed for right-handed bowlers.

She tucked the ball into the crook of her arm. "Before we do this, I need to tell you something. I know the odds of you remembering this are slim, let alone *believing* it. But I need you to try, okay?"

He frowned at her. "What are you talking about?"

"This is real. I'm really here, and I really do need your help. The crystal you gave me, the white... whatever."

"White chalcedony."

"Right. I need you to get one and come to the morgue at Lady Sabri's Hospital. You know where that is, right?"

"The *morgue?*" Des wrinkled his nose. "What's going on? Are you in trouble?"

"Yes. And if I don't get out of it, a lot more people are going to be in trouble. Okay?"

He nodded uncertainly. "Can we play now?"

Ash sighed, and both of us started to doubt her genius plan. A lot of people didn't remember their dreams when they woke up, and the ones they did remember often faded quickly. The chance of him remembering and *then* getting up in the middle of the night to drive all the way to Crystal Caverns and get her a rock? Extremely unlikely.

Ash had been correct about not being a good bowler. Her first ball barely nicked the pin on the far left side, and her second went straight into the gutter. Des did much better, even with his non-dominant hand. He took out six pins on his first throw, then picked up the spare with ease.

After three frames of this, I started silently begging Ash to do something to change the game. I hated watching her lose. Having been a silent passenger in her life for so long, it felt like *I* was losing.

When her next ball drifted toward the gutter, I waited to see if Ash would do anything about it, but she only watched with her lip caught between her teeth. If she wasn't going to do something, I would. I pushed the ball so it curved inward and took down five pins instead of missing completely.

The next time, I guided the ball right into that sweet spot between the headpin and the one beside it. Pins scattered, leaving only one wobbling upright. I gave it a nudge, and it toppled over.

"Whoo! That's what I'm talking about!" Des called from behind her.

Ash grinned as she stepped down from the lane. She accepted his offered high five, but her smile dimmed once he had turned his back. She looked around the bowling alley, not at the other bowlers but in the nooks and crannies where one usually wouldn't expect to find something.

Like she was looking for me.

I watched curiously, wondering if she would manage to spot me, but her eyes passed right over me. Of course. She was looking with her eyes, but my presence didn't have physical form. I was almost disappointed.

The crash of bowling pins brought her attention back to Des. He had left two pins with a sizable gap between them. The bowling animation mocked him with a banana split.

For a short time, Ash was able to forget about everything else. About me, about the morgue, about TJ and Cat in potential danger. She allowed herself to tuck her worries away for a while and just have fun. I didn't know the last time that had happened. She had been spinning her wheels, friendless and directionless, for so long that there had been no time for activities like bowling.

I found myself forgetting as well. My every thought for eight years had been consumed by Sebastian, the Committee, and the need to escape and take revenge. Something about watching Ash enjoying herself brought my mind away from it all. The burning anger was a distant memory that belonged in the waking world. For now, there was only Ash, the pins, and that guy I didn't care about but who had made this possible, so I guessed we could keep him.

I could have given Ash a clean game following the rough start, but I sensed she didn't want that for some reason. Des might dream of bowling a 300, but Ash's idea of fun wasn't perfection. She was messy and unpredictable and liked laughing at the ball tumbling down the gutter now and then.

When the game ended—fairly evenly matched, thanks to Des using his right hand and my interferences—Des tried to talk her into another, but Ash firmly declined.

"I need you to wake up now," she said. She had wasted enough time. "I need you to *remember.* The white chalcedony. Lady Sabri's Hospital morgue. Promise me you'll try."

"I promise," he said, though he still sounded confused. "I had fun. We should do this again so—"

Ash shoved him backward, toward a line of seats. They vanished before he hit them, along with the floor, so Des fell into dark nothingness. Ash hoped it would help him wake up, the way Cat had shoved her out of TJ's dream. She didn't stick around to find out, and neither did I. The last thing I needed was to get stuck again, this time in a cartoonish dreamscape of bowling and video game music.

Chapter 30

D URING THE GAME, ASH had forgotten where she'd left her body. Waking up to the inside of the drawer felt like plunging into icy water. Her mind could move freely to nearby dreamers, but her body was stuck.

And worse, all she could do was wait. And wait some more. She had to pray that Des would come through, that her faith in him wasn't misplaced. With every passing hour, she grew more worried that he hadn't remembered her request, or had dismissed it, or maybe he had never even woken up.

She was left with far too much time alone with her own thoughts. She spent that time dwelling on everything that had happened. The realization that I had been the one in her dreams all along and she had walked eagerly into my trap. In trying to prevent me from escaping, she had been the one to free me. She tried to hold onto her anger at both me and her uncle, but left alone in darkness, guilt started to seep in.

I could have left her and gotten the sleep I desperately need-ed. Something kept me there, though: the all-consuming need to know what happened next. I stayed with her while every piece of hope slipped away, until it dangled by that last thread too stubborn to let go.

Finally, a masculine voice came from outside, muffled by the thick metal. Her own name, barely recognizable. "Ash?"

"I'm here!" she called. The words echoed around the small chamber and made Ash's ears ring. She banged her palm against the door above her head. "Help me! I'm here."

The latch released, and the door opened, letting light fall onto her face. But when she looked up, it wasn't Des she found staring down at her.

It was Tiernan.

His face was blank, the expression somehow worse than anger. He pulled the drawer out so she could sit up, then he took a step back. She hardly recognized the man who regarded her with tired eyes. I did, though. The mask was slipping, and I could see the Tiernan I knew eight years ago seeping through.

"Tell me what happened," he said.

Ash really had tried to stay angry at him for keeping secrets. If he had told her the truth, maybe none of this would have happened. She would have known not to trust the stranger in her dreams. She would have stayed far away from the hospital. This was *his* fault.

The furious words clung to the tip of her tongue, but when she opened her mouth to spit them out, all that escaped was a sob. Tiernan's stern expression shattered, and he pulled her into his arms. The warmth of his embrace was familiar to both her and me, and welcome after the frigid interior of the cadaver drawer. I remembered what it was like to be cared for by someone like Tiernan.

Ash pulled her knees up and leaned into him, shivering. It shook loose the pain and regret that had been building up since we left her behind in that morgue, and she let her tears flow freely.

"He's awake," she said when she found her voice again. "And it's my fault. Everyone said not to look for him, but we didn't listen. I just... I wanted to keep him from escaping. I wanted to do something *important* with my life. Now he's free, and it's all my fault."

"Oh, Ash..." Tiernan brushed her hair out of her face. "You are not to blame for any of this. If anyone is, it's me. I should never have done what I did. At the time, it seemed brilliant, but now... I promised your parents I would keep you safe. Instead, I put a murderer in your mind."

She pulled free and scooted away from him. For the first time, Ash realized another person hovered near the door. Raisa inched closer, her eyes wide and apprehensive. "Cat?" she asked quietly.

Ash gave her head a small shake. "He has them."

Raisa's face fell. Her dismay radiated through the room in a visceral wave that Ash felt as clearly as her own emotions. Another by-product of my living in her mind for eight years. Tiernan probably felt it too.

"I'm so sorry. I tried... the things he can *do*. I thought the legends were ridiculous, but it's true." Ash looked back at Tiernan, and tears burned her eyes again. "Why me? Why choose my dreams?" It wasn't only me he had hurt when he'd turned Ash's mind into a prison.

Tiernan rubbed his forehead, then dragged his hand down his face. "There are people whose minds work differently from most. There are dreamwalkers, and then there are our opposites. It's harder to enter these people's dreams. Nearly impossible to control them. Your mother was one of them. By the time you were seven, we were pretty sure you were, too. You never showed any sign of being able to dreamwalk, and it took me years to be able to enter your dreams. Your mother didn't want you getting wrapped up in the Committee and dreamwalker drama, so after your father died, she made me promise to keep you separate from them if anything happened to her. I kept that promise... until eight years ago when Griffin threatened to kill all of us."

"So you decided to turn my dreams into a prison."

"In retrospect, a selfish and brash idea." He looked away, his expression rife with shame and regret. It was nice to know he regretted what he had done, but it didn't change anything. He had still done it. "To understand, you have to know everything that happened eight years ago. Griffin's real name is Zain Remington."

"Remington? Like James and Zahra Remington?"

Correct, Ash. So much for me being raised by the mafia.

On second thought, that legend wasn't so far off.

Tiernan nodded in confirmation. "His parents brought him to me when he was fifteen, after they realized he showed more power than they knew what to do with. They were afraid of what he might do if he didn't learn to control it. It went beyond what either of them could have imagined, though. He wasn't just gifted. He was... *extraordinary.* There are things I can do that the Committee doesn't even know about. I can sense feelings, sometimes even thoughts, when people are conscious. But Zain surpassed even me."

"He can control what people see and hear and feel," Ash said. "Even when they're awake."

"He *what?*" Raisa broke in. She sounded spooked, and rightfully so.

"What he can do should be impossible. And it's dangerous," Tiernan said. "He was an angry young man, prone to lashing out, and I was worried what he might do if he lost his temper. I tried to teach him to control it. Like my own abilities, I didn't know how the Committee would react to his. But my concerns grew along with his power, and eventually I confided in a friend. Robert Knight."

He grabbed a rolling stool and sank onto it, his shoulders hunched. It brought me a cold sort of satisfaction, to see how much the story pained him. He deserved to suffer for the suffering he had caused.

"His reaction was... different from what I'd expected," Tiernan went on. "Where I saw danger, he saw potential. He told the others, despite my pleas to keep Zain's powers a secret. Garcia was running for senator at the time. They wanted to use his ability to manipulate conscious minds to sway people. To change not only what they saw and heard but what they thought and felt. Their emotions. So the Committee took over his training." Tiernan took a deep breath. I could sense his weariness growing with every word. "Charlotte was against it, but the two of us weren't enough to stop the rest of the Committee. Then my worst fears came true when Zain killed Walter Edgeworth. An accident, I'm sure, but that didn't matter to the others."

Ash and Raisa listened in silence now, entranced by the story. Even I found myself drawn in, despite the fact that I had lived it. I already knew how it ended.

"They turned against him. They had unwittingly created a weapon, and if they couldn't use it, then they would destroy it. Sebastian Knight tried to defend him and died doing it. That was the end of it. Any hope of bringing Zain back from the brink was lost. All he cared about was getting revenge.

"Even after he killed Moreau and Garcia, I couldn't bring myself to let them just *execute* him. No prison could hold him, but I realized you would be the perfect way to contain him. I could bring him with me into your mind, and he wouldn't be able to escape by changing the dream. Except you could never know. That was important. If you ever encountered him in your dreams, you had to believe he existed only in your imagination."

Ash thought back to the drawings that littered her walls, images that she didn't know where they had come from. My house, my face, other memories of mine that had leaked into her head. "And I did," she said. "Until I found myself in someone else's dream."

"It shouldn't have been possible," Tiernan said. "When I trapped Griffin, I didn't consider the potential side effects. You might be the first person with shielded dreams who is also able to dreamwalk. The way brains with these different abilities are structured... they're just incompatible. But I think somehow having him in your mind let you siphon his abilities and use them for your own. The longer he was there, the stronger the connection between you became. It seems that eventually he found a way to change your dreams and actually talk to you in a way he couldn't before."

"And change his appearance," Ash murmured.

Now Tiernan looked curious. "He didn't appear as himself?"

"He used Sebastian's face to get me and the others to trust him," she said. Bitterness welled up inside her, at both me and herself. "I probably would have fallen for it either way, but TJ and Cat were so desperate to have their brother back. He chose his ruse well."

I did feel a prickle of guilt at that. I would have been furious if someone had used Sebastian against me, but my deception had been necessary. He would have understood.

"I'm so sorry I dragged you into this," Tiernan murmured. "For what it's worth, I don't think he plans to hurt TJ and Cat. He might use them, but his vendetta is against the Committee. Against me."

"You still care about him," Ash said.

"I feel responsible. I should have protected him better. I should have been able to stop the others from following through with their plan. If I had, Sebastian would be alive and Zain wouldn't be intent on destroying all of us."

"You couldn't have known what the Committee would do," Raisa said. "We're not to blame for the actions of others. Griffin might be able to control people, but you can't."

"She's right." Ash pushed down her own regrets and met her uncle's gaze. "You're not to blame for this any more than I am."

"Ash?" A new voice interrupted them, and they all turned toward the door to find Des staring at them in confusion. He eyed the drawer that Ash still sat on and said, "You're not a zombie, are you?"

Despite everything, her eyes still red from crying and her heart heavy with worry for her friends, Ash laughed. "No, I'm not a zombie. It's okay, you can come in. I promise not to eat your brains."

Des still walked toward them with abundant caution. "What's going on? Why are we in a morgue?"

"It's an extremely long story," Ash said. And she hadn't known half of it five minutes ago. "You brought it?"

Des bobbed his head and reached into his pocket to produce a white rock. I still didn't understand why Ash had asked for it. From their expressions, neither did Tiernan and Raisa.

"What is it?" Raisa asked.

"The way I'm going to stop Griffin, I hope," Ash said. Des held the chalcedony out to her, but she didn't take it yet. Instead, she turned to Tiernan. "He told me he doesn't want to manipulate me anymore, but that's not true, is it? He can't."

"He may have gained the ability to manipulate your dreams while you're asleep, but no, I don't think he's strong enough to control your thoughts while awake."

My spark of irritation clashed with Ash's relief. "Which is why I have to do this alone."

"Ash..." Tiernan protested.

"If you or Raisa come, he'll be able to use you against me." She looked at Des, who hovered awkwardly nearby. "I think he can still see inside my mind, though. I can *feel* him. He's watching me. Which means whatever I plan to do, he'll see me coming." She smiled then, which made me nervous. What could she have to smile about? "Des told me that rock might help me sleep. I didn't believe it at first, but then I gave one to TJ. I didn't think anything of it at the time, but I couldn't feel TJ's mind while he slept in the car. I think that thing prevents dreamwalkers from getting in."

Tiernan's expression walked the line between skeptical and intrigued. "I've never heard of such a thing, but it would be foolish to think I know everything about the world, given what I've seen Griffin do."

"The strength of our connection might make it so he can get past my natural defenses, but I think this will block him out." She held out her hand to Des. "Only one way to find out."

Des still looked baffled, but he passed the white chalcedony to her. The moment it settled into her palm, something pressed against my mind, a barrier slamming down and forcing me out.

Chapter 31

"**N**o!" I SHOUTED AS the last strands of the vision slipped away. I could still feel her at the back of my head, the faint hints of emotion, but when I tried to look into her mind, I found a roadblock. *How?* Like Tiernan, I had never heard of something able to block out a dreamwalker, but clearly it worked.

I needed to know her plans. She hovered in my blind spot now, frustratingly out of reach. How could I do what needed to be done if I had to watch my back for a sneak attack?

I slammed my fist against the table beside me, hard enough to make the lamp shade rattle.

A derisive snort from across the room made me stiffen. I turned slowly and narrowed my eyes at Cat, who stared at me again with her dark, judgmental gaze.

"Do you have something to say?" I asked.

"What's wrong? Bad dream?"

"Cat," TJ said quietly. He was scrunched up beside her with his knees tucked against his chest. His arms, which were looped around one of the desk legs, rested atop them. Unlike Cat, he avoided looking at me. "Please don't antagonize the sociopath."

Anger twinged at that word. It wasn't the first time someone with the last name Knight had called me that.

Garcia is right. Do you realize what we could do with some-one like him at our disposal?

Are you insane? He's a psychopath. We should put him down before he kills someone else. Aaron had been all for using me until he learned I could literally kill him with my mind. *Actually, his anti-social tendencies are more sociopathic than psychopathic, even if both are outdated terms.*

Leave it to Robert to be precise about these things.

"I never thought you one for name calling," I said.

"It was an observation, not an insult." His calm voice didn't match the way he stared at the faded carpet.

"You think you're pretty smart, don't you? All those degrees. They don't do you much good, though, do they? Your father still doesn't respect you. *Either* of you. At least Sebastian had the sense to cut ties."

"You do a lot of talking, do you know that?" Cat said. "I guess I shouldn't expect anything less from an egotistical super villain."

I stood so fast it made my head spin, and my vision went blurry for a moment. I almost fell face-first onto the floor, but I reached blindly for the bed and guided myself back down. Some super villain I made. I couldn't even stand on my own.

"I'm not the villain," I murmured. Or maybe I was. I didn't even care anymore. They could cast me as the villain in their story if they wanted to. I was done playing by other people's rules, playing the role *they* assigned. I wasn't the hero or the villain. I was just a man who had nothing left to lose.

I was also a man with limited time. With no idea what Ash had planned next, I had to act quickly.

I made TJ drive us to the house while I slumped in the backseat, the hum of the road threatening to lull me to sleep. Focusing on altering TJ's reality helped keep me awake. I changed the names on street signs, blurred or altered other landmarks, and simply told him where to turn. It left him confused and uncertain of where we were going. I didn't think he would keep driving if he knew.

As for Cat, I had to hope whatever affection she might feel for the man-shaped garbage that had adopted her was trumped by her love for her brother.

She had to know where we were going, but she sat silently in the passenger seat, staring stoically ahead. Sulking or scheming? I had no way to know. Either way, she offered no protests about our destination. Perhaps in the end she would see I was doing her a favor. Maybe she already did.

"This one here on the left," I said. I redesigned the house in TJ's mind, making it a rather ugly shade of yellow with white trim. I changed the color of the flowers in the garden and the front door, but I didn't waste energy on anything more. TJ still stared at it, his muddled mind telling him something was wrong, but he couldn't push past the illusion I had created.

Cat helped me out of the backseat and into the wheelchair. She still didn't speak as she pushed me up the driveway. I kept waiting for something from her, anything at all. Was she really going to let me stroll in there and do this? Or roll in, technically.

"Open the garage," I ordered Cat. I wasn't going to ring the doorbell and wait for an invitation to kill him, though that did sound like it could be some fun. What would I have to say and make him see to convince him to let me in?

My chair barely fit between the two cars parked in the garage. We squeezed through, then TJ and Cat worked together to lift my chair up the few steps that led into the house. When TJ saw the interior, he finally realized where we were. It was far too late to do anything about it, though, so he only shook his head and whispered, "*No.*"

Yes, I thought. He would thank me later. The whole city would be better off without this man in it.

The moment the door shut behind us, a light flicked on in the living room, revealing Robert on the couch with a golf club resting across his lap. Tiernan must have warned him. Hopefully Celia was still fast asleep upstairs. She wasn't a part of this.

"So you did come here first," Robert said. His voice was calm, but I didn't miss the flash of fear in his eyes when he glanced at TJ and Cat behind me. I'm sure I was a sight to behold, sunken and fragile and sitting in a wheelchair, but at least I could still elicit fear.

Only a fool would think me harmless.

Robert rose from the couch, the club clutched in his hands. Maybe he was a fool after all, if he thought that would protect him. "Let them go," he said. "They're innocent in this."

"I'm only interested in you," I replied. "Accept your fate, and they won't get hurt."

He took a few slow steps toward us. I watched, curious what he had planned. When he sprang forward, the golf club poised to strike, I decided he was indeed a fool. I let him reach the line where the carpet met the hardwood of the hallway before I seized his mind.

His chest convulsed as water started filling his lungs. It choked off his shout as it bubbled up his throat and poured out of his mouth, splattering the wood floor. The useless weapon slipped from his fingers and landed with a muffled thud on the carpet behind him.

Robert coughed, trying to expel the liquid that didn't exist. All he had to do was breathe normally, but when your body is convinced you're drowning, it's difficult to do anything else.

In a dream, his muscles would have been inert, the atonia preventing him from flailing in his sleep. His breathing would have remained measured, controlled by the automated part of his brain. When you die in your own dream, you wake up. But this was a nightmare he couldn't wake up from.

He fell to his knees, one hand grasping at his throat. I savored the panic on his face, the knowledge that he was going to die and there was nothing he could do about it.

"Dad!" TJ ran forward and knelt beside him, placing a hand on Robert's shoulder. "Dad, what's wrong?"

I noticed Cat remained where she stood.

TJ looked up at me, his eyes brimming with tears. "Stop it! What are you doing to him?"

"Making him pay," I said softly. "You can't help him."

I didn't expect TJ to tackle me straight out of the chair, but that was exactly what he did. The back of my head hit the floorboards hard enough to daze me and break my connection with Robert. He gasped for breath, his lungs no longer flooded, while TJ aimed a punch at my face.

I reached up to grab TJ's wrist, but my movements were sluggish, my muscles still not responding readily. I missed, but so did he, my arm deflecting the blow so his knuckles met the floor instead of my nose.

"TJ, stop!" To my surprise, Cat took TJ's arms and pulled him off me. He fought to break her grip, all flailing limbs and blind rage.

I struggled to sit up and scooted away from them until I found the wall and could lean against it. The moment I touched TJ's mind, his anger and fear plowed into me like a wrecking ball. I had to push it aside so I could focus. "Sleep now," I murmured, and TJ went limp in Cat's arms.

"TJ!" She lowered him to the ground and cradled his head in her lap, her fingers pressed against his neck to find his pulse.

"He's fine," I assured her. "Just sleeping. Can't have him interrupting us again." I didn't want Cat suddenly deciding to be a hero, either, so I pushed the thought of being sleepy into her mind as well. She slumped against the wall, her eyes closed.

By the time I looked back at Robert, he was on his feet, but he made no move toward me. Terror had leached the color from his face, but his voice was steady when he spoke. "Do what you want but leave my children alone."

"Your children?" I pressed my palms against the wall and used it for support as I struggled to my feet. My legs barely held me, so I stood there trembling like a newborn fawn learning to walk for the first time. But I was upright, and that was better than staring up at him from the floor. "I bet you think you're some kind of savior, don't you? Running around rescuing poor little orphan kids and giving them a better life. If only those poor orphans knew you were just building your army. And what a defective army it is. TJ can't control his nightmares, Cat dreams in darkness, and Sebastian... we both know what a huge disappointment *he* was to you."

Robert's wince almost made me think he cared about the son he had cast aside. "Don't talk about Sebastian. You corrupted him."

"I corrupted *him*?" I regretted laughing because it made my whole body hurt. "What if we talk about who corrupted me? Who took a boy and turned him into a weapon? Who told him he was dangerous and needed to be controlled?"

"Garcia's plans died with her," Robert said. "You don't have to do this."

"Did they? And what if another comes along just like me? Who can do what I do. Who's to say you won't try to control them too? You're all so obsessed with power, you don't care who you use to get it." Cat had been right about that. They were all too blinded by ambition, even Byrne, who didn't seem like a half-bad person overall. I couldn't help but wonder if she would have gone along with everything, if she had been on the Committee back then.

Robert held up his hands. "Please, Griffin. She was the one who did this."

He took a step forward, but I held up my thumb and index finger like a gun and said, "Bang."

Robert cried out in pain and fell to one knee, clutching his completely uninjured leg in both hands. He knew it wasn't real and tried to push through the pain, but he still stumbled when he stood.

"Do you know the great thing about having been shot?" I asked. I rubbed my finger against the spot on my hip where I knew the bullet had left a scar. "It makes it that much easier to simulate the pain of a gunshot wound." I would never forget that feeling, but getting shot hadn't been half as bad as watching Sebastian bleed out in front of me. "Do you even care that your own son died that night because of what you did?"

"What Garcia did," Robert said through gritted teeth. His eyes were unfocused. He looked like he might pass out, so I let up on the pain a little.

"You might not have pulled the trigger, but don't pretend that you didn't have a hand in his death."

"And what about you, *Griffin.*" He said the name with such derision. He probably didn't even know that Sebastian had come up with it. "I suppose you think you're entirely faultless in that."

My hand twitched, then curled into a fist to keep it from shaking. I could still remember the slick warmth of his blood on my hands. Sebastian attempting to speak as his life slipped away between my fingers. I still didn't know what he had tried to tell me. Forgiveness or blame?

No. Sebastian would never have blamed me for what happened, just like he hadn't blamed me for Edgeworth's death. "I never asked for *any* of it," I spat. I took a step toward Robert, which proved to be a mistake, because I almost fell to the floor as well. I retreated again and kept my hand against the wall for balance. "You forced me into it, the five of you." Tiernan and my parents, as well. I could have led a normal life if it weren't for their actions. Their choices. They had paved the path that had led me here.

And I still had so much work to do before the night was done. The time for talking was over.

I brushed aside the thought of the gunshot and refocused on the water that would stifle the life from his body. He could drown in his own denial.

"Hello, Griffin."

The voice broke my concentration. *Her voice.* I knew it as well as my own, if not better at this point. I kept my eyes on Robert, who no longer looked afraid. He was smirking a little, even. *Do you think the girl is going to save you?* I asked without speaking. I couldn't read thoughts, not really, but I could put mine in other people's heads.

"I think Tiernan's niece is going to defeat you," he said. "Look at you. You're as weak as a sickly old man. Without your mind tricks, you're nothing. And you can't play your games with someone like her."

I hated him for being right. The truth didn't look good on him.

"You knew, didn't you?" Ash said. "You knew who I was and what my uncle did."

"I suspected," Robert replied. "He refused to tell me whom he had chosen as the cage for Griffin's mind, but I knew you took after your mother. It made sense. When you showed up at my door... I had to pretend I didn't recognize you. The less you knew the better. But you *idiots* had to keep digging, even after I'd explicitly told you not to."

"Maybe you shouldn't have underestimated your own children," Ash said. "Stop this, Griffin. No one else has to die. Do you think this is what Sebastian would have wanted?"

"You don't know what he would have wanted," I said. "You never even met him!"

"And yet I still feel like I know him. I think that means, deep down, you know he would tell you not to do this."

I thought about Sebastian and his tranq gun. The way he had begged for the violence to end. He had asked his father to simply let us go. *He wouldn't want this.*

Well, maybe *he* wouldn't. "You're right," I admitted. "The problem is, I don't really care." Sebastian was gone, and what he would have wanted was irrelevant. "For once, it's going to be about what *I* want."

"Oh, please," Robert scoffed. "You were always a selfish bastard."

"Don't even get me started on you," Ash snapped. "You indirectly got your son killed and were terrible to your other two children when they came to you for help. So sit there and shut up."

Despite the situation, I felt a flicker of pride. My lips twitched into a smile, but it vanished when Ash took a step toward me. "Stay back or I'll kill him," I ordered.

"You're going to kill him anyway," she said, but she heeded my threat. She stopped, her eyes going from me to the pale-faced Robert, then to TJ and Cat on the floor. She could sense their sleeping minds, without having to check for breathing or a pulse to know they were still alive.

I suddenly wished I hadn't knocked them out. They would be much better leverage against her than Robert, but it was easier to put people to sleep than wake them back up. When she took another step, testing me, I seized Robert's mind and summoned the memory of the bullet hole again. He cried out, but Ash kept coming.

I saw her hand go into her pocket. I realized her intentions when I saw the flash of the needle. In other circumstances, I would have had plenty of time to stop her, but by the time my fingers wrapped around her wrist, the needle was already in my neck. I only had time to force Robert into sleep before the drugs blurred my mind too much to focus.

Ash gave me a small smile that was more than a little worrying. Scary, even. "I thought maybe we should level the playing field. See you on the other side." Her quiet words guided me into oblivion as the drug took hold and my vision went black.

Chapter 32

T HE DREAM FORMED ON the beach. Deep sand under my bare feet, the sun blazing against the back of my neck. The ocean was calm, no movement other than the tide lapping at the wet sand. Venice Beach. Sebastian and I used to love it here. We would find a relatively quiet spot away from the rest of the people and hide out until it was time to return to our separate lives.

There was no need to hide now, though. The expanse of sand seemed bigger devoid of people. I thought I would prefer it that way, but there was something eerie about the deserted beach. No one standing in the surf, no laughter or hum of voices in the background. The emptiness made the truth glaringly obvious, that this wasn't reality.

"Interesting choice," Ash said behind me. I spun in the sand. "I never took you for a beach guy."

"As you've already stated, you don't know me very well." She was right, though. The beach had been Sebastian's choice. My favorite place had always been wherever he was. The backdrop hadn't mattered.

She stepped around me and walked closer to the waterline. She kept her distance, though taking her eyes off me at all seemed bold. "It's nice. A little too bright for my tastes."

"I prefer your sunset," I said quietly. Her shoulders stiffened, but she still didn't look at me. "You know you can't win here. You had a better shot in the real world."

Ash nodded. "True. I can't beat you in your own dream."

"Then why—"

I cut off when a hand grabbed my wrist and yanked me backward. It was the only warning I had before I found myself falling between dreams. When an image reformed around me, I didn't know where Cat had brought me. Not her own dreams, obviously. Not Ash's, either. I knew the feel of her dreams as distinctly as I knew my own.

I wrenched my wrist out of Cat's grasp and took a step away. Before she could dream-hop me anywhere else, a powerful gust of wind pushed her back and knocked her to the floor. "Stay away from me," I snarled. Last time someone had taken me to unknown dreams, I had gotten stuck there.

I kept an eye on her while I took stock of my surroundings. Instead of any familiar place, we stood in an impossibly long hallway. Speckled linoleum tiles, fluorescent lights overhead, closed doors every few paces on either side. Benches sat in the spaces between doors, spots for students to sit while waiting for their classes, though the hallway was empty.

I had never been to college, but I knew the sight of one anyway.

Ash stepped through the only open door, the one that had brought me there. It looked like all the others, simple wood with a silver handle. Ash shut it behind her, closing off my view of the classroom on the other side.

"Where did you bring me?" I asked. I had a guess, but ultimately this could be anyone's dream.

When Ash didn't answer, I said, "You must think you're clever." I'll admit, it wasn't a terrible idea, taking me away from where I was most in control. In someone else's dream, at least they could fight back. That wouldn't be enough, though. "You still can't beat me."

"Are you sure?" She pushed open the same door we had emerged from, but this time only a classroom waited on the other side, not the portal that would bring me back to my own dream. She stepped through, and the door swung closed on its own.

I glanced at Cat to make sure she didn't try anything, but the other girl had vanished. Unease crept up my spine. What were the two of them planning? They had brought me here for a reason. Ash might be foolish for thinking she could defeat me, but she wasn't an idiot. She had some scheme up her sleeve.

The sensible thing would have been to find Cat or to avoid them both until I was able to wake up. Ash clearly wanted my focus on her, so maybe they planned to have Cat attack while I was distracted. If I were *sensible,* I wouldn't have played along.

Instead, I pushed through the door and followed Ash into a massive lecture hall.

It was too big to be a real place, more of a stadium than a classroom. Some of the largest could seat around a thousand students, but this place had to have room for *ten* thousand. The seats wrapped around the middle of the room in a ring, while a second level balcony added another dozen rows.

Ash stood on the raised stage in the center of the room, beside a balding white man who had to be Tycho Brahe. The fake nose kind of gave it away. His pointed mustache and frilled white collar betrayed his era. Of the thousands of seats, only one was occupied, a spot in the front row. A boy scribbled in a notebook, glancing up every now and then at the deceased lecturer.

Only TJ would have *good* dreams about being in school, lectured by a dead scientist.

Neither lecturer nor student noticed the intruder on the stage, not even when she spoke over Brahe's droning voice going on about supernovas. "You think you're so powerful," she said. "The big, bad Griffin. But you're just that same scared, angry boy."

"I'm not scared of anything anymore." I started down the aisle but stopped halfway to the bottom. "Now everyone fears me."

"And what would Sebastian think of that?"

That was so cool, he had said in my dream, the memory I had rewritten. He wouldn't have, though. The real Sebastian would have been horrified at the carnage I'd left behind. But Sebastian hadn't lived long enough to see what the Committee was capable of, how far they were willing to go.

"The Committee deserves it," I said. They deserved the ax that had been hanging over their heads for eight years, and they would deserve it when it finally fell.

"That sounds familiar." Her figure blurred and vanished, reappearing behind the railing of the balcony across from me.

"Showing off, Ash?" I shouted, though I needn't have raised my voice for it to carry throughout the room. "That's not like you."

"How would you know?"

"I told you. I know you better than anyone. I know your aspirations, your insecurities, your regrets. I know what drives you, and I know the fears that shut you down. I know you're terrified of letting down the people who believe in you. People like Tiernan. You think that someday they'll finally stop believing."

"Did you let him down?"

I narrowed my eyes. In the background, I could still hear Brahe's voice, but the words had lost all meaning. "He let *me* down," I said. "I trusted him, and he betrayed me. He told Robert about me. Tiernan was supposed to be the one person I could confide in, but he was the one who set all of this in motion."

"He was afraid for you."

"He was afraid *of* me," I snapped. "He sold me out. If he'd wanted to help me, he would have kept my secret."

"He cared about you," she said. "I think you cared about him, too. But that hurts too much to accept, so you choose to hate him instead. Is it so hard for you to admit you were wrong?"

My rage simmered, growing stronger with her every word. How could she take his side, after he had betrayed her too? She should understand better than anyone. "Why are you saying these things?"

"Maybe I want you to fight me."

"You have a death wish, dreamer."

Ash vanished again, and next time she spoke, her voice came from behind me. "Perhaps I want to see if you're as powerful as you think you are."

I spun around, but Ash wasn't there anymore. I searched the room with narrowed eyes. "Or maybe you want to prove how powerful *you* have become." I knew I had hit the truth on the head when she didn't respond. "Just remember, everything you can do is because of me. My power, my guidance. What makes you think you can defeat me?"

"Why don't we find out?" Her voice projected from all sides, and I couldn't tell where she had gone. She was getting better.

"I don't want to hurt you."

"Too bad, because I really want to hurt you." She materialized in front of me, dangerously close. "You kidnapped my friends. Threatened to torture them. You're planning to kill my uncle. He's on your little hit list, isn't he?"

I didn't answer. She already knew the truth.

"Maybe they were right all along. You really do need to be controlled. It was only a matter of time before Sebastian realized you weren't good enough for him and left. Is that why you let him die?"

"*Let* him?" I said. "He was taken from me!"

"All your power, and you really couldn't save him?"

My building rage burst out of me in a roar as I threw myself forward to tackle her. I went right through her, and when I spun around she had vanished.

Her voice came from all around me again. "Is that really the best you've got? Come on, Griffin. Show me that power that made everyone so frightened of you."

I focused, searching for her presence. She was the one thing, aside from me, that didn't belong in the dream. I found her on the balcony again, directly above me. After watching her jump around, it was easy to imagine myself vanishing and reappearing in front of her. I hoped for a look of surprise, but Ash had been waiting for me. The moment I solidified, she grabbed my arms and shoved me back, right over the balcony railing. I teetered on top of it for a second, but then my weight tipped back too far. Gravity claimed me.

But what gravity? My free fall toward the seats below halted. I righted myself so I stood on thin air, then I walked up a flight of invisible stairs until I stood level with the railing.

I leaned forward and shot toward her, my arms outstretched. Ash didn't react fast enough to dodge or simply vanish. I slammed into her and drove her backward into the wall. Drywall and splinters flew as we crashed through, leaving a gaping hole behind us.

I pinned her against the wall of the hallway that looked identical to the one a level below. "You don't know anything about me," I said in a low voice. My face was mere inches from hers. The memory of kissing her flashed through my mind, but I shut it down. Ash had chosen her side. She was my enemy now. Everyone in this world was against me. I needed to stop believing someone might stand by my side.

If she was going to stand in my way, then I had no choice but to get rid of her.

Ash didn't look the least bit frightened, staring back at me with defiant green eyes. "I know enough." She lifted her arms, breaking my grasp on her, and pushed me away with incredible strength. I staggered across the hallway. By the time I regained my balance, Ash was halfway into the wall behind her, passing through it like a ghost.

"Catch me if you can," she said before her face disappeared, leaving behind only a blank white wall.

I plunged after her, my body passing through the wall like it didn't exist. She had learned quickly. I had wanted to unlock the potential I'd known existed in her, but now that altruism was going to bite me in the ass.

When I emerged on the other side, Ash was already across the room, a classroom much smaller than the lecture hall. She stood in front of a series of windows with dark green treetops visible through the glass.

I launched myself into the air in a massive leap that brought me in a high arc over the desks. I collided with Ash and sent us both smashing through a window. It shattered, shards of glass flashing in the sunlight as we fell from the second story.

I braced myself for the impact, blocking the pain and preventing any potential damage to my dream body. I lost my grip on Ash, though, and she rolled away from me over the pieces of glass that littered the ground.

She sprang to her feet with the unnatural grace of a martial arts master in a kung fu movie and flashed me a smile. "Is that all you've got?" Then she turned and dashed into the dense forest that surrounded the massive school TJ had dreamed up.

Instead of getting to my feet, I rolled onto my hands and knees and willed my body to change. If I could make myself look like Sebastian, why not something else? When I chased after Ash, I did so on four paws, in the form of a wolf with fur the color of Sebastian's hair. I lost sight of her almost immediately, but I could sense her nearby. I could feel her exhilaration, the pure *joy* hanging the air in her wake.

She was having fun. This wasn't a *game* to me.

I moved faster than her with my four legs, but when I drew near enough to catch her in my sight, she bent her knees and launched herself into the air. She landed on a thick branch and leaped effortlessly to the next. She sprang from branch to branch like a lemur, while I raced along the ground below, weaving between tree trunks and leaping over bushes. When I was almost directly under her, I bent my legs and jumped twenty feet into the treetops.

I shifted back into a human midair. When she realized I was no longer on the ground, she glanced over her shoulder, just in time for me to catch her look of surprise before I tackled her. We fell again, but this time I kept my arms locked around her. We grappled on the ground, Ash trying to escape while I kept her arms pinned against her sides, her back against my chest.

"Stop. Fighting. Me," I said.

She didn't listen. A bolt of lightning flashed through the foliage and struck my shoulder. My mind responded instinctively, and my muscles convulsed as electricity sizzled through my body. It was enough to weaken my hold on Ash, and she slithered free like an oiled snake.

She remained crouched a few feet away. She looked like an Amazon warrior, red hair wild and adorned with leaves. "Just let it go, Zain."

I got to my feet. "Don't call me that."

Ash rose with me, her eyes tracking my movements. "The Committee didn't do this. A small group of people did, and three of them are already dead. Let the rest live."

"Tiernan and my parents—"

"Made mistakes. The way anyone does. That doesn't make them bad people."

"You met my parents. They *are* bad people." She had said she wanted to hurt me, so why was she still trying to talk me out of it? Why didn't she attack?

"Would Sebastian really be okay with you killing his father?"

"He wasn't his real father. Sebastian hated Robert."

"You didn't answer my question. I'm starting to think your goal is to make Sebastian hate you as much as you hate yourself. Is that why you're doing this, Zain?"

"Stop. Saying. That name!" I threw out my arm, a knife appearing in my hand a moment before I released it. The blade flew through the air, straight at Ash, my aim true despite never having thrown a knife in real life.

She gasped as the knife sank into her stomach. We stared at each other, my anger dissolving into horror. Blood bloomed over her shirt, and she collapsed, a motionless heap on the forest floor.

Chapter 33

"**A**SH!" I RAN FORWARD and dropped to my knees beside her. "No. I'm sorry. I didn't mean it. Please, I didn't mean to." My hand hovered over the knife while I struggled over whether to pull it out, but Ash's eyes were closed. She wasn't moving, wasn't even breathing.

This wasn't how it was supposed to go. She had goaded me into it, had intentionally taunted me until my temper snapped. I hadn't wanted this! I hadn't—

Her eyes snapped open. She yanked the knife from her own chest and drove it upward into mine. I didn't react fast enough to prevent it from sinking into my flesh, but I did shut out the pain my mind automatically created in response.

I didn't bleed. I didn't have blood here. I didn't have a body, and the knife didn't really exist. I wrapped my fingers around the handle of the knife and willed it to vanish. My torn shirt shimmered and repaired itself.

When I looked up at Ash, the blood had disappeared from her shirt. She looked the same as she had minutes ago. Better, even. I had always thought Ash's self-image in a dream dulled in comparison to reality, but in that moment, she looked like herself. Every detail about Ash remained the same as the image I had memorized in the hospital, right down to the freckles dusted over her cheekbones, though her curls were free from their usual bun. She looked *real.*

She looked stunning. And she wanted me dead.

"I told you that dying outside your own dreams is a lie," I said. She had listened. She had *believed* me. Something about that stunned me. For most dreamwalkers, the rules are so deeply ingrained that telling them the truth wouldn't change anything. But Ash hadn't been brought up as a dreamwalker. Their beliefs hadn't been instilled in her since she was a child. She wasn't limited by their teachings.

For the first time, I worried that might get me killed.

"I guess you were right," she said. "I can't beat you here. But you can't beat me, either."

"Maybe not you," I agreed. "But what about Cat? Or maybe we'll have a little fun with TJ. How about a change of scenery?"

The forest blurred and darkened, and when our surroundings sharpened again, we stood in the graveyard that haunted TJ's nightmares. I didn't think I would have to summon the creatures that always lurked between the headstones. His mind would do that part.

I glanced around us, searching for TJ and Cat. They couldn't be far, and there was nowhere to hide in this place. I found the top of Cat's head poking up from behind a headstone and started toward her, unhurried.

"Griffin, wait," Ash said. She sounded nervous, finally.

I ignored her and kept walking, my shoes crunching on the frost-coated grass. When I rounded the headstone, I found Cat crouching with her arm around a younger version of TJ, who had his face buried in his arms. She glared up at me, refusing to show any fear. I could admire that, at least.

Cat let out a startled scream when the earth turned to liquid beneath her. It swallowed her whole, then solidified over her head. I summoned a new stone for the graveyard, one that read *Catalina Knight: Loving sister, disappointing daughter, failure.*

"Cat!" Ash fell to her knees in the spot where Cat had vanished. She started digging at the earth with her hands while young TJ pressed his back against his mother's headstone, his eyes squeezed shut and his face streaked with tears.

I felt their presence the moment they manifested in the dream. The monsters had come out to play.

"About damn time," I murmured. I knelt in front of TJ, my gaze focused on him. I could sense the shadows moving around me—the mysterious creatures designed to give TJ nightmares so his parents would come rescue him. "If I don't look, they won't kill me. Isn't that right, TJ?"

Ash had a pile of dirt beside her, bigger than should have been possible, but the result was still nothing but an empty hole. She didn't stop digging, even as she shouted, "Bring her back, Griffin!"

"I will if you bring Sebastian back," I said softly.

She froze, her hands buried in the earth. "He's gone. No one can fix that."

"No?" I said. "That's a shame. I guess Cat will finally get what she wants. She'll see him again soon, if you believe in that kind of thing."

Ash threw herself at me, but I swept my arm toward her before she reached me. Ash went flying through the air until her back struck one of the headstones. She landed on the grave and went limp aside from her fingers curling into the grass.

"Stop it," came TJ's whisper from behind me. He looked at Cat's headstone, then lifted his gaze to me. His face was still that of an eight-year-old boy, but suddenly his eyes were so much older. "I won't let it happen again," he said. "I won't let you hurt my family."

Something grabbed me from behind and yanked me backward. Claws like jagged icicles pierced my shoulder, and pain shot through me as my mind reacted instinctively to the dream. A force pressed down on me, not a weight exactly, but something able to pin me to the ground all the same. A shadow hovered over me, a twisted, leathery face a few inches from my own. It had no eyes, no nose, just a gaping mouth that blew rotted air against my skin. Its breath rattled through the graveyard.

"I didn't look," I gasped. I instantly regretted opening my mouth, because I could taste the creature's foul breath on my tongue.

It didn't care. Something had changed the rules that bound the creature, if only for a split second. Now that I had seen its face, its only job was to tear me apart.

I blocked out the pain, but when I tried to focus on banishing the creature, it felt like running headfirst into a brick wall. Trying to fight off TJ's nightmare was like trying to change Ash's dreams. Worse, even, because it *hurt*. I could ignore my shredded body, but the harder I tried to affect the monsters, the more the pain inside my head grew.

Hands reached right through the creature and pulled me upright. Cat and Ash stood on either side of me, each holding one of my arms. Dirt still clung to Cat's hair and face, but she was alive. Why was it that these Knights were so hard to kill, all except the one I *wanted* alive?

"You—" I started, but I only got the single word out before they shoved me backward. I staggered through an open door and landed on my back in the middle of a forest. The thick foliage blocked out most of the sunlight, but the change from the darkness of the graveyard still stung my eyes. When they adjusted, I found Ash standing over me.

I scrambled to my feet and backed away from her. Both the door and Cat were nowhere to be found.

The forest around us was different from the one in TJ's dream. Different trees, brighter colors, the sweet scent of maple in the air. I realized then that TJ had been a pit stop. I didn't understand how Cat could travel between dreams, how she could bring people with her, or how Tiernan was able to do the same thing. Still, it made sense that moving from my dreams straight to Ash's would be difficult. It was impressive Cat managed to find her way into Ash's dreams at all. A strong connection made it easier to get into dreams, so perhaps it also provided an anchor point for moving directly from one to another. Cat knew TJ better than anyone, which meant she could use him as a stepping stone to bridge the gap between my dreams and Ash's.

The goal had always been to bring me here, where I was at a disadvantage. When I tried to escape back to my own dreams, I found I couldn't. It was different than when Tiernan had trapped me here by moving my body. Back then, when I'd tried to leave, I'd had nowhere to go. This time, Ash constructed a barrier around her own mind, locking me inside. I was trapped *again*, an animal in a cage.

But this time I had claws. I wouldn't go down without a fight.

When she stepped toward me, I summoned a wall of flames and pushed it toward her. It dissipated before it reached her, leaving only wisps of smoke behind. I lifted my hands to try again, but vines shot down from the trees and wrapped around my wrists like whips. They pulled my arms to the sides and dragged me backward until I slammed against a tree. Branches sprouted from the trunk and curled around my torso. More coiled around my arms and legs, immobilizing me.

I pushed forward with strength that should have snapped the branches, but they held firm. I might have found a way to alter her dreams, but with my will pitted directly against her own, she came out on top.

She stopped in front of me, close enough to touch if my arms weren't tangled in branches. I waited for her to have the branches snap my neck or tear me limb from limb. She only stared at me, her face unreadable.

"What are you going to do, dreamer?" I asked. "You going to kill me? The Committee won't let me live now. Not even Tiernan will defend me this time."

She watched me, her eyes a dark evergreen in the shadows cast over her face. I could feel her uncertainty. As usual, she hadn't planned that far ahead.

"I don't want to kill anyone," she said finally. "There's been enough death." She stepped closer and cupped my cheek in her hand, and for a strange moment I thought she might kiss me. Then she closed her eyes, and I felt something *tug* against my mind, my body, every fiber of my being.

"What are you doing?" Stark terror crept into my voice. I had a guess, but the thought was too sickening to even think. She couldn't, could she? I had seen her do a lot of things, but no one could do *that*.

"I'm taking away what makes them fear you."

I could feel every stitch in the seam snap as she tore away something vital to my very identity. Griffin was a legend. Griffin was powerful. Griffin could make you see or hear or feel whatever he wanted.

Now Griffin slumped in restraints made of branches and vines, as weak and vulnerable as his physical body in the real world.

Ash's fingers slid away from my cheek. They took with them the last shred of my power. I could feel its absence in every inch of my being. Whatever gift I'd possessed that had let me infiltrate people's minds... It was gone.

The dream flickered around me. It didn't vanish like I expected it to, though. Maybe the connection forged between Ash and me persisted, our minds woven together so tightly I didn't need dreamwalking to see her dreams.

"Ash, please... Please." I felt empty. She had reached inside and scooped out something I needed, leaving me slumped there like a hollow, uncarved jack-o-lantern. "You can't do this to me. You should kill me." I would rather be dead than *this*.

She shook her head. "Don't you see? I'm giving you a second chance. To live your life without the burden of this power." She curled her fingers, a look of wonder crossing her face. She hadn't only torn my power away from me. She had taken it for herself. She could feel it humming inside her, the ability to force her will upon others.

"You think taking away what made me *great* is going to somehow fix what's wrong with me?" I said. "Did you ever consider that maybe they were right? Maybe I'm just broken."

"The thing about everyone treating you like a villain is you start to believe them," she said. "You're not evil, Griffin. I think you're still the same lost teenager who was told his only purpose was manipulating people. You made mistakes, and you did your time. Now you deserve a chance to prove them wrong."

"The Committee won't agree to this. They won't let me walk away."

"I think Robert will be inclined to convince them, seeing as I saved his life tonight. I probably saved all of their lives, in the long run."

I lifted my head, a motion that took all my strength. "Why are you doing this? Why do you care?"

"Do I need a reason?"

"Yes. Everyone needs a reason."

Her eyes wandered, a frown on her lips, and I realized she hadn't thought about the *why*. Ash acted on instinct, forging ahead.

"I spent a lot of time letting people tell me what I could do, who I could be. I was waiting for someone to believe in me. What I really needed was to believe in myself." She brushed her fingers against the branch curled around my wrist, and it retreated like a fleeing snake. My arm fell to my side. After the rest of my restraints had slithered away, I dropped to my knees, unable to remain standing on my own.

She knelt in front of me. "I thought it was just guilt I carried over what happened with my friend. But I think I was angry, too. I was mad that he wouldn't believe me. I was scared he would think I was crazy if I told the truth." She brushed her fingers against my cheek again, a gesture so tender I thought maybe she did still feel something for me, the *real* me, but when I looked into her eyes, it wasn't affection I found.

It was pity.

"I focused on my guilt. You focused on your anger," Ash said. "The other emotions were still there. We have to accept all of them. And then we have to let them go. It's time to move on from the past. You were hurt, you made mistakes, but you get to choose who you get to be moving forward."

Who was she to talk about moving forward? She had been stuck for a full year, circling in a holding pattern and waiting for something to change. At least I had *acted*.

She pulled away and straightened. I remained on the ground at her feet, nothing but a husk of myself. "Cat?" she called. "I think it's time for Griffin to go back to his own dream."

Cat appeared from behind the trunk of an ancient oak tree and stepped to Ash's side. She eyed me like she was considering finishing the job and killing me herself. "Are you sure about this?"

"I'm sure," Ash said.

Cat sighed and reached for me. I didn't fight her as she hauled me to my feet. She started to tug me away, but I moved faster than I knew I still could and caught Ash's wrist. I pulled her closer, which I was only able to do because she came willingly.

"You think they will let you walk free now that you have this power?" I asked, keeping my voice low enough that Cat couldn't hear. "You can't keep the secret forever. And once they know, they'll either try to use you too, or they'll get rid of you before you can become a danger to them. It's only a matter of time, dreamer."

Her eyes flickered over my face. Then she gently pried my fingers off her wrist. "That's for me to worry about now." She took a step back, out of my reach. "Goodbye, Griffin."

Cat summoned Ash's blue front door. We stepped through, back into my own dreamscape.

"The drugs should wear off soon," she said. "Enjoy it while it lasts."

Cat left me exactly where they had found me, alone on a deserted beach. The world had gone still, even the ocean. The tide had pulled away from the line where wet sand met dry beach and didn't sweep back in. Sunlight reflected off the motionless waves, the ridges suspended in time. No breeze ruffled my hair, no sound reached my ears. The fluffy clouds were fixed in place on an expanse of blue sky.

I was frozen inside an afterimage of reality.

I sank down onto the sand, which was neither cold nor baked warm by the nonexistent sun. It had no temperature at all, as if I had gone numb, though I could feel the granules beneath my fingertips.

I remained there, as still as the world around me. I didn't blink. I didn't breathe. Doing so felt wrong when the dream itself was holding its breath. Finally, it faded away as I slipped into a deeper, dreamless sleep.

When I opened my eyes, waking up no longer felt like a gift.

Chapter 34

"**I**'M SORRY... I THINK my brain liquefied," Des said. He sat with five other people, crammed around Ash's kitchen table designed for four. The gentle light of early dawn seeped through the windows. It had still been night when Ash had begun telling the story, the room gradually brightening as the minutes ticked by.

For a short time after our fight, Ash had been riding high, giddy with adrenaline and exhilaration, not to mention the thrum of new power coursing through her. Now, though, the fatigue had started to set in. Weariness laced her voice, gravity dragged at her posture, and she had trouble even keeping her eyes open. She had over-exerted herself, tapping into power she hadn't known she possessed, exercising a muscle previously undiscovered. She would probably be feeling it for weeks.

Across the table, Des folded his hands together. "So you all can enter people's dreams, and that Griffin guy could mind control people while they were awake?"

"It's not mind control," Ash and Tiernan said at the same time. They exchanged a glance, and one corner of Tiernan's lips curled up.

"Griffin simply had the same ability we do, but more powerful," Tiernan said. "When you change someone else's dream, you're telling them what to perceive. Griffin could do this when people were asleep *or* awake. He was one of only two people I've ever heard of with that level of ability."

That caught my interest. I had thought I was the only one. *Who?* I screamed into Ash's mind. Her back straightened, confusion flickering through her. She could still hear me.

She shook her head and asked the question she had already planned to. "Two people?"

"There was one other. Like Griffin, she did horrible things while she was alive. Many thought the stories about her were myths and exaggerations, but I always believed it was possible."

"Who was she?" Cat asked.

"Dahlia Remington. Griffin's great-grandmother."

"That's why his parents were so worried," Ash murmured.

I couldn't believe what Ash was hearing. I had thought my father would be proud when he learned how much potential his son had. I had never understood why it had been met with such fear. But if I had an ancestor who had abused such power, then suddenly his reaction made sense.

Was it possible I hated my father a little less?

"And after everything he did, you decided to just turn him loose on the world?" Des said, putting them back on track.

"He doesn't have his powers anymore," Ash said. "That doesn't necessarily mean he's not a threat to anyone, but I took away what made it so easy for him to hurt people."

"He can still hurt people the old-fashioned way," Des said.

"Maybe. But that's why Raisa is keeping an eye on him."

"Thanks for that, by the way," Raisa said. "I love babysitting sociopaths."

"Don't call him that," Ash said softly.

Tiernan watched her from across the table. She reached out to touch his mind on impulse, wanting to know what he was thinking, but she recoiled the moment she realized what she was doing. All she got was a sense of curiosity and a glimmer of pride before she severed the link between them.

"It is perhaps true that he's on the anti-social spectrum," Tiernan said. "I could see the signs in him as a boy. But whatever sickness he struggled with didn't make him a killer. His own circumstances and choices drove him to that. Ash is right—maybe now there's a chance he can figure out how to fit in with society. He was never given that, not really. Without his powers, he'll have to learn there are better ways to get what you want."

TJ tore his eyes away from Des to look over at Ash. I wondered if he even knew he'd been staring in a rather obvious way. "How did you know you could take away his powers like that?"

"I don't know... I guess I just knew. I had already stolen some abilities from him. That's why I can dreamwalk. It wasn't my power to begin with. It was his."

"The important thing is now he can't hurt anyone with it," Cat said. "No one should have that kind of power. It makes people think they can do whatever they want."

"Right... No one should have it," Ash murmured.

A question floated around Ash's mind. A question she was too afraid to voice. Would I have become what I had if my parents hadn't been so afraid of me? Their fears had become a self-fulfilling prophecy. That, coupled with the Committee's scheme, had paved the path to where I'd ended up.

Or maybe it didn't matter. We didn't know my great-grandmother's story. It was possible she had done terrible things just because she *could.* Maybe Ash and Tiernan were wrong, and that sort of power corrupted a person, no matter how they started out.

Which of course begged the question, what would it do to Ash?

My parting words to her replayed in her head. *Once they know, they'll either try to use you, too, or they'll get rid of you.* The fact that she hadn't told anyone, that she had let them assume she had drained my power and released it into the ether, said she believed me.

She tried to shake off the worries that swirled in her mind, but the sense of dread remained.

"It's possible he'll never be a 'good person,'" she said. "But I think he deserves the chance to find out. Maybe a little help and better guidance will make all the difference."

"I still don't know why I have to be the guidance," Raisa muttered. "You're the one who did this. Why can't you take care of him?"

Ash's chest tightened, but whatever thoughts or feelings caused it, I couldn't sense them. Somehow, she had figured out how to hide them from me. "It can't be me because he thinks he's in love with me." She clenched her hands together under the table. "I don't think I'm what he needs right now."

Again, Tiernan gave her that look that made her feel like he was digging through her thoughts and emotions. I didn't think he could do it to her, though, not with her shielded mind. It kept him out of her waking mind the way it kept others out of her dreams.

Cat's chair scraped against the hardwood as she pushed it back and stood. "We should get going. We have some consequences to sort out."

"Yeah," TJ said miserably. "We can't avoid Dad forever."

Ash was glad she wouldn't have to be present for that conversation. "Good luck."

"We're going to need a hell of a lot more than luck," Cat muttered. "Come on, TJ. We'll stop at the bakery for some coffee cake on the way home." TJ perked up a little at that. Apparently, cake made everything better. Raisa gave the rest of the table a little wave and went with them.

They would *all* need a lot more than luck. I had a feeling they would be dealing with the fallout from their actions for months to come. Secrets revealed and trust broken on all sides. Ash still held tightly to a new secret, one she wanted to keep hidden forever. Ideally, she would forget about it herself.

But secrets had only hurt her, and she couldn't keep them from the people she loved any longer. She just had to figure out how to tell them, and it wouldn't be easy. Nothing worth it ever was.

Despite wanting nothing more than to curl up in her bed and go to sleep, Ash rose and followed the others to the entryway. "Hey, wait." They paused and glanced back in unison, Cat's hand still on the doorknob. "I wanted to thank all of you. I know I made some mistakes along the way but... you still trusted me. You stood by me. That means a lot."

"You weren't the only person he tricked, Ash," TJ said. "We all fell for it."

But you didn't fall for him. Ash tried to stamp out the thought before it floated through her mind, but I heard it anyway.

Shockingly, Cat slid her fingers from the doorknob and gave Ash a small nod. "You fixed it. That's what matters. And you saved us from Griffin. I guess that matters, too. A little bit." Ash gave her a dry smile. Cat glanced away awkwardly and pulled open the door. "Anyway, bye. I'll be in the car."

Raisa grinned at Ash before following her girlfriend out, but TJ remained behind. His eyes had drifted past Ash, back to the kitchen where Des still chatted with Tiernan.

"Maybe he doesn't care about football as much as some people," Ash said lightly. TJ gave her a shocked look that she rolled her eyes at. "It's not like you were doing a good job of hiding your interest. You won't know until you talk to him, right?"

TJ gave an unenthusiastic nod.

Ash stepped forward to wrap her arms around her new friend. Her new *best* friend, she dared to think. "You're amazing, and someday you're going to meet the right person who realizes that. Okay?"

After a brief hesitation, TJ hugged her back. "Thanks," he murmured.

Ash released him from the hug, but she kept a hand on his arm. She took a deep breath and lowered her voice so the two in the kitchen couldn't hear, even if they decided to eavesdrop. "TJ?"

He must have picked up on her tone because he eyed her with concern. "Yeah?"

"I... I need to tell you something. And you can't tell Cat or Raisa or anyone else yet, okay? I'll do it. I just have to figure out how and when." She *would* do it, she promised herself. She couldn't keep the secret buried. Not again.

"Okay," he said hesitantly. "I won't."

Ash clasped her hands together to keep them from shaking. She didn't know how he would react. I personally thought she was making a mistake, but as with every other mistake I had ever watched her make, I was powerless to stop her.

"I didn't just take away Griffin's abilities," she said when she finally found the courage. "I stole them. I have them. I can feel it... I could do what he did, if I wanted to."

Anxiety rushed through her when he didn't respond right away. She couldn't read his expression, which wasn't typical with him. She had grown used to his openness.

Then he smiled, and though it was strained, there was no fear or mistrust in his eyes. "Unlike Griffin, you won't misuse it.

If anyone should have that power... it should be someone like you."

"I won't use it at all," Ash said, a promise to both him and herself. "I don't want to."

TJ slid his hand into hers and gave it a squeeze. "It will be okay. I promise I'll keep your secret. But you need to tell them soon. Cat, Raisa, your uncle."

Ash grimaced and nodded. She could already imagine how that conversation would go with Cat. Probably nowhere near as well as it had with TJ, which was exactly why she had told him first. Tiernan, however... She had no idea what to expect from him anymore.

"I'll text you soon, if we survive Dad's wrath," TJ said. "Maybe we can go to trivia." Ash gave a weak laugh. Then he darted one last glance at Des and followed Raisa and Cat.

Ash closed the door behind him and stood there for a few seconds. She had found new people to fill the void her old relationship had left behind. She had TJ and Raisa. Maybe had even won over Cat, just a little bit. But she wasn't done with her old best friend yet. There was still something she had to do.

Five weeks later, Ash pulled into the small lot beside the apartment building. She had spent the last month mulling over what she would say when she got there, but she still only had a half-baked plan. She would have to make up the rest as she went. She followed the familiar path her feet had walked many times and stopped in front of a white door. She took a deep breath and let it out slowly, trying to calm her racing heart.

If Ash could block out the last year, this would feel like coming home. She could walk through that door, and they would spend the night making dinner and then watching their latest TV show addiction.

But the last year had happened, and Ash wouldn't change it for anything, even if she could. All she could do now was move forward.

She lifted her fist and knocked three times. It felt weird to her, knocking on a door that had once been her own. She waited for a long time—so long she feared he wasn't home—but then the deadbolt clicked and a face appeared through the cracked door.

It was a face both familiar and unfamiliar, changed by time and other factors. His features were thinner and more angular, with faint stubble along his jaw. It wasn't quite what he had looked like in the dream that had sparked the fuse of their eventual downfall, but close enough.

He opened the door wider, and his initial surprise flattened into a dead stare. "What are you doing here?"

His voice was deeper than Ash remembered. Like everything else about him, more masculine. "Hi, Ezra," she said pitifully. "Can we talk? I owe you a real apology, and the truth. All of it."

He narrowed his eyes, but he didn't slam the door in her face. That was a good start. "I'm listening."

"I'm sorry," she said. "I did invade your privacy. Not intentionally, but it happened. It wasn't your phone, though. I couldn't tell you the truth because I thought you wouldn't believe me. I guess I thought it was better to let you hate me than think I was insane. But I realized recently that you deserve to know, and keeping secrets doesn't protect anyone. It's up to you whether you want to believe or not."

Ezra didn't say anything. He stared at her for a few seconds, then took a step back to pull the door open, a wordless invitation to enter. She would take it.

Not this part, Griffin, she thought. She couldn't know for sure I was watching, but it was a solid guess. She took the white chalcedony, now fashioned into a pendant, from her pocket and slipped the string over her head. She tucked it under her shirt so the white rock rested against the skin of her chest. I felt that pressure against my mind, forcing me out. I tried to cling to her, because I cared a lot more about what happened with Ash and her friend than what awaited me back at my own body, but the tension grew until the connection eventually snapped.

Chapter 35

"**R**EMINGTON!"

I opened my eyes and turned a stare on Jacob that would have made anyone who knew what I was once capable of quake in their awful turtleneck. I mean, really, a turtleneck in California? Jacob looked wholly unintimidated.

I hated the sound of my own name, more than I ever had. At least they had let me put "Griffin" on my name tag.

"Those dishes aren't going to bus themselves," he said.

"Yes, sir." I tried to sound respectful, but derision dripped from my words anyway. This man, at least four years younger than I was, probably assumed I was some high school dropout whose only future prospect was bouncing between menial jobs. If only he knew I had not only graduated but had been top of my class. I had such plans before the Committee had taken it all away from me.

I grabbed the bus bin and headed out to the recently vacated table. The customers had left it a mess, not just the dishes but food dropped on the table. Someone had spilled a drink and left a pile of sopping wet napkins at the table's edge. I stared for several seconds, lamenting what my life had become. Was this to be my future? I didn't think I could live this way. I would go crazy. Purposeless, worthless, alone. At least when I carried vengeance in my heart, I'd had something to strive toward. My life had held meaning. Now what did I have? Wet napkins and meager wages.

I piled the dirty dishes into the bin, then wiped the napkins and food scraps in as well. I trudged back to the kitchen and placed the bin in the sink. Jacob waited there with his arms crossed.

"I'm keeping my eye on you, Remington. I've seen your type before."

What type? I thought. It didn't even matter. There could be a dozen reasons he didn't trust me, from the way I talked to the color of my skin or my haircut. I ignored him and started working on the dishes.

"Hey, Remington, I'm talking to you!" A shadow moved on the wall as he stepped up behind me.

My shoulders tensed. Rage blossomed in my chest. An image flashed in my mind, him choking on water that bubbled up from inside his own chest.

You should respect me. You should fear me.

But I wasn't the world's most powerful dreamwalker anymore. I was *nothing*.

"Sorry, sir," I said flatly. I set the dishes in the soapy water and scraped the rest of the contents from the bin into the trash. I still didn't look at him, but I saw him give a satisfied nod out of the corner of my eye.

How long before I snapped? Maybe I couldn't flood his mind with terror, but I still had my fists. Everyone had always been so eager to tell me my temper would get me into trouble, and Sebastian had been the only one who could calm me. Nothing had changed there. I was still a ticking time-bomb. And Sebastian was still gone.

I dunked my hands in the water to start scrubbing a plate. Jacob moved away, and I let out a breath of relief. His presence had been like a hot poker jabbing at my temper. With him gone, I could see straight again.

Unfortunately, there was still nothing to see but soap bubbles and dirty dishes. I squeezed my eyes shut and bowed my head, trying to see into Ash's mind again, but she had blocked me out. My connection to her was all I had left, and right then it felt like I had lost that too.

My hands curled into fists, still submerged beneath the water. *Three more hours.* Three hours until closing, and then I could go home. I could find some peace. I would go to sleep, and Sebastian's face would haunt my lonely dreams. Then I would wake up and have to do it all over again.

I got through those last three hours without breaking anything. Not a plate or a glass or Jacob's face.

It was a short walk back to my tiny studio apartment. I had one room with a bed shoved in the corner, bare kitchen cabinets, and a freezer full of microwave dinners.

But it was mine, I supposed. I wasn't a backseat passenger in someone else's life anymore. If I were being honest, part of me missed that. I missed *her.*

When I entered my apartment, I almost stepped on the envelope that had been slipped under the door. The front only had my name written on it in looping cursive letters. Ash's handwriting. I bent down to pick it up and slid my fingers under the flap. The envelope wasn't sealed, just tucked in, and I pulled out a *second* envelope from the first. It was addressed to me—Zain Remington—but had Ash's address instead of my own. The return address said UCLA.

"What are you up to, Ash?" I muttered as I tore open the letter. She allowed me glimpses into her life on occasion, but it felt weird not knowing everything she had been doing for the past few weeks. For eight years I had known her every action, her every thought.

Dear Zain:

Congratulations! It is our great pleasure to offer you admission to UCLA for the Fall Quarter. You have been admitted to the UCLA School of the Arts & Architecture with Architectural Studies as your academic major.

The letter went on for several paragraphs, but I noticed something written on the back of the envelope, so I set the letter aside to read the four words Ash had written to me: *Don't mess it up.*

I stared at the words for a long time, there in the entry way to my apartment, the door hanging open behind me. She had submitted an application for me? How had she even gotten my records? It was so surreal that it felt like a dream, but no, I definitely wasn't dreaming.

I folded the letter, slid it back into its envelope, and closed the door behind me. Then I walked to the window to peer through the curtains at the dark street. Ash had said she was giving me a second chance, but I hadn't believed her. After all, what was I without my abilities? Without Sebastian, without *her.*

Fierce like a lion but free like a bird.

I had been a slave to my powers. Because of what I could do, people had always feared me or wanted something from me. After I'd lost Sebastian, rage had burned inside me, fueled by the knowledge that I could take my revenge and no one could stand in my way. *Second chances. Freedom.*

With that letter in my hands, I thought maybe she was right. Maybe they both were. *Don't mess it up.* "I'll try, Ash," I murmured. "I'll try."

Acknowledgments

Thank you to everyone who supported me through drafting and editing this. For my sister: your perfectionism is annoying but appreciated. This book wouldn't exist without you. My writing group and friends: Audrey, Cassie, Clayton, Rachel, and Raylee. You kept me going and helped me brainstorm, fix issues I couldn't figure out on my own, and put up with my constant need for validation when the impostor syndrome kicked in. My wonderful beta readers helped turn the mess of a first draft into something coherent. Thank you to Sophie Edwards for the amazing cover design.

For everyone who supported the Kickstarter: You made publishing this possible. Thank you so much for your support and patience.

About the Author

Nicole Aisling is equal parts biology nerd, animal lover, and story enthusiast. She studied biology in college, but an incurable thirst for knowledge led her astray to philosophy and psychology classes, which inspired stories like *Chasing Nightmares*. She loves merging magic with science, creating worlds grounded in physics and biology... but still fantastical. When she's not outside enjoying nature, she can be found cuddled up on the couch with her dogs, settled in for either a good book or the latest TV episode.

https://nicoleaisling.com/

Made in the USA
Middletown, DE
09 September 2024

60067910R00175